Simone rested an elbow on the tabletop, turning flirtatiously toward Paul. "Do you know Tom and Jerry over there?" she asked softly. She reached a hand out, trailing her fingers against his arm.

Her touch proved just distracting enough to him that Paul didn't turn abruptly to stare back, drawing even more attention in their direction. His focus shifted slowly from her toward the duo at the bar. He eyed them briefly before turning his attention back to Simone. He shook his head. "Should I?"

"It might be nothing, but they seem very interested in you."

Paul's gaze danced back in their direction and he took a swift inhale of air. One of the men was on a cell phone and both were still eyeing him intently.

"We need to leave," he said, suddenly anxious. He began to gather his papers.

"What's going on, Paul?"

"I don't think we're safe, Simone."

* * *

Don't miss future installments in the To Serve and Seduce miniseries, coming soon...

* * *

If you're on Twitter, tell us what you think of Harlequin Romantic Suspense! #harlequinromsuspense

Dear Reader,

I wish I had something profound to say about this story. Something that would have bells ringing and angels dancing. But I really don't. This story, based in fact, made me a little sad. Medical and pharmaceutical abuse against patients is very real. Too often it flies under the radar, the public completely unaware. I appreciate being able to fictionalize and bring awareness to what is a very real problem. I wish I could do more.

I loved fleshing out Simone Black. She's fire and her love affair with Dr. Paul Reilly made my heart sing. The two together are oil and water, and they mingle so perfectly, it made writing their story one enjoyable adventure. I absolutely adore the two, and I really love his philanthropic spirit and her devotion to her man! I hope you will enjoy them together as much as I enjoyed writing them!

Thank you so much for your support. I am humbled by all the love you keep showing me, my characters and our stories. I know that none of this would be possible without you.

Until the next time, please take care and may God's blessings be with you always.

With much love,

Deborah Fletcher Mello

www.DeborahMello.blogspot.com

REUNITED BY
THE BADGE

———

Deborah Fletcher Mello

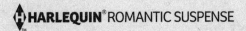

HARLEQUIN® ROMANTIC SUSPENSE

Recycling programs
for this product may
not exist in your area.

ISBN-13: 978-1-335-66220-0

Reunited by the Badge

Printed in U.S.A.

A true Renaissance woman, **Deborah Fletcher Mello** finds joy in crafting unique story lines and memorable characters. She's received accolades from several publications, including *Publishers Weekly*, *Library Journal* and *RT Book Reviews*. Born and raised in Connecticut, Deborah now considers home to be wherever the moment moves her.

Books by Deborah Fletcher Mello

Harlequin Romantic Suspense

To Serve and Seduce

Seduced by the Badge
Tempted by the Badge
Reunited by the Badge

Harlequin Kimani Romance

Truly Yours
Hearts Afire
Twelve Days of Pleasure
My Stallion Heart
Stallion Magic
Tuscan Heat
A Stallion's Touch
A Pleasing Temptation
Sweet Stallion
To Tempt a Stallion
A Stallion Dream

Visit the Author Profile page at Harlequin.com for more titles.

To all my Jewels in The Reading Room

Know that you are much loved and valued!

You all make my heart sing!

Chapter 1

Dr. Paul Reilly stood in front of his business-class seat, waiting anxiously to disembark the airplane. He'd been traveling for some thirty-plus hours, having started with an Air France flight from Accra, Ghana, to Paris, France, and ending with a Delta flight into Chicago. He was past the point of exhaustion and all he wanted was to be on firm ground, and home.

The cell phone in his hand began to beep and vibrate, an influx of incoming messages finally getting through after he'd taken the device out of airplane mode. He stole a quick glance at the lengthy list to determine the urgency of his responding, or not, and then he dropped the unit into the inner breast pocket of his blazer.

The line out of the aircraft began to move slowly. When he spied his first opportunity to make an exit, Paul stepped into the aisle. He reached for his carry-on bag out of the upper storage compartment and pushed forward, beating a woman who was whining about the heat and a couple with four unruly kids out the door. He moved swiftly down the Jetway to the terminal, exhaling a sigh of relief as he shifted out of the crowd toward the baggage reclaim area.

As he waited for the airlines to engage the luggage carousel, he pulled his cell back into his hands and dialed one of the first numbers in his call list. His brother Oliver answered on the second ring.

"Where are you?" Oliver questioned, a hint of stress in his tone.

Paul took a deep breath. "The airport. I just landed."

"Did you get my text message?"

"I got a few dozen. I haven't had an opportunity to read any of them since I left Ghana."

"I sent you the lab results for those tissue samples you gave me. I haven't had a chance to start testing the drug samples yet."

"And?"

"And, something is definitely not right. But you have a bigger problem."

"What's that?"

"The samples have disappeared. All of them. The tissue samples and the drug products."

"What do you mean, *disappeared*?"

"I mean someone took them and now they're gone."

"But you have the results?"

"No. *You* have the only results. I emailed them to you first thing, before I even looked at them. Once I did read them, I needed to do some additional testing, but before that could happen it all vanished. Including the original first round of test results!"

"So, they got both shipments?"

"Both? You sent more than one shipment of samples?"

"Yeah. I mailed one to your office and I mailed the other to the house in Windsor, since I knew you had plans to be there."

"The Windsor shipment might be waiting for me, as long as no one knew you were sending it there."

Paul blew a soft sigh, his mind racing as he tried to make sense of what his brother was telling him. Dr. Oliver Reilly worked for the federal government. He was a cancer research scientist reporting to the Centers for Disease Control and Prevention. Like his brother, Paul had a medical degree, but specialized in emergency care and family practice. He'd chosen to be a public health practitioner over private practice.

Paul trusted Oliver, one of only a few people he knew who would have his back, whatever the situation. "Did you discuss this with anyone?"

"No. Not a soul. Which is also why I didn't file a police report. Whoever knew the samples were here, also knew you sent them. Whoever took them has access to the government labs because there isn't an ounce of evidence to point toward a break-in. Now, I'm not one for conspiracy theories, but something's going on."

Paul took another deep breath. The carousel had just begun to spin, the passengers from his international flight crowding around like a herd of cattle waiting for something to happen. As the first bags appeared out of a hole in the rear wall, the group drew closer, preparing to snatch their possessions as quickly as they could.

Oliver called his name. "Paul! You still there?"

"Sorry, yeah. Just trying to think."

"Look, I'm here to help any way I can. But, this feels like it might be more than either one of us can handle. Have *you* talked to anyone? The police? An attorney, maybe?"

Paul shook his head, oblivious to the fact his brother couldn't see him through the telephone line. His eyes were skating over the crowd, a sense of unease beginning to swell in his midsection. He was suddenly feeling slightly paranoid, like he needed to be looking over his shoulder. "I've got to run. I'll call you as soon as I get to the house."

"Be careful, please," Oliver admonished as the line disconnected in his ear.

Minutes later, Paul sat in the back of an Uber. His

preferred driver, a grandmother from the island of Haiti, was chatting him up about his trip. The older woman had been driving him back and forth for the last year, her wide smile always a welcome sight whether he was coming or going.

"You need a wife," she said, the comment coming out of left field.

Paul laughed. "Why would I want to do something like that?"

"God didn't make man to live his life alone. That's why he gave Eve to Adam. Someone to be your helpmate. A partner to help carry some of the burden and provide comfort when you need it. It's why you need a wife. God has ordained it!" she professed with an air of finality that suddenly had Paul considering the possibilities.

He thought about the women in his life—one woman in particular—then shook his head. "I don't foresee that in my immediate future, Mrs. Pippin."

"What about that beauty queen you were dating? Was she not wifey material?"

"No!" he exclaimed, his head waving from side to side. "She was *definitely* not wife material." For a moment he thought about the Miss Illinois contestant he'd met in the hospital waiting room. She had captured his attention and then all focus had been lost two weeks later when she accused him of cheating because he hadn't answered her call or returned it in a timely manner. She had keyed his car, stolen his phone and had poisoned his fish tank with bleach. He discovered later that he had fared better than her last boyfriend. That poor guy had suffered immeasurable damage when she'd superglued his junk to his leg after discovering he'd slept with her friend. Any man willing to make her his wife would have to sleep with both eyes open at night.

Mrs. Pippin interrupted his moment of reverie. "Your heart is still with that lawyer woman. The one you talk about, but don't talk to," she concluded, grunting slightly as she gave him a look through the rearview mirror.

The faintest hint of a smile lifted across Paul's face. "She broke my heart, Mrs. Pippin. And she left it in a million pieces."

The old woman grunted a second time. "She is still under your skin. She never leaves you. Like a bad juju. That is why all the other beauties you date don't stand a chance. You should call her."

Paul suddenly found himself pondering her suggestion, smiling at the thought of any woman being some kind of mystical charm that could sway him from other relationships. Maybe Mrs. Pippin was right, and he had himself a case of bad juju. He remembered how smitten he'd been, so possessed that he couldn't begin to imagine his life without the beauty who'd felt like home in his small world.

That woman she referred to was Simone Black, daughter of Chicago's illustrious police superintendent Jerome Black and his wife, federal court judge Judith Harmon Black. The last time he had spoken with Simone, their conversation had been tense, and he'd felt battered by the end of it. There had been an ultimatum, or two, and the predictable battle of wills when the two disagreed. Their communication had failed, and both had shut down.

He could barely remember who had started that fight or what they'd even fought about, just that it had been the end for their relationship and months of conflict between them. They had agreed to part ways, choosing to let go of each other, instead of battling for a happily-ever-after that could have lasted a lifetime.

A mission trip to Northern Thailand to treat the indigenous people of the Akha tribe, high in the Chiang Rai mountains, had kept him from falling into a fit of depression and crying into his cornflakes for months. Being able to provide medical treatment to patient populations that included local migrant workers, as well as refugee populations from bordering Myanmar, had kept him sane and balanced and unconcerned with whether the woman he had loved was moving on without him. He had regained focus and come back with a renewed sense of purpose. The spiritual journey that had been so much about expanding his horizon and answering a calling, had become a much needed balm, a bandage of sorts on an open wound. There had been five more mission trips since and no wailing over the loss of his woman.

Now, thinking about her was adding to the frustration he was already feeling. But calling Simone, a prominent lawyer with the state's attorney's office, suddenly made more sense than not. Despite their problems, he trusted her and right then, he needed counsel from someone he could trust.

Mrs. Pippin was rambling, sharing a story about one of her many grandchildren. Paul listened with half an ear as he considered his options. He needed help and Simone might be willing to point him in the right direction. She also had connections who might prove to be beneficial in helping him solve his problem. He knew he'd fare better with her than without her, if only to get a hint or two of advice.

Paul shifted forward in his seat. "Mrs. Pippin, change of plans. I need to grab a bite to eat. Do you mind taking me to West Bryn Mawr, please? Down near North Clark Street."

"No problem at all. Just change the destination in the app for me."

"Yes, ma'am."

Minutes later she'd turned the burgundy Avalon he was riding in about and headed toward the North Side of town. He pushed the speed dial for the first number in his phone contacts and waited for it to be answered.

Simone Black answered just as he was about to hang up. "Why are you calling me, Paul?" Her tone was wary as she said hello.

Hearing her voice sent both a rumble of anxiety into the pit of his stomach and a blanket of calm across his back and shoulders. The conflicting emotions caused him to struggle to stay focused. He took a deep breath before he spoke. "It's important, Simone. I really need your help."

There was an awkward pause as the woman on the other end took time to ponder his comment. When she finally responded her voice was thick with attitude. "This better be good, Paul Reilly. Do not waste my time!"

"Can you meet me, please?"

"Now? Do you know what time it is?"

"I know it's late, Simone, but I wouldn't ask if it weren't important. And I mean life-and-death important. I really need to talk to you."

There was another lengthy pause before she answered. "If it's that important, I guess I can make the time. But you'd better not be playing games with me!"

He blew a soft sigh of relief. "I'm headed over to our place now. I should be there in ten minutes."

"We have a place?" she replied sarcastically.

Paul shook his head. "I'll be waiting, Simone. I'll see you when you get there."

As he disconnected the line, Paul noted the look Mrs. Pippin was giving him. The old woman eyed him with raised brows. Bemusement furrowed her forehead and there was a hint of hubris in her eyes. He was sure something snarky teased the tip of her tongue, but she bit back the quip, giving him an easy smile instead.

Paul chuckled. He hated admitting when the old woman was right and in the short time he'd known her, her instincts had often been spot-on. This time was no different. Because Simone Black did have his heart on lock. Even with the distance between them, and the young woman's sometimes contentious demeanor that had him wanting to pull his hair out, Paul still loved Simone more than he had ever loved any other woman in his life.

Simone Black had needed to park her car around the corner from their favorite local restaurant. Walking the length of the block in high heels was proving to be quite the chore and she was kicking herself for choosing cute over comfort. But it had been quite some time since she and Paul had been in a room together and she was determined that he saw cute when they next met.

Just hearing his voice over the telephone had sent shivers of excitement down her spine. She hadn't wanted to admit just how much she missed him, because admitting she missed him meant admitting she might have been wrong about breaking up with him. Simone had lost count of the number of times she'd kicked herself for that decision.

Since their separation almost one year ago and him leaving the country, Simone often claimed she'd been abandoned, left pining after a man who had loved his career more than he had loved her. She conveniently left out the fact that Paul had begged her to leave with him, wanting her to follow his dreams as they worked together to fulfill her own. She had always admired his humanitarian spirit but had been ill-prepared the day he announced he wanted to serve patients overseas in developing countries. It had been a calling on his heart that she'd found admirable, but she hadn't been able to see how she might fit in the life he imagined.

But Paul had wanted a future together that included whatever they both needed, and Simone had just been too scared to commit, not wanting to admit that at that time, she didn't have a clue what she had wanted or needed.

She and Paul had met in college, becoming fast friends in a few short weeks. He could make her laugh with little effort and his energy was infectious. Paul's enthusiasm for life had brought out the best traits in Simone and where she was often snarky and difficult with others, with Paul Reilly she was like the easiest breeze on a summer day.

They had absolutely nothing in common, not even a shared interest in the same foods. He was altruistic, and she was often self-centered, thinking only about herself. He believed in a higher power and she proclaimed herself an agnostic. Where he was willing to venture through life all willy-nilly, she was more restrained and guarded and not a risk taker. Paul had treated her with kindness in a way no other man had before. And there had been other men. Casual acquaintances who never quite measured up to the father and brothers she compared them with. The male members of Simone's family had set a standard others had found insurmountable. Paul had surpassed the challenge.

Paul had never tried to control her, allowing her the freedom to find her own way as it suited her. He was nonjudgmental, even tempered and compassionate to a fault. The friendship that had evolved between them had taken on a life of its own. Their intense physical attraction to each other and a willingness to simply trust the process had created a bond that even they didn't understand. It worked, even when it shouldn't have.

Paul leaving after weeks of begging her to join him had been devastating. It had left a hollow void in her life that she'd been unable to fill. She'd regretted the decision more times than she cared to count, and she had never told him, hating to admit that she had simply been too scared to step outside of her comfort zone. Her pride had been the biggest wall standing between them. Now, here she was, racing to see him, and trying to be cute when she got there.

Her heel caught in a crack in the concrete sidewalk and she almost tripped, barely stopping herself from falling forward. She came to an abrupt halt, pausing to take a deep breath to calm her nerves as she steadied herself. The air was crisp, evening temperatures predicting snow in a forecast that was warm one day and practically cataclysmic the next. She sucked in oxygen like her life depended on it.

The two men entering Little Bad Wolf caught her attention. They wore matching black suits and when one shoved his hands into his pants pockets, she spied a holster beneath his jacket. They had an odd, *Men in Black* vibe that felt strangely unnatural. The duo gave her reason to pause, something about them feeling out of sync with the neighborhood. Each tossed a look over his shoulder before moving through the entrance, which made her uneasy. She wanted to dismiss the emotion, her nerves already on overdrive as she thought about Paul and his telephone call and her excitement about meeting him. But there was something that suddenly had her imagining terrorist attacks, hostage situations or something else bringing harm to a host of innocent bystanders.

She would wonder why later, but instinct moved her to

reach for her cell phone and dial the number to the local police station. Two rings and an officer Simone didn't recognize answered the phone.

"Good evening. Is Captain Black available, please? It's his sister calling."

Parker Black answered the line a few seconds later. "Hello?"

"Hey, it's me, Simone."

"What's wrong, Simone?"

"It might not be anything, but can you roll a patrol car out to Little Bad Wolf? I feel like they need to do a safety check of the area."

"Because…?"

"I'm here to meet Paul and two really shady-looking guys just went into the place. One's carrying a gun under his jacket. I'm not sure about the other. But they're not regulars and they don't look like they're visiting Chicago for our pleasant tourist sights. It's just a feeling I get. Something's just not right about them." She didn't bother to tell her brother that Paul had said his problem was a matter of life and death and that something in his voice had been concerning. She doubted the two had anything to do with each other, but she would rather be safe than sorry.

"So, you're meeting Paul the doctor? Your ex-boyfriend Paul? I heard he was back. So, are you two reconciling or is this just a late-night booty call?"

"Just send a car, please?"

"He's a good guy, Simone. Go easy on the brother."

"Thank you, Parker!" she answered, her singsong tone belying her anxiety.

Her brother persisted. "It wasn't cool how you ended things. You're lucky…"

Simone disconnected the call, not even bothering to

say goodbye. She took another deep breath and moved through the door into the space.

Little Bad Wolf was a neighborhood favorite. The gastropub was often packed, a lengthy line waiting to get inside during prime dinner hours. She and Paul had been regulars, eating there at least three, sometimes four times, per week.

The young man who greeted her at the door looked discombobulated, although he tried nicely to mask his distress. He smiled, recognition washing over his expression. "Attorney Black, long time no see!" he exclaimed as he leaned in to give her a warm hug.

Simone hugged him back. "Jacob, hey! Is everything okay?"

The man named Jacob nodded, but there was something about the twitch over his eye that said so much more. "I'm good. Really good," he said as he tossed a look over his shoulder.

Simone smiled. "I've missed this place," she said casually.

"Dr. Reilly is in the back," Jacob said as he grabbed a menu and turned, gesturing for her to follow. "He's been waiting for you."

Simone's gaze skated around the room, eyeing the patrons who sat in conversation, laughter ringing warmly through the space. It was a nice crowd for a late hour.

The boys in black were seated at the oversize bar. The bartender was trying to make conversation, but neither was interested. One sat with his broad back to the polished, wooden structure, staring toward the other end of the room. Simone shifted to see where he was staring, her eyes finding Paul seated at their usual spot in the rear. The sight of him triggered a host of alarms she hadn't been expecting.

Simone gasped slightly, the man lifting her lips in the sweetest smile. He was still a beautiful specimen of manhood with his hazel eyes, warm beige complexion and meticulously trimmed beard and mustache. He had always been fastidious with his grooming and lifted weights regularly to maintain a fit physique. He wore a formfitting gray sweater that looked molded to his muscles and denim jeans. He was as dashing as she remembered, her heart skipping a beat, or two, as she gawked.

His briefcase rested on the seat beside him, a pile of papers on the table that he was shifting awkwardly back and forth. His brow was furrowed, and he seemed completely lost in thought, oblivious to his surroundings. She glanced back toward the two men, shifting to put herself between them and their view of Paul. She bumped Jacob's shoulder, her voice dropping to a low whisper. "Do you know the two men at the bar?" she questioned.

"You mean the two *brutes* at the bar?" He shook his head. "No, and they feel like they might be a problem. You won't believe how they pushed their way in!" he said, squarely in his feelings about their interaction at the door.

Simone gave him a nod. "I thought so, too. It's why I called my brother and asked for a patrol car to come by and do a safety check. When the cops get here, point them in my direction. If those two do anything before they get here, just dial nine-one-one."

"Thank you," Jacob said, relief flooding his face.

They came to a stop at the edge of the table. Paul looked up, startled out of the trance he'd fallen into. He tossed Jacob a polite glance, then settled his gaze on Simone. His eyes widened, and joy shimmered in the light orbs.

"Simone, hey," he said, standing abruptly. He moved to wrap his arms around her, pulling her against him in a warm hug. He pressed his lips to her cheek, allowing them to linger there a second longer than necessary. His hold tightened, his arms like a cashmere blanket in a vise-like grip around her torso.

Simone felt her whole body welcoming him home as she hugged him back. "Hey," she answered, her voice a loud whisper.

Jacob dropped her menu to the table. "Thank you, again," he said before hurrying back to the front of the restaurant.

Paul finally let her go, a warm smile filling his face. "I appreciate you coming," he said.

"You said it was important."

Paul nodded as he gestured for her to take a seat. Sitting down, Simone stole another quick glance toward the bar. The two strangers were both staring blatantly, not bothering to hide their interest in the two of them.

Simone rested an elbow on the tabletop, turning flirtatiously toward Paul. "Do you know Tom and Jerry over there?" she asked softly. She reached a hand out, trailing her fingers against his arm.

Her touch proved just distracting enough to him that Paul didn't turn abruptly to stare back, drawing even more attention in their direction. His focus shifted slowly from her toward the duo at the bar. He eyed them briefly before turning his attention back to Simone. He shook his head. "Should I?"

"It might be nothing, but they seem very interested in you."

Paul's gaze danced back in their direction and he took a swift inhale of air. One of the men was on a cell phone and both were still eyeing him intently.

"We need to leave," he said, suddenly anxious. He began to gather his papers.

"What's going on, Paul?"

"I don't think we're safe, Simone."

"What do you mean we're not safe?" she snapped, her teeth clenched tightly. "Why are we not safe?"

"I'll explain, but I think we really need to leave."

Simone took a deep breath and held it, watching as he repacked his belongings into his briefcase.

"We're not going anywhere until you explain," she started and then a commotion at the door pulled at her attention. She turned to see two of her brothers, Parker and Armstrong, and two uniformed police officers standing at the entrance talking with Jacob. Their chatter carried through the room, the conversation casual. They all appeared to be old acquaintances greeting each other warmly.

The two strangers suddenly began eyeing each other nervously. Their earlier bravado seemed to be momentarily eliminated. Simone shot Paul a look but said nothing. They continued watching and another quick minute passed before the duo finally rose from where they sat at the bar and moved toward the exit door. Sighs of relief seemed to billow throughout the whole room.

The Black brothers were slowly moving toward their table, both eyeing the other two men as they passed each other. Parker acknowledged them with a nod of his head but there was no response. As the two men exited the building, the uniformed cops followed behind them.

Detective Armstrong Black greeted them with a wide grin. "Well, well, well. Isn't this a pleasant surprise!" he said. He extended his hand in greeting and the two men bumped shoulders. "How's it going, Paul?"

"It's good to see you, Armstrong."

Armstrong winked an eye at his baby sister. "Simone."

"Armstrong."

Parker shook his head as he leaned to kiss Simone's cheek. He and Paul shook hands. "Everyone okay?"

Simone nodded. "You two didn't need to come. You could have just sent a patrol car."

"We just wanted to make sure everything was good."

"You two just wanted to be nosey."

"That, too!" Parker said with a chuckle. His phone rang, pulling his attention as he stepped away to answer the call.

Armstrong took a seat at the table with them. "So, one of you want to tell me what's going on? Why the concern?"

Simone turned toward Paul, folding her arms over her chest. Raising her brows, she gave him a questioning look.

He heaved a deep sigh, closing his eyes for a split second. "I made a mistake. I should never have called Simone. I just…well…" He paused. Then shrugged, as if unable to find the worlds to answer the question being posed.

Simone rolled her eyes skyward. "It's nothing," she said. "Those two just looked sketchy and I didn't like how pushy they were being. I was worried that something might jump off and figured we were better safe than sorry."

Armstrong looked from one to the other, perhaps sensing a half-truth and a blatant lie being told. Before he could question them further, Parker rejoined the conversation.

"My guys ran their license plate. It's a rental car that came back to a man named Thomas Donald. That ring any bells?"

Paul and Simone both shook their heads.

Parker continued. "We didn't get a hit on anyone named Thomas Donald and we don't have any reason to hold either of them."

"What about the gun I saw?"

"He had a valid FOID."

"What's that?" Paul questioned. "FOID?"

"Firearm Owners Identification card. It makes it legal for him to carry a concealed weapon," Simone answered.

Parker nodded. "They're gone now, so I wouldn't be overly concerned. I think you may have just overreacted."

"Simone? Overreact? Not my little sister!" Armstrong said facetiously as he pressed his palm to his broad chest. "My little sister *never* overreacts!"

"Don't you two have someplace to be?" Simone said, annoyance painting her expression.

Armstrong shook his head. "Nope. We're officially off duty!"

Paul chuckled, a moment of amusement washing over him. It passed quickly but Simone was the only one who noticed. She met his eyes and held the gaze a second longer than necessary before turning back to her brothers.

"You're intruding on my date."

"So, it is a date?" Parker asked, his grin widening.

"Mom will be very excited. I can't wait to tell her," Armstrong added.

Paul laughed out loud. "How is your mom?"

Simone tossed him another look. "Please don't entertain them. If you talk to them, they won't go away. And they need to go away!" She looked from one brother to the other.

"My feelings are hurt, Simone!" Armstrong said. He pushed his full lips out in a full pout.

"Mine, too, but the hint is taken," Parker said. He rose from his seat, adjusting the jacket of his navy-blue suit.

"I need to get home anyway," Armstrong added. "I have a wife waiting for me!" He grinned smugly as he waved his ring finger, like they needed to be reminded that he was a newlywed, having recently married another detective on the Chicago police team.

Parker laughed. "I have someone waiting for me, too, but she's not a wife."

"Not yours anyway," Simone quipped.

Laughter rang around the table.

"It was good to see you guys again," Paul said, the trio shaking hands one last time.

"Good luck," Armstrong said, his voice dropping to a loud whisper. "She's still mean as hell!"

"I heard that!" Simone exclaimed, her eyes rolling skyward.

The brothers grinned, both leaning to kiss their sister's cheek one last time.

"Stay out of trouble, Simone," Parker said.

"Please," Armstrong echoed.

The couple watched as the two men strolled back toward the door, pausing briefly to chat with an elderly couple who sat near the front of the room.

"I see things haven't changed much," Paul said casually.

"You don't get to do that," Simone snapped. "You don't get to pretend nothing's wrong when clearly something's not right. Now spill it! Why did you call me? Why are we not safe, and who were those two men?"

Contrition furrowed Paul's brow. "I shouldn't have called you, Simone."

"But you did, so tell me why. What's going on, Paul?"

Jacob interrupted the conversation, dropping two drinks onto the table. "Courtesy of Captain Black," he said, smiling brightly.

Simone shook her head. "What is this?" The beverage was a beautiful shade of pink, topped with a fluff of cotton candy and skewered raspberries.

"We call it the Honeymoon Special."

Paul laughed again, relieving the tension between them. "Your brothers have a keen sense of humor."

"They really are not funny," Simone responded, though she felt the slightest smile pulling at her mouth.

"Are you ready to order?" Jacob asked.

"I think we're going to have to take it to go, Jacob," Paul said. "I hope that's not a problem."

"Not at all, Dr. Reilly. Your usual?"

"Yes, sir. The Bad Burger with a side of fries, please."

"I'll take the mac and cheese," Simone said. "Also to go."

"Yes, ma'am. I'll put that order in for you. And I'd like to throw in a dessert on the house. We have a spectacular carrot cake tonight. I'd also highly recommend the vanilla brownie."

"The carrot cake sounds good," Simone said. "Thank you, Jacob."

"And for you, Dr. Reilly?"

"Whatever the lady is having sounds good to me," Paul said.

"Two slices of carrot cake to go. I'll be back shortly with your food," Jacob said as he backed away from the table and headed toward the kitchen.

A pregnant pause bloomed full and thick between them. Simone stared, the look she was giving him so intense that Paul felt his stomach flip as the air was sucked from his lungs. She was even more stunning than he remembered, and he remembered everything about Simone.

Her hair had been freshly cut, her lush curls cropped short in a style that flattered her exquisite face. Chocolate-chip freckles danced across her nose and cheeks, complementing her warm copper complexion. Her dark eyes were large and bright and light shimmered in her stare. And she had the most perfect mouth, her full, luscious lips like plush pillows begging to be kissed. It took every ounce of fortitude he possessed not to lean over and capture her lips with his own. He took a deep breath and held it, hoping to stall the emotion that had swelled between them.

If anyone had asked, Paul would have had to admit to falling in love with Simone at first sight. She'd been the most beautiful woman he had ever seen as she had skipped across the university's quad. He'd stepped into her path and had introduced himself, asking for directions he hadn't needed. Simone had walked him to the destination, talking a mile a minute, which she later admitted had been to calm her nerves about a class that had her concerned. Their friendship had been like spun sugar: threads deeply entwined, intensely sweet and delicately fragile. Simone treaded cautiously, wherein he was always ready to take risks.

After spending a decade together, he had never imagined life without her until the day she'd told him to leave, unwilling to follow where he needed to go. He was still in shock, still hurt by the loss, still hoping for a reconciliation, even if he never said the words aloud. There was just something about the two of them together that worked, making it feel like all was well in the world, even when they were off-balance with each other.

He finally spoke, Simone still waiting patiently for him to say something. "I think Lender Pharmaceuticals is poisoning patients who are taking their drugs."

Simone blinked, her lashes fluttering as she processed the comment. "That's a serious accusation, Paul," she said finally.

He nodded. "I know, and I don't make it lightly, but I

believe that I have irrefutable proof that Lender Pharmaceuticals is purposely providing contaminated medications to doctors and medical facilities here in the United States and abroad."

Paul continued to explain. "I've been working in a clinic in Ghana. In Accra. It's not a large facility but it supports the local orphanages in the area and has been a refuge for the community. I have patients that I had treated for a measles-related virus on a previous trip who should have been well by now, but they're either still symptomatic, showing rapid deterioration or have succumbed to the illness. And not one or two patients, but dozens! The disease is spreading too quickly in communities that should be thriving when you consider the preventive and curative medications that Lender Pharmaceuticals has been providing. On this last trip I think I may have poked a bear by throwing accusing questions at them that the company wasn't expecting."

"What's the drug we're talking about?"

"It's a synthetic drug called Halphedrone-B, which is being used worldwide to treat patients with autoimmune diseases, most especially in impoverished communities, because allegedly Lender is practically selling it at cost. But I think it's the drug that's killing them."

"What kind of proof do you have?"

"The drugs. The patients. The fact that since I called BS on their products, I feel like someone wants to stop me from going public with the information."

"How? What's happened that you haven't told me?"

Paul took a deep breath. He hadn't given the series of mishaps while he'd been abroad any thought until he'd spoken with his brother. He'd experienced several minor accidents that could have been potentially devastating. There had been a car traveling too fast that had just missed hitting him, and a fire, the cause unknown and devastating the hut he'd been sleeping in. Lastly, the close encounter at the airport in Africa with a stranger he'd dismissed as mentally ill, a man swinging a machete haphazardly in his direction until security had taken him down. Considering all of it together, and now the two strangers who'd clearly had him in their sights, had him concerned.

When he finished detailing the incidents, Simone shook her head, the gesture slow and methodic. "What else?"

Paul took a deep breath and blew it past his full lips. "I overnighted blood and tissue samples, and drug samples to my brother. I asked him to run some tests for me. The samples have disappeared."

"Define *disappeared*."

"Someone took them. They knew he had them and they stole them right out of his lab."

"Do you think that someone is tracking you?"

"I don't know what to think, Simone. Hell, I'm not even sure what to do with what I do know."

"So, you called me?"

"I trust you."

There was a moment that passed between them as Simone remembered what that trust meant to them both. How important it had been to protect and nurture each other. To have complete and total faith in what they shared. She suddenly resisted the urge to wrap her arms around him, wanting to pull him close to tell him everything was going to be okay. To say it, even if she wasn't certain that it would.

"You probably shouldn't go back to your apartment. Not until we're sure it's safe. You can stay with me while we figure it out," she said instead.

"I need to go to the hospital. I need to follow up on patients I have here."

She started to argue and then she didn't. "I need to do some research. I also have a sorority sister at the FDA. I'll call her tomorrow to see if they have any open investigations against Lender. I hope you're wrong, Paul, but if you're not, I'll do whatever I can to help you take them down."

Paul reached for her hand, his palm sliding warmly against hers as he entwined her fingers between his own. For as much as he trusted her, he knew Simone trusted him, too. He'd spent most of his adult life assuring her that he would never walk her into trouble he couldn't get her out of, and until now, he'd been certain that he could do that. Now he had doubts and that uncertainty felt like a sledgehammer to his abdomen. "Thank you, but I don't want to drag you into this. Especially if it looks like it might get ugly."

"You should have thought about that *before* you called me."

"I honestly didn't think you'd come."

"You knew I'd come."

Paul held the look she was giving him. He didn't bother to acknowledge that she was right. Nor did he admit that he hadn't really thought it through. He knew he didn't need to tell her that he was suddenly feeling like he was out of his element, or that he was scared. But with her by his side, he had faith it would all work out. He didn't need to say it because Simone knew. She knew him better than anyone.

Minutes later he had paid for their meals and they were walking back up the block toward her car. Neither had spoken, nothing else needing to be said. Both had fallen into their own thoughts, planning what needed to come next, or not. Paul carried the bags of food and Simone had looped her arm through his, lightly clutching his elbow as she steadied herself on her high heels.

The car lock disengaged when Simone pressed her hand to the door latch. Paul opened her side door, closing it after she was settled in the driver's seat. He moved around the back of the vehicle to the passenger side, pausing to rest their dinners on the back seat. He had just opened his door when a gunshot rang loudly through the late-night air. The windowpane in the storefront behind him shattered, glass sounding like breaking chimes against the concrete sidewalk. The building's alarm rang loudly, the harsh tones loud enough to wake the dead. A second shot shattered the car's back window.

Panic hit Paul broadside, rising fear holding him hostage where he stood. He was discombobulated, but he ducked, his gaze sweeping the landscape for an explanation. Simone shouted, the words incoherent as she shifted the car into Reverse. Paul jumped awkwardly into the passenger seat as she pulled forward, grazing the bumper of the car parked in front of her. A few quick turns and they were driving seventy miles per hour on Highway 41 until both were certain they weren't being followed. When she finally slowed to the speed limit, Paul cussed, the profanity moving Simone to toss him a quick look.

"What now?" she asked.

"Whatever it takes," Paul answered, still trying to catch his breath. "We'll do whatever it takes to shut these bastards down.

Simone nodded. "Let's not get killed trying to do it."

Paul took a deep breath into his lungs and held it. His mind was racing, his thoughts a mishmash of questions with no answers. Confusion had settled deep into every crevice in his head; it felt like sludge was weighing down his thought process. "We should find somewhere to lay low," he said. "Until we can figure it all out."

"We can go back to my house..." Simone started.

"No. Now that they've seen us together, I don't trust that they won't find us there."

"Then we should go to the police station."

"Let's just get a hotel room. I don't think we should involve the police just yet."

"Someone shot at us, Paul! We need to file a report! My brothers need to know!"

"I know that, Simone! But I need to think this through. Please, just give me a minute to think!"

"We might not have a minute, Paul!" Simone's voice rose an octave and the tension between them suddenly increased ten-fold. Before either could blink, the conversation took a sharp left turn and they were yelling back and forth, each determined to prove a point when there was none. It was Bickering 101 and reminiscent of when their relationship had gone all kinds of wrong.

Chapter 2

The no-tell motel they'd found by the highway was fetid, reeking of debauchery and sin. The smell of cigarettes, marijuana, sex and body odor was pungent through the late-night air. Simone distorted her face with displeasure as Paul closed the door to room thirty-eight and tossed the key card on the laminated dresser. He sat down on the foot of the mattress beside her and exhaled his first sigh of relief since leaving the restaurant. Simone had finally stopped shaking and Paul felt like he could breathe normally again.

Neither spoke. Both were still reeling from the fight they'd had in the car. Simone had wanted them to drive straight to the police station. Paul had refused, insisting that it would only make things worse. He was adamant that they needed additional proof to substantiate his claims and the only way to get that was if no one knew where they were or what they were after. Simone knew her family wouldn't take them disappearing lightly and she trusted her brothers would look for them. They still hadn't come to an agreement. The argument had been contentious, the intensity of their emotions palpable.

"It doesn't make any sense," Simone finally said, breaking the silence. "No one we know would think our not going to the police is a smart thing to do." There was still an air of hostility in her tone.

And a hint of defiance in his as he responded. "No

one knows what we're up against. Even we don't know yet, Simone."

"Which is why going to the police would make sense. I know my brothers would back us up."

"I don't agree. All that's going to happen is that the police will dismiss my concerns because the proof I have is shaky at best. The preliminary test results Oliver sent me still need to be analyzed and there's more testing that needs to be done. Lender will be tipped off that we're on to them and we won't be able to prove what they're doing or stop them."

"In the movies when people don't go to the police, they die. They fall off cliffs, demons get them, all kinds of horrors," Simone said facetiously.

"In the movies I've seen the police get it, too."

"You're watching the wrong movies."

"You watch too many."

Simone tossed up her hands in frustration. "I'm an officer of the court, Paul! I have a responsibility to uphold the law. I have a damn badge, for heaven's sake!"

Paul cut his gaze in her direction, a smile pulling at his mouth. "Why do they issue you a badge anyway? You're a prosecutor."

Simone shifted her body, turning to stare at him. "Are you making fun of my badge?"

"I just asked the question!"

Her tone was laced with attitude. "It makes me official. It says that I represent the courts of the state and that I took the Attorney's Oath and I've promised to honor its tenets. Don't you dare make light of what I do, Paul Reilly. It's as important to me as the Hippocratic Oath that you doctors take."

"I'm not, Simone. I was just curious about the badge. They don't give us doctors one."

"No, they give you those white jackets with your names embroidered over the breast pockets. Same thing, different medium."

"I cannot believe we're sitting here arguing over a tin emblem." He lay backward on the bed, pulling his arms over his head.

"We're arguing about involving the police. Don't change the subject."

Paul blew a soft sigh as another wave of silence swept between them. Both sat listening instead to the noise in the room. An alarm clocked ticked loudly from the nightstand next to the bed and water leaked from the faucet in the bathroom. There was a steady rhythm of clicks and plops, both just loud enough to be annoying. Minutes passed before he spoke again. "I'll do whatever you think is best, Simone."

"You will?"

"Yeah," he mumbled as he folded an arm over his eyes.

She nodded. "I'll call my brother. We need to at least tell him that we're safe. We can also tell him what we know in an unofficial capacity. If they can help work it from their end, it can't hurt. Until we figure out what the hell we're doing, we can use all the help we can get."

"Okay."

"Okay? Really?"

"Yeah, baby, okay."

A noise outside the door pulled Simone upright. "Did you hear that?"

Paul mumbled, "No. I didn't hear anything."

Simone stood and moved to the window to peer through the blinds. Outside, three working women were gathered in the parking lot changing their clothes. Bare asses and boobs were on full display and no one seemed to be concerned. Laughter rang through the late-night air, their good time fueled by the bottle of booze being passed between them. Simone exhaled, turning back toward the bed. "I don't know if I can stay here..." she started.

The rest of her comment stalled in midair, warm breath the slightest whistle past her lips. Paul had fallen into a deep sleep, jet lag and exhaustion fully claiming him. He snored softly and for a quick moment Simone realized just how much she missed hearing him beside her at night.

Shaking the thought, she grabbed her cell phone from her purse and her food from the meal bag. She took a seat on a cushioned chair in front of the small desk and dialed Parker's number. As she waited for someone to answer, she took the first bite of her macaroni and cheese.

"Where are you?" Parker questioned. "I'm sending a patrol car."

"We're fine, big brother. You just needed to know what happened. I also took the bumper off some guy's car, I think. You'll handle that for me, too, right?"

"If they knew Paul was at that restaurant, they're probably tracking his cell phone. They may even be tracking yours."

"We thought that, too, so we tossed the sim card in his phone and powered it off. I'm using my other phone. The one that's in mom's name. My primary phone was dead, so I left it at the house on the charger."

"You need to come in, Simone. Until we figure out who shot at you, we can't trust that either of you is safe."

"We can't, Parker. Paul truly believes this company is killing patients and he's determined to stop them. If we come in, we might lose our window of opportunity to prove his theory."

"I wasn't asking, Simone. That was an order."

"I stopped taking orders from you when I was ten."

"Then I'm calling Mom and Dad."

"Don't you dare! I just need you to trust me."

Parker yelled, "You don't know what the hell you're doing! Neither of you has a clue what you've gotten yourselves into! Now, where are you?"

Simone sighed. "I love you. And I'll be okay. I promise."

"Don't you dare hang…"

Simone disconnected the call abruptly. She took another bite of macaroni and sat in reflection as she polished off the last of her meal. She didn't have the words to explain to her brother what she was feeling or why they were suddenly acting like fugitives. She honestly wasn't sure what the hell they were doing. But they were together and she instinctively wanted to do whatever necessary to support Paul. He needed her and it had been forever since she'd felt like she added value to his life. Wanting each other had never been the problem between them. Needing each other, and admitting to it, had been a whole other animal neither had been willing to claim. But now necessity had put them together, if for nothing more than to hold on to each other for emotional support, and Simone had no intentions of failing him.

Paul was now snoring loudly, and she instinctively knew that it had been days since he'd last rested well. She was reminded of those days after medical school, during his residency, when his shifts at the hospital seemed to last for days before he was able to come home and fall out from exhaustion.

She dropped her fork and empty container back into the bag. After reaching for her phone she dialed again.

Her brother Mingus Black answered on the second ring. "What's wrong, Simone? And why is Parker texting me to ask where you are?"

"I need you. I'm at the Karavan Motel on Cicero Avenue."

"Karavan? On the South Side? What the hell are you doing there?"

"Someone tried to kill us tonight," she said, explaining all that had happened since Paul Reilly had called her.

"So, you two check into the city's seediest motel?"

"We're not planning to stay, and they take cash," she continued, hoping to rationalize why the no-tell motel had been a good idea and why Paul felt going to the police was not. Even after saying it out loud Simone knew it sounded like she and Paul had lost their collective minds. And she definitely couldn't tell any of them that she just needed to be with Paul because she had missed him terribly.

Mingus listened, taking it all in. A private detective by profession, he heard his sister's dilemma with a different ear than their police officer brother. He didn't yell or give her orders he knew she wouldn't heed like Parker did. Instead, when she was done talking, Mingus said, "Sit tight. I need to put some things in place. I'll be there before breakfast tomorrow. Are you carrying?"

"Yes," she said, taking a moment to check the weapon in her handbag. The Glock 43 had been a gift from her father, the patriarch ensuring she and her sister both knew how to handle a firearm just as well as their brothers. Regular visits to the gun range kept her shooting and safety skills honed.

"Keep it close, and if you need to use it, don't hesitate to pull the trigger. You can always ask questions later."

"What are you going to tell Parker?"

"That I didn't put your leash on you this morning. That he should check with whoever did."

"Thank you," Simone responded, chuckling softly.

"Get some rest. I'm sure you're going to need it," Mingus concluded.

After disconnecting the call, Simone moved back to the bed and kicked off her heels. Laying her body beside Paul's, she eased an arm around his waist and shifted herself close against him. She nuzzled her nose against his back, inhaling the scent of his cologne. The familiar fragrance reminded her of their last trip together, a two-week excursion on the island of Jamaica. They had walked hand in hand along the beaches of Negril, had swum beneath the cascading waters of Gully Falls, and had danced under a full moon in Montego Bay. They'd fallen asleep in each other's arms and woken each morning making love. It had been as magical as any holiday getaway could possibly be. Weeks later, they were no longer a couple, barely talking to each other about the weather.

Taking deep breaths to calm her nerves, Simone closed her eyes and settled into his body heat. She couldn't begin to know what he had gotten her into and despite trusting that Paul would have never purposely put her in harm's way, running from gunfire added a whole other dynamic to his situation. The nearness of him only put her slightly at ease, not enough that she could fully relax.

Sleep didn't come as quickly for Simone as she lay listening to the occasional sound outside the door and the steady rhythm of Paul's heavy snores. Simone hated showing any vulnerability, but she was scared. This was bad and had the potential to get worse.

Her mind continued to race as she thought about what she might need to do to help her friend. Thinking how much she had missed him when he'd been gone and being grateful to have him back, even under the dire circumstances they found themselves trapped in. Wondering if she should heed Parker's advice and run for the security of the police department and shelter with her law-abiding family. Her father was, after all, Jerome Black, the Superintendent of Police, leading the entire Chicago Police Department. Her mother, Judith Harmon Black, was a federal court judge, and both were well respected in Chicago's judicial system. With two brothers on the police force, another who was an attorney in private practice, the baby boy in the family a city alderman, her favorite sibling a private investigator, and her only sister front and center in state politics, law-abiding protection was a given.

Despite her best efforts she couldn't turn her brain off. For another two hours she lay pressed against his back, not wanting to disturb his rest and needing him near, even if they weren't a couple anymore. Thinking about the past and the present, Simone's thoughts ran the gamut from sane to senseless until sleep finally slipped in and delivered her from her misery.

Chapter 3

Outside, the morning sun was just beginning to rise. Paul stood at the foot of the bed staring down at Simone's sleeping form. Fully clothed, she was curled in a fetal position around a pillow. Her mouth was open, low gasps expelled from her lush lips. Her freckles were like stardust across her nose and her skin shimmered under a layer of light perspiration. Simone was a beautiful woman, but there was something about her when she slumbered, where she seemed most angelic and at peace. In those moments her beauty was extraordinary, leaving him to wonder what he had done to get so lucky.

In that moment though, he was wondering what he needed to do to ensure she was protected. How to get her, and himself, out of the mess he'd pulled them into. He sighed, feeling as if things might implode if he didn't tread cautiously. But he had neither the time or the wherewithal to play nice with Lender Pharmaceuticals.

The knock on the door pulled him from his reverie and startled Simone out of a deep sleep. She sat upright, clutching at the well-worn spread atop the bed. Bewilderment furrowed her brow. Rubbing the sleep from her eyes, she threw her legs off the side of the bed as Paul moved to look out the window. He heaved a deep sigh as he sidestepped to the door and opened it, greeting Simone's brother Mingus. The two men embraced like old friends, an exchange of shoulders bumping and chests grazing.

"You two good?" Mingus questioned as he entered the room, carrying two large duffel bags over his shoulder and a tray of coffees from Starbucks.

"No," Simone muttered as she flipped her hand at him. "I need to pee, and I want a shower."

Mingus and Paul exchanged a look, both smirking slightly. Her brother shook his head at her as he extended the duffel bag in her direction.

"Well, I brought you some things from your house. Clothes, your toothbrush…"

"My toothbrush!" she exclaimed, jumping up and down like a four-year-old. "I love you, big brother!"

Mingus laughed. "Until you see what I packed for you. Knowing you, I'm sure it's all wrong."

"As long as you brought me clean panties, I'll be a very happy woman."

"Panties? Ohhh…well… I didn't…"

Simone's eyes widened, a hint of saline suddenly pressing against her thick lashes. "Please, don't tell me you didn't get me any clean underwear. How could you not think to pack me clean underwear? I can't believe you…"

Mingus held up his hand to stall the rant he knew was coming. He winked an eye at her. "Vaughan packed clothes for you. I'm sure you're good."

Relief flooded Simone's expression. "You talked to my sister?"

"She had the spare key to your town house."

Simone nodded. "Excuse me, please, while I go freshen up."

Mingus dropped to the chair, his clasped hands resting in his lap as he gave Paul a look. "Don't rush," he said.

Simone looked from one man to the other and back, then rolled her eyes skyward. "Don't hurt him, Mingus."

Mingus narrowed his gaze and pushed his shoulders skyward. "No promises."

Paul chuckled, dropping his large frame to the bedside. He clasped his own hands together in front of his face as he rested his elbows on his thighs.

She gave them both another look, then moved into the bathroom, shutting the door behind her. "You two work it out," she muttered under her breath. "Not my problem." The pipes rattled loudly as the shower was turned on in the other room. When the rain of water sounded steadily on the other side of the door, both men shifted forward to stare at each other.

"I talked to your brother. He packed that other bag for you. He said to tell you he's headed north to lie low for a few days. That you would know where to find him. He doesn't like how folks are looking at him. He also said he has enough equipment there if you need it. He said you knew what that meant, too."

Paul nodded. "Did he tell you where *north* was?"

"No, and I don't want to know. And, if that's where you're planning to go, you don't need to tell Simone until after you get there."

"I don't know if I can keep her safe, Mingus."

"You better," the other man said with conviction. "She's already a target. They know she's connected to you. If they can't get to you through regular channels, they'll get to you through her. I know I would."

Like all the members of the Black family, Mingus was just as dedicated to the municipality. But he usually worked alone, sometimes in the dregs of the community, beneath the cover of darkness, getting his hands dirty. He sometimes did what others weren't willing to do and he did it exceptionally well. Paul had no doubts he knew what he was talking about.

"I need to go to the hospital. I have patients there I need to check on. I also need to get my hands on some of my files and maybe a new sample or two."

"I don't think that's a good idea."

"I don't have a choice. I have to go, but I'm not taking Simone with me. She can stay here until I get back."

"*If* you get back."

"Such faith!"

"In my line of business, we deal in facts, not faith. And the fact is someone is gunning for you. And maybe it's because you know something about that pharmaceutical company that they don't want you to know. Or maybe not. For all I know, it could be a spurned lover out for revenge."

"Your sister had an alibi. She was with me, so she didn't have a reason to try and kill me."

Mingus chuckled. "Touché!"

Paul sighed. "I need to print the emails my brother sent me so I can study the results from the tests he was able to run. I'll swing by a FedEx office first and then head over to the hospital. I'll be in and out in thirty minutes. Forty-five max. Then Simone and I'll get on the road."

"The print shop is going to want a credit card. Go here," Mingus said, jotting an address down on the hotel notepad that rested on the desk. "Ask for Liza. Tell her I sent you. She'll print whatever you need. You can also use her computers. She can back-door you into any system you need to get into. Tell her what you need, and she'll find it for you."

"And she can be trusted?"

Mingus shot him a narrowed look but didn't bother to answer. Instead, he passed him a set of keys. "I'll take Simone's car," he said. "There's a black BMW parked outside beside it. The registration won't come back to either of you. If you get stopped, the car belongs to Black

Investigative Services. Tell them to call and I'll confirm you're authorized to be driving it. But don't get stopped. I did a little digging last night and the men at the restaurant were a professional team. They didn't miss by accident. They wanted to scare you, not kill you. But if they had wanted you dead, you would be."

The sound of the shower suddenly came to an abrupt halt, Simone cursing loudly about there being no more hot water. The two men exchanged a look and shook their heads.

Mingus continued, "Lender Pharmaceuticals has deep pockets. They can afford to pay well to silence you. If you keep digging and they get pissed off enough, whomever comes next might not miss."

Paul rose from his seat and Mingus stood with him. Both stole glances at their wristwatches.

"One hour," Mingus said. "Go to the hospital. Get in, get what you need and get out. Simone and I'll meet you at that address I gave you in one hour. Then you two need to put some distance between you and Chicago."

Paul nodded and the two men shook hands. "Thank you," he said. "I really appreciate your help."

Mingus chuckled. "Don't thank me. Thank the nuisance in there. If she didn't love you, I'd kick your ass for getting her in this mess. I still might. No telling about me!"

Paul hesitated as he pondered Mingus's comment, wondering if it were possible that Simone did still love him. If they might be more than old friends. If when all of this was finished, Simone would still find favor with him. He suddenly wanted it more than he'd ever admitted to himself previously. He felt a mist of saline press hard against his lashes and he swiped at his eyes with the back of his hand.

Paul gave Mingus a wry smile and then he turned to leave, his hand on the doorknob. For a split second he thought about telling Simone goodbye. Just in case they didn't make it back to each other. Then he reasoned there was no point in tempting fate.

He turned back to face Simone's brother. "I really love your sister. I hope you know that. I never meant for any of this to happen," he said.

"Yeah, I know," Mingus replied. "We all do."

Paul spun back toward the exit, then he stepped out into the early morning chill, closing the door behind him.

Chapter 4

It was the new day shift change, the hospital employees focused on updates about patients and not on him. Paul managed to enter the building and make his way to his office with only two nods of his head and one *good morning* to an elderly man rolling his way down the corridor in a wheelchair. Paul stole a quick glance out the glass partition before closing the blinds.

There were manila folders resting on the center of his desk and a boatload of pink message slips. He didn't bother to look at either pile, instead reaching to unlock the bottom drawer with the smallest key on his key ring. At first glance, it appeared that the drawer held indexed files and nothing more. What Paul was after was duct-taped to the underside of the inner drawer. He pulled the flash drive from its hiding spot and slid it into the back pocket of his denim jeans.

Just as he relocked the drawer, after pausing to grab his calendar from the desktop and sliding it into his briefcase, there was a knock on the door. Paul froze, his eyes skating from side to side. There was a second knock, someone calling his name. He took a deep breath and held it as he considered his options.

Paul secured the zipper on the briefcase and rested it in the seat of the chair. He moved from behind the desk to the door and pulled it open. The voice that greeted him was overly exuberant for such an early morning hour.

"Dr. Reilly! You're back!" The nurse standing before him looked relieved. "Kelly said she thought someone was in here, but she wasn't sure. I wanted to make sure we didn't have another intruder."

"Good morning, Grace. *Another* intruder?"

She nodded. "Someone was in here yesterday, rifling through the files on top of your desk. We called security but by the time they got here, the men were gone."

"Men? There were more than one?"

"There were two men actually. Both white, dark hair, wearing dark suits," she said.

Paul nodded his head slowly. "Do you know what they were looking for?"

"No, sir. I checked everything afterward and nothing was missing. All the files there for you were exactly as you left them. They made a mess, but they didn't take anything. At least I don't think they did."

Paul paused in reflection. He had a good idea who'd been there and what they were after. He also knew that the flash drive was now in his possession and he needed to ensure it stayed with him. He gave his nurse a slight smile. "Well, I'm glad it wasn't more serious, and I appreciate you looking out for me, Grace. Actually, I was just headed out the door. I only stopped in to check on a few of my patients. I'm not officially back for another week."

"Well, we can't wait to have you back with us."

"How are you doing?"

"I'm good. It's been busy around here. We've been short staffed, so you've really been missed. You're one of the only doctors who'll roll up his sleeves to pitch in and help out."

Paul smiled. "I appreciate that."

Grace took a deep inhale of air. "Did you hear about the Lukas kid?"

"David Lukas?"

She nodded. "Poor little thing died last week. We were all heartbroken. Parents brought him into the emergency room suffering from seizures. He didn't recover."

There was a moment of pause as Paul took a deep breath and held it, his eyes closed as he recalled the youngster who had touched the hearts of everyone who knew him. The child had been six years old when he'd first been admitted. His symptoms had mimicked those of influenza, hepatitis and yellow fever. Weeks of testing hadn't been able to find a cause for his symptoms until Paul and his medical team discovered the child had been away on a tropical holiday twelve months earlier. Paul had ordered another round of tests and little David had been diagnosed with malaria. The rashes, high fevers, anemia and subsequent seizures had been consistent with the disease, but the parasites had been missed in the initial testing due to malaria's rarity in the United States.

The treatment plan and prescribed drugs Paul had ordered should have had him back to climbing trees and playing games with his little friends. Learning that the child had died felt like a punch to his gut. The antimalarial drugs sold by Lender Pharmaceuticals were used worldwide and Paul had been confident about their capabilities before he'd learned of Lender's duplicity. Now, that baby was dead, and the guilt was suddenly consuming. Paul no longer had any confidence in any product with the Lender name attached to it.

He opened his eyes and took a second breath. "Did they do an autopsy?"

"The official ruling was complications from pneumonia. I can get you a copy of the autopsy report if you'd like me to."

"I'd really appreciate that. He was doing better when I left. I need to know what happened."

"I understand completely. Dr. Hayes was attending when he was admitted. He may be able to answer some of your questions, as well. Would you like me to see if he's in yet?"

Paul shook his head. "Don't worry yourself. I'll run down to the morgue and see what I can find out myself. I appreciate your help, though."

The iPhone that rested on the woman's hip suddenly chimed. "Duty calls," she said as she reached for the device.

Paul smiled. "Don't let me keep you from your rounds."

"It was good to see you, Dr. Reilly," she said as she exited the room to answer the call.

"It was good to see you, too, Grace."

Paul moved back to the desk to claim his briefcase. He exited the office, locked it behind him and headed down the corridor. Grace had been called into a patient's room and she waved one last time as he passed by the door.

As he neared the nurses' station Paul saw them before they saw him. The two men from the night before stood with a hospital administrator, questioning one of the staff members. He made an abrupt turn as he heard them speak his name, asking about his whereabouts. As he made it to the opposite end of the hallway and turned toward the stairs, they spied him, the administrator pointing in his direction.

Without giving it an ounce of thought, Paul took off running, descending three flights of stairs and tearing out a side door, through the emergency room bay, to the car parked in the back lot. As he pulled the vehicle onto the main road, the two men stood outside the hospital building, spinning in circles as they tried to figure out where he'd disappeared to. Paul kept driving, not bothering to give a second look behind him.

Simone stepped out of the bathroom. She was drying her damp hair with a thin white towel. Her brother was on his phone, texting intently as he sat waiting for her.

"Where's Paul?" she questioned as she moved to the window. She pushed the drapes aside to peer out at the parking lot.

"Hospital," Mingus answered, never lifting his eyes from his cell phone screen.

She blinked. "Why didn't you stop him?"

"Why didn't you?"

She winced, her hands falling to her hips. "If I'd known he planned to leave, I would have."

Her brother shrugged his broad shoulders, his gaze still focused on his phone. "He said he had patients to see."

"And you didn't think that might be a problem?"

"Should it be?"

"Uhhh, maybe? Or did you forget someone was shooting at us last night?" she quipped.

Mingus finally lifted his eyes to give her a quick look. "It's doubtful anyone will take a shot at him in broad daylight," he said.

"And you know this how?"

"I don't really. It's just a hunch," Mingus said as he slid his cell phone into the inside pocket of his leather jacket. He changed the subject. "You need to finish getting dressed. We need to meet your boyfriend in forty-five minutes."

"Meet him where?"

"You sure do ask a lot of questions, Simone! Can you just get ready to leave, please?"

"I ask questions because I need answers and you're not telling me anything."

Mingus blew air past his full lips. "You two need to get out of Chicago. I don't know where you're going, and it's best no one knows, but I trust Paul is going to keep you safe. Now, let's get moving, please. You need to call your job so they're not looking for you. And, you need to call our mother. Tell her Paul is taking you away for a few days to reconcile. I'm sure she'll be very excited! Throw something in there about grandbabies and she won't worry about you for at least a month!"

A wave of panic hit Simone like a gut punch to her midsection. She and Paul were leaving Chicago and the uncertainty of what lay ahead for them suddenly felt daunting. She had a lengthy list of what-ifs and no sustainable answers about the future filling her head and she knew it showed in the angst-filled expression on her face. Her brother picking at her didn't help the situation.

"Talk about planning a wedding and that might buy you two months of freedom from parental interference," Mingus was saying.

Simone's lips twisted and turned, her face burning hot with annoyance. She shook her index finger at her brother. "I really don't like you," she said as she shuffled back in the direction of the bathroom.

Mingus laughed. "I love you, too, Simone. You're the best little sister in the whole wide world."

"And don't you forget it," Simone muttered as she slammed the bathroom door closed after her.

Paul's mind was racing as he searched out a parking space in the West Loop neighborhood. His anxiety level was at an all-time high and he took two deep breaths to calm his nerves. After shutting down the engine of the luxury vehicle, he checked and then double-checked the address Mingus had given him before stepping out of the car.

Paul paused at the chain-link fence that bordered the property. He looked left and then right, assessing his surroundings before he stepped through the latched gate, then reclosed it behind him. He took the steps two at a time and depressed the doorbell. As he waited, he paced, his eyes darting back and forth across the landscape.

The elderly woman who answered the door eyed him with reservation. "What'cha want, baby?"

"Good morning, ma'am. I'm here to see Liza? My name's Paul Reilly. Mingus Black sent me."

The woman didn't respond, still staring at him intently. She was petite in stature, wearing a floral housecoat and a full-length apron that stopped below her knees. There was a dishcloth in her hand and a light brush of white flour dusting her chubby cheek. Her gaze swept over him, running the length of his body from head to toe. After sizing him up she finally unlocked the door and pushed it open to allow him entry.

"Come on in, baby. I'm Pearl Hill but e'erybody calls me Mama. You want somethin' to eat? I got a pan of biscuits 'bout to come out the oven. I got some fatback and bacon, too, but Liza don't eat no meat. You ain't one of them vegans, too, are you?" she asked, her words laced with a Southern drawl and coming in what sounded like one long, drawn-out sentence before she took another breath.

Paul smiled. "No, thank you, ma'am. I'm good."

She sized him up a second time. "You know you hungry," she said with an air of finality. "I'm gon' make you a plate." She pointed down a flight of stairs. "Liza's down in the basement. She's expecting you."

Paul nodded as she continued toward the back of the home and the kitchen. The stately greystone, an architectural staple in Chicago since the 1890s, was built from Bedford limestone and named for its color. It was oversize, the craftsmanship evident in the exterior detail. The interior of the duplex featured wide-plank oak flooring, high ceilings and an abundance of natural light. Moving down the steps Paul discovered the lower-level bonus room with walls of computer screens and a young woman who looked like a bag of Skittles candy had exploded over her.

Liza was very young. Much younger than he'd expected, and he hadn't known what he might have been walking into. Her royal blue hair had a streak of white in the front that was swept across her brow and was pulled into a high ponytail adorned with a barrette of yellow flowers. She wore an orange, yellow and pink tie-dyed sweat suit with red Converse sneakers. She was the Rainbow Brite character on steroids, and she made Paul smile.

"Hey! Mingus didn't come with you?" she said, her hands coming to an abrupt halt atop the keyboard she was typing on.

Paul shook his head. He couldn't help but wonder what she did for Mingus and how they knew each other. "No," he answered, "but I think he's coming."

She shrugged and resumed her typing. "Mama Hill's going to be pissed. She's up there cooking bacon for him right now and she knows how much I hate the smell of pig cooking in the kitchen. He better come."

"He…well…it's…"

"No worries. We'll see him when we see him. Until then though, you'll have to eat the bacon."

Paul took two steps forward. "Is Mama Hill your grandmother?"

Liza shot him a look. "She's everyone's grandmother. So, what do you need?"

"I just have messages on my phone that I need to print out."

Liza gestured for him to take a seat beside her. "What's your email address?" she asked.

Paul reached for his phone, stopping when she asked him again.

"I just need your email address, not your phone." She pushed a pad of paper and an ink pen toward him.

After writing down his personal email address, Paul pushed the pad back to her. "I just need any messages that might have come in the last three days," he said softly.

A few short minutes later paper was spewing from a Xerox multifunction printer in the corner of the room. Liza gestured with her head, pointing him toward the ream of documents filling the output tray.

"So, you're a hacker," Paul said as he began sorting through the papers for those he needed and the ones he didn't.

"I prefer 'skilled computer expert.'"

"You just look so young."

Her brows raised but she didn't look in his direction, studying the screen before her instead. "I'm older than you think," she muttered.

"Can you get into anyone's computer system?"

"What do you need?"

"Everything you can get on a company called Lender Pharmaceuticals and what they have on a drug called Halphedrone-B. Not sure where you'd look, but maybe start in their research and development department? Maybe any communications about the drug between their management team?"

Liza typed, her head shifting from side to side as data

filled the two screens on the desktop and then more information began to cover the larger screens on the walls. Liza stopped typing and stared from one screen to another, deciphering code that looked like a foreign language to Paul.

He was impressed with Liza's expertise as he watched pages of emails and reports begin to fill the computer screens and he wasn't sure why because what they were doing was highly illegal. If he didn't already have enough problems, this might top his list and send him straight to prison. But curiosity had gotten the better of him. And Simone wasn't there to play devil's advocate and make him change his mind about asking for the information. He knew Simone would not be pleased, and he was sure she'd have his head when she found out. He took a deep breath as he imagined the choice words she would spew.

"This may take a minute," Liza said finally, pulling at his attention. "They have some serious firewalls up to keep people like me out."

"But you can get in without them knowing?"

She gave him a look, her expression twisted with evident annoyance at his question. "Go eat some bacon. I'll call you if I need you." She reached for a remote that rested on the table and music suddenly filled the room. It was something classical, a poetic blend of flutes, violins and a piano. She threw him one last glance as she turned the volume up high, then she resumed typing, her blue hair swaying with the music.

Upstairs, Mama Hill had set the kitchen table with five places. A feast for twenty sat table center. There was a platter of hot biscuits, crispy bacon, buttered grits, blueberry muffins, scrambled eggs, a bowl of sliced fruit and a pitcher of freshly squeezed orange juice.

The old woman winked an eye at him as he entered

the room and pointed him to the chair. She stood at the stove, stirring something in a large cast-iron pot. The aroma wafting around the room was mouthwatering and a hunger pang rippled through his midsection. Paul stole a quick glance toward his wristwatch, noting the time he was quickly running out of. Wondering if Simone was on her way, or if perhaps she'd changed her mind.

"Sit!" Mama Hill snapped, seeming to read his mind. Her dark eyes narrowed slightly. "You need to eat!" She stopped stirring the pot she was standing over. "Answer the door first, though. Make yourself useful."

Paul hesitated for a moment, then turned on his heel. He hadn't heard the doorbell, but the look the old woman threw in his direction had him thinking there might be a problem if he protested. He made his way back to the front of the home and pulled open the door. Simone and Mingus stood on the front porch. As Mingus brushed past him, entering the living space, he rolled his eyes skyward. Paul instinctively knew Simone was not a happy camper. He didn't know if he should be scared or not, but the sight of her instantly calmed his nerves.

"Hey," he said, greeting her softly.

When Simone didn't respond, instead giving him a dirty look before she followed her brother, Paul figured it probably wasn't a good time to tell her about the two strangers being at the hospital. Laughter suddenly rang loudly from the kitchen, the matriarch in high spirits as she greeted Mingus. Paul blew a soft sigh. He closed and locked the door and moved back toward the kitchen.

Mingus was making introductions. "Mama Hill, this is my baby sister Simone. Simone, this is Mrs. Pearl Hill, but everyone calls her Mama. Mama has helped me out with a few cases in the past."

Mama Hill pulled Simone into a warm hug. "Any family of Mingus's is family here. Y'all sit down. We was just 'bout to have us some breakfast." She pointed them toward the table.

"It smells good, Mama. And you made your special candied bacon!" Mingus chimed as he pulled out a chair at the head of the table and sat down.

The older woman grinned, her toothy smile gleaming under the morning light. "Made it just for you. I know how much you like my bacon."

Simone looked all kinds of confused as she sat down next to her brother. She clearly had questions, but she sensed she needed to wait before asking. She was also tense, her nerves feeling like she might explode. She was angry at Paul and relieved and all she wanted was to throw herself into his arms and then slap his face for making her worry.

For the briefest moment she stared in Paul's direction, then snatched her eyes away when he sat down and stared back. There was a hint of relief in her gaze and then that sliver of anger revved back up to full throttle. Paul smiled, vaguely amused by the wealth of emotion she was struggling to contain. Mama Hill suddenly tapped him against the back of his head, snapping him back to attention.

"Ouch!" he exclaimed as he reached to rub the offending bruise.

Simone and Mingus both laughed.

"Mama was asking you a question," Mingus said.

"Sorry," Paul responded. "I wasn't paying attention, Mama Hill. What were you saying?"

The old woman chuckled, her head shaking from side to side. "Liza is calling for you. She needs you to come downstairs."

"Who's Liza?" Simone suddenly questioned, giving him another look.

Mingus grinned, eyeing him with a raised brow.

Paul shook his head, looking slightly flustered by the sliver of jealousy that blew over her spirit. "She's a friend of your brother's. She's helping us out."

Mama Hill looked from him to Simone and back. "Take Simone downstairs with you and introduce her. Then the three of you come back up dem stairs and get you some breakfast. Tell Liza Mingus is here."

Paul nodded. "Yes, ma'am."

Simone sat for a second too long before the older woman admonished them both. "Y'all ain't got all day now!"

Mingus laughed, a deep belly guffaw that made Simone shift her annoyance in his direction as she stood and followed Paul to the basement.

Chapter 5

"**D**ude! Did you know that the pharmaceutical industry raised prices on thousands of drugs this year? Including medications to treat arthritis, high blood pressure and diabetes? Some of these guys hauled in over $25 billion in profits last year. That's some serious price gouging!" Liza looked astonished as Paul and Simone went downstairs.

Paul nodded. "Americans routinely pay more for prescription drugs that are just a fraction of the cost in other countries. The bigger question is why we're the only industrialized nation that allows pharmaceutical executives to raise prices with zero consideration for public health."

Liza pointed her index finger at him. "This really is some shysty mess!" She shifted her gaze toward Simone. "Who are you?"

Paul tossed a look over his shoulder. "Liza, this is Simone. Simone, this is Liza, Mingus's friend." He emphasized the word *friend* so there was no doubt in Simone's mind about his association with the young woman.

"You a friend of Mingus's, too?" Liza questioned.

"Mingus is my brother. He's upstairs, by the way. He got distracted by the food."

Liza's excitement shimmered across her face. "Cool beans! It's nice to meet you."

"It's nice to meet you, too," Simone said, her eyes sweeping the room and taking in all the technology in the space.

Paul could see the questions that caused her brow to furrow. "Liza is trying to find some information for me."

"I see. And how many laws are we breaking right now?"

"You really don't want to know," Liza answered, shooting her another look.

"Were you able to find anything?" Paul asked.

Liza pointed to the printer. "You know none of this is admissible in a court of law, right?"

Paul nodded, moving swiftly to the stack of paper spilling out of the machine.

Liza stood. "The CEO of Lender Pharmaceuticals is a freak, too. He has all kinds of porn on his computer."

"Porn?" Simone questioned. "What kind of porn?"

"Golden showers seem to be his perversion of choice. Some real nasty stuff. But his emails make for interesting reading." She suddenly jumped up excitedly. "And do you know that if he leaves the company his severance package will pay him over eighty million dollars? How crazy is that mess!"

Paul was shifting through the printed documents, having barely heard Liza's last comments. His focus was singular, his attention distracted. He was surprised by the volume of information Liza had managed to obtain and a lab report had him crunching data in his head.

Liza shrugged her shoulders and headed for the stairs. Simone started to follow but Paul suddenly called her name, looking up abruptly from the documents he was reading. She turned around to see what he needed.

Paul was staring at her intently, emotion flooding his face as he struggled with how to make things right between them. How to assuage her anger and get her to understand how much he appreciated her help. He was searching for the right words and struggled with finding them. How best to give her an out before they were both too deep in the midst of it to find their way out.

"Yes?"

"I would understand if this is too much for you to handle. If you didn't want to see this through with me."

Simone bit down against her bottom lip, twisting her hands together anxiously. "Does that mean you don't want me to help?"

"It means I understand if you think it's too much for you to handle."

She gave him a nod and turned, her hand on the railing. He called after her a second time.

"Simone?"

She took a deep breath before turning back a second time, her brow raised ever so slightly. Her tone was soft, just a hint above a whisper. "Yes, Paul?"

"I still love you. I never stopped. I don't know what may happen, but I needed you to know that."

When Paul admitted his love for her, time seemed to come to an abrupt halt, the minute hand on every clock stalling. Words caught in Simone's chest, a wealth of emotion smothering her thoughts. They stood staring at each other, something shifting in their relationship that clearly neither had anticipated. Unable to find the words to respond, Simone could only give him a nod of her head and then she turned, almost running back up the stairs.

Hearing his declaration had been everything Simone had wanted. He still loved her. He had never stopped. Despite the time that had separated them, they had slid back into sync with each other and all she needed to do was say the words back. He needed to know she felt the same way, and she needed to ensure she didn't screw it up like the last time.

When Paul finally joined them at the breakfast table, Simone was regaling the two women with a story about Mingus and one of his many exploits as a child. Mama Hill and Liza were both laughing heartily. The matriarch gave him a stern look as she passed him the plate of bacon.

"Sorry, Mama. I didn't mean to take so long."

The old woman tossed Mingus a look and he was grinning like a Cheshire cat. "I like this one," she said, nodding eagerly. "Yes, I do. I like him a lot." She shifted her gaze toward Simone. "He's a keeper. Not that you asked my opinion, but if I were you, I'd hold on to him. Hell, if I were a few years younger I'd give you a run for your money!"

"No, we're…just…" Simone started, suddenly unsure how to identify the two of them. There was still so much they needed to figure out and even more that needed to be said. Telling people she'd barely known for a hour that Paul was the love of her life had her feeling completely out of sorts.

"Friends. We're just friends," Paul concluded.

Simone gave him a quick look, then dropped her eyes down to her plate.

Mama Hill looked from one to the other and then she burst out laughing, her head waving from side to side. "Friends my ass!" she said. "You young people kill me! Even a blind man can see the kind of *friends* you two are!"

As soon as the meal was finished Paul headed back to the basement with Liza and Mingus. Simone hesitated just long enough for Mama Hill to point her toward the sink and the pile of dirty dishes. Her eyes widened and for a moment she almost balked, catching herself when the old woman pressed a wrinkled hand against her cheek.

"Why are you so sad?" she asked, eyeing Simone intently. "You know that young man has deep feelings for you."

Simone felt a tear slip past her lengthy lashes and Mama Hill brushed it away with a calloused thumb. She nodded. "I do. He's a great guy, but it will never work out. We're too different."

Simone hated saying those words the minute they left her mouth. Hated that she'd even had the thought and had given it life. Every ounce of doubt and fear she had about their relationship manifested in those words, already rationalizing why them being together was destined to fail. Instead of thinking how to tell Paul she loved him back, Simone was reasoning why they shouldn't be together.

Mama Hill fanned a dismissive hand. "Girl, please! If you want it badly enough, you make it work. My late husband and I were like oil and water. That man worked my good nerve on a regular basis, but I loved everything about him. I fought hard for our marriage. Giving up would have been easy but the fight was so much sweeter."

"So how long were you two married?"

"Thirty-eight years. He passed on back nine years ago. Was sitting right here in this kitchen fussing at me when he had a heart attack and never woke up."

"I'm so sorry."

Mama Hill passed Simone a dry towel and then she turned toward the sink. "We was good as gold while we lasted, even with the challenges we faced. I missed him something awful. Wasn't sure I was going to make it when I happened upon Liza. She was just a little bitty thing and smart as a whip. Her mama was lost out here in these streets and her daddy was incarcerated. I became her foster mother and she's been here raising hell ever since." The woman chuckled, joy shining in her eyes.

She continued. "I fostered a few other strays over the years. Then last year they said I was too old. So, now it's just me and Liza and I can't get her away from them computers long enough to meet a man. I keep telling her I want to see some grandbabies around here before I die." She laughed as she rinsed suds from a dinner plate.

Simone smiled. "My mother says the same thing. My brothers will probably give her grandkids before I or my sister do."

"How long have you and that pretty doctor been playing games with each other?"

"Games?"

"Yes. Loving on each other one day, then mad about absolutely nothing the next day."

Simone blew a soft sigh. "Since we were in college together. It's been off and on over ten years now."

Mama Hill shook her head. "Like my Douglas use to say, that's enough time to piss or get off the pot. What are you waiting for?"

Simone pondered the question, dropping the dishrag in her hand down to her side. She had often asked herself that question. When Paul had been overseas the answer had seemed obvious. Now he was back, proclaiming to still be in love with her, and she had no answer that would make an ounce of sense to anyone else.

If Paul had been solely responsible for their future, they would have been married with a dozen kids. He had always been open about wanting marriage and a family to balance his medical career. Simone hadn't needed either and earnestly believed she would be happier without the picket-fence fantasy. She had routinely stalled his quest to move their relationship forward, convinced she didn't need a piece of paper to validate her commitment to him. She had fought him at every turn and he had still loved her. She was feeling pretty crappy about the whole thing as she brushed a fall of moisture from her cheek.

She lifted her eyes to find Mama Hill staring at her. Simone shrugged, forcing a smile to her face. She couldn't find the words to answer, struggling once again not to cry.

Mama Hill clasped a hand to her hip, the look she gave Simone scolding. "Let me give you another bit of advice you didn't ask for," she said. "Love ain't easy. In fact, it's damn hard work! But as long as that love isn't toxic, it's worth every ounce of effort you can give it. You love him and he loves you. Stop fighting it and just let yourself enjoy whatever it has for you."

Mama Hill untied the apron from around her waist. She crossed to the other side of the room to hang it on a hook near the door that led out to a rear deck. "I think I'm going to go watch me some Dr. Phil. I may fall asleep and if I do, don't y'all wake me up. Whatever trouble you two done found yourselves in will work itself out. Just trust your instincts and hold tight to each other and everything will be okay."

"Thank you, Mama," Simone said softly. "Thank you for everything."

The matriarch laughed. "Baby, thank the Lord! Pay me—advice ain't never been cheap!"

Simone laughed with her and when she disappeared behind a closed door at the end of the hallway, Simone turned toward the basement.

"How do you not test a drug? Federal regulations demand they test any product they put on the market. There have to be test results and research data somewhere besides the damn brochure!" Paul snapped, irritation blessing his words.

He was sorting pages into individual piles and then

slipping them into manila folders. With a permanent marker he jotted notes on the front of each, his scribblings only making sense to him. He met Simone's stare as she eased her way to his side, her expression questioning as she peered down at the papers in his hand. He gave her a slight smile as he turned his attention back to Liza.

Liza tossed her hands up in frustration. "I've looked in every file I could get into. There's nothing there before it hit the market."

"And you looked everywhere?"

"Everywhere I could without setting off any alarms that would let their IT department know I was there snooping. I ain't interested in going to jail!"

Paul closed his eyes, falling into thought. Clearly, what he had fathomed was turning out to be true. But there were still questions that needed to be answered. Things that didn't make sense and he wasn't sure if he was even asking the right questions or searching for the correct answers. Mostly, he needed to understand why.

Mingus cleared his throat. "You two need to get a move on it," he said. "It's starting to get too hot for you to hang around here much longer. The police superintendent wants to see you both for questioning."

Simone gasped. "Daddy called you?"

"Not yet. Parker messaged me so it's just a matter of time."

"Where should we go?" Simone asked, a wave of anxiety washing over her.

Her brother tossed Paul a look. "I'm told it's handled. Just send me a text when you get there to let me know you're safe."

Paul had opened his eyes, looking from Simone to Mingus and back. "You can still stay here with your brother," he said. "I'd understand. It might actually be the best thing for everybody."

"That's not an option," she snapped.

Silence rose full and thick between them. Paul finally nodded. "We'll be okay," he said, throwing Mingus one last look. Despite his uncertainty about what might come next, he was happy to know he hadn't run her off and Simone was as determined to be with him as he was determined to be with her.

He changed the subject. "Liza, can you give me all the info they have on the drugs they've manufactured over the last ten years?"

Liza nodded. "That's a lot of paper but if you want it, I can get it for you."

"Please," he said. "I would really appreciate it."

"You know I can put it on a flash drive."

"I know. I'm going to need hard copy. And this, too, please." He reached into his back pocket for the storage device he'd taken from the hospital. "If you can print out everything on here and then give it to Mingus for safe-keeping."

"What's on it?" Mingus asked, eyeing them both with a raised brow.

Paul took a deep inhale of air. "Proof. Data I've been collecting since I first suspected something wasn't right."

An hour later Simone moved to the opposite end of the large work table. She leaned in to her brother's side, wrapping her arms around his waist as she hugged him goodbye. Mingus was on his phone with their mother, purposely avoiding answering questions about her and Paul. He wrapped an arm around her shoulders and hugged her back before pressing a light kiss to the top of her head, then pausing to push the mute button on his phone. "Take this," he said, pulling a roll of one-hundred-dollar bills from his pocket and slipping it into the pocket of her jacket. "Do not, under any circumstances, use your credit cards," he said. "If you need more, you call me."

Simone nodded, her fingers wrapping tightly around the wad of cash.

"I mean it, Simone! If you use your cards anyone looking for you will find you."

"I get it," she replied. Tears suddenly misted her eyes and she blinked to stall them from falling.

Mingus turned his attention toward Paul. "Keep her safe," he said, as they punched fists.

"With my life," Paul answered.

Liza jumped from her seat, moving to hug them both. "I'll keep digging. If I come up with anything, I'll message you," she said.

"Thank you," Paul responded.

"Give Mama a hug for us," Simone said.

"Mama is not the hugging type, but I'll tell her you said goodbye," Liza said with a hearty laugh.

After the couple went outside and settled down in the car, Paul told her, "You know you don't have to do this, Simone." He was giving her one last chance to change her mind and back out.

"Do what?"

"You don't have to come with me. Especially since we don't know what's going to happen."

"I know that. Do you want me to drive?" Her eyes were wide and she gave him a bright smile. Without saying it aloud she was committed to running away with him, determined to make the best of a bad situation. Because being with Paul was the best of anything she could possibly imagine.

Paul shook his head, a slight smile pulling at his full

lips. "No, I'm good," he said. He buckled his seat belt and started the engine. Shifting the car into gear, he pulled out of the parking space and into traffic.

"So where are we going?" she asked.

Paul cut an eye in her direction. "Canada," he answered.

"Canada?"

"Yeah. My brother and I have a cabin there."

"Since when?"

"Since our mother willed it to us. It was her family home. We invested a little money to restore it and now Oliver spends more time there than I do."

Simone stared as he pulled the car onto Interstate 94 east, headed toward Detroit. She suddenly had questions but figured she'd wait until there was too much distance between them and Chicago for him to consider turning around to bring her back. Because she had no intentions of coming back if he wasn't coming with her.

Simone had thought she knew everything there was to know about Paul. But this was the first time hearing he owned a cabin in Canada. When Paul's mother died his second year in medical school, he'd been devastated, the loss unexpected. After the funeral his brother had handled the estate and Paul had thrown himself back into his studies, leaving himself no time to mourn. There had been moments when Simone had been concerned. He'd been moody: zealously happy one minute and bitterly sullen the next. She had suggested counseling, passing him the telephone number of a therapist her mother had recommended. Weeks later he seemed to find a new normal and life had gone on without skipping another beat.

Now there were things between them that she didn't know. Experiences they hadn't shared. A lifetime lived without each other. Thinking about it made Simone all kinds of sad.

Simone reached for the radio and pushed buttons until she found the satellite station. Beyoncé was lecturing in perfect pitch, the lyrics harmonizing with a decadent Caribbean beat. Paul had gone quiet, falling into his own thoughts. Simone eyed him a second time, sensing that he was working through something in his head. She knew this mood and also knew she needed to give him space. She would ask her questions later, when he was ready for conversation. Reclining the seat slightly, Simone settled in for the ride.

Chapter 6

Paul slowed the car as he met a line of traffic on the Michigan freeway. Simone had been snoring softly and she woke with a start. Her eyes were wide as she sat upright and looked around.

"Where are we?" she asked, stretching her arms in front of her.

"Just outside Battle Creek, Michigan. We're a little more than two hours from Detroit."

Simone looked down at her watch. "You've been driving for over three hours. You need a break."

"I'm good, actually. It's given me some time to think. Do you need me to stop, though?"

"I could use the bathroom. And you really do need to stretch your legs, Dr. Reilly. Didn't you lecture me once about preventing blood clots?"

Paul chuckled. "I don't lecture." His laugh was light and easy, making him feel like old times.

Laughing with him, Simone rolled her eyes skyward. "Not much you don't!" she muttered.

Traffic was still crawling slowly. Paul shifted his buttocks against the seat to ease the tension tightening in his limbs. Simone reached for her phone, searching for restaurants near their location.

"There's a travel plaza right off the next exit. They have a diner and a McDonald's and we can fill up the car."

"That'll work. I really want to cross the border before

it gets dark. By the way, you do still carry your passport with you, don't you?"

Simone nodded. "You know I do. But it's a little late to be asking, isn't it? What if I didn't have it?"

"I'd have to leave you in Detroit," Paul said matter-of-factly.

"You would not leave me."

He cut an eye at her, but he didn't respond, and the moment gave them both pause.

Simone took a deep breath. "I was wrong," she suddenly said, her eyes fixed on the roadway in front of them. "I should have gone with you to Africa."

The comment surprised him, and Paul tried not to let it show on his face. Simone saying she was wrong was life-changing, and he wasn't sure if he should send up a flare to celebrate or find shelter and wait for an impending lightning strike. He took a deep breath, blowing it out slowly as he responded. "You did what you thought you needed to do, Simone. There wasn't anything wrong with that."

"I was scared. I was afraid that in chasing you and your dreams I would lose myself."

"I wouldn't have let that happen."

"You don't know that."

"I knew that I loved you enough to want to make sure that your joy was as bright as my own. I still do. But you never trusted that. What kind of man would I be if I didn't do everything I could for you to love me and live in your purpose, too? You always felt like you had to choose one or the other and you didn't."

Simone shifted her gaze to look at him, meeting the glance he was giving her. "I did trust it, Paul. But I let my own insecurities and fears get in the way. I made the biggest mistake of my life. Because I did love you. I still love you, too."

Paul reached for her hand and tangled his fingers with hers. His palm was heated, and his touch was comforting. Simone exhaled loudly, the sound of it like music to his ears. Relief washed over him, and Paul knew that no matter what happened from that moment forward, he and Simone would be better than okay. He trusted that more than he ever had before.

Once they pulled into the Te-Khi Travel Court, Paul found an empty spot, parked the car and shut down the engine.

"So, what now?" Simone asked.

"You and I have a lot to talk about," Paul said finally. The list in his head was lengthy, including wanting to hear what *she* wanted for their future. But the past few hours had begun to wear on him. He was tired and they still had a ways to go before they could rest and she could feel completely safe. Because he desperately needed her to feel that things would be okay. "But I need the men's room first and then we need to grab something to eat so we can get back on the road."

Stepping out of the vehicle, they both cast their gazes around the landscape. Despite the distance between them and Chicago, they were still on edge about being followed. Paul had been reluctant to share what had happened at the hospital, not wanting to alarm Simone any more. He was worried for her. He wanted only the best for them both. Loving Simone fueled his actions and insuring she was protected was foremost in his mind. Protected and happy. At the moment though, that was far from their reality. Simone wasn't content or cheery and she couldn't be until he could get them out of harm's way. He still had his own questions that needed to be answered, so he could only imagine the mayhem spinning in her head trying to make sense of it all.

The truck stop was old but established. It was average at best and the convenience store supplied basic staples. After using the restroom, Paul headed over to the diner and ordered them two daily specials to go. By the time he returned Simone was at the register paying cash for chips, water, a chocolate bar for him and her favorite gummy bears.

He stepped in behind her, dropping his hands against her shoulders. His fingers slid down the length of her upper arms, up and then across her back. He noted the tension beneath his palms. Simone leaned against his chest as she waited for the clerk to bag her items and count out her change.

"Junk food, Simone?"

"Road-trip food. How do you travel?"

Paul grinned. "Fried chicken and French fries, baby," he said, pointing toward the diner. "With two slices of homemade chocolate cake to go. Our food should be ready for us as soon as we're done here."

"They do make the best cake!" the young woman behind the counter interjected.

Simone laughed. "Please, don't encourage him."

The other woman laughed with her. "You two are so cute together. Is he your husband?"

Simone shot a quick glance over her shoulder. Paul was gently kneading the stress out of her shoulders. "Something like that," she said, blushing slightly.

Paul leaned forward and pressed a kiss to the top of her head. The familiar scent of her perfume and the airy aroma of her jasmine-scented shampoo teased his nostrils. As he savored the sweetness that reminded him of so many beautiful moments between them, he felt conflicted.

Wanting to relish the joy they shared despite knowing the challenges they still faced. But he had missed those moments, when the nearness of her gave him pause and everything felt right in their small world. He kissed her a second time before releasing the hold on her shoulders. He said nothing as Simone thanked the woman for her help and then they turned toward the door.

An hour later their stomachs were full, and Simone was trying not to speed. Paul sat in the passenger seat flipping through the papers in one of the many files he'd brought with him. Between intermittent admonishments for her to slow down, he kept his attention focused on the documents in his hands.

"What are you reading?" Simone questioned, giving him a curious glance.

"Trying to make sense out of the drug data Liza pulled off the Lender computer. There's a definite trail with some of their drugs. Research studies, FDA approvals, sales. With Halphedrone-B, there's no data before the sales data. And I mean nothing. There's an amended FDA approval and sales, nothing about the research prior to that."

"Any other drugs follow that pattern or seem skewed?"

"There are three that don't show ever going into mass production or having ever been sold to the public. Not sure why, though. And dozens are still in various phases of testing."

"You probably need to focus on the drugs that don't have a clear data pattern of production and sales history. That might help you figure out what you're looking for."

"When we get to the house, I need you to call your friend at the FDA, please."

"I will. And if I can get to a computer, I can do some research, as well. If we know where they do most of their business, I can search the state court records to see any current or previous lawsuits against them."

"That might be a bit of a problem."

Simone shot him a quick look. "A problem?"

"It's complicated."

"How complicated can it be?"

"The last time I was up here, there was no electricity. Oliver has wanted to keep it rustic and isolated, with no outside distractions. That's why I asked Liza to print everything. Just in case."

"No electricity?"

"We'll be deep in the woods. There's a generator but it's used sparingly."

"So, you're taking me deep into the woods with no electricity?" Her gaze narrowed. Rustic with a hint of luxury she could handle, Simone thought. Rustic with archaic accommodations was not her idea of a good time.

"And spotty cell phone service. There's a house phone, though."

"No electricity, no cell phone service, no internet and your reclusive brother?"

"Oliver's not a recluse. And don't get there picking on my brother. I don't want to hear you two bickering the whole time we're there."

"Is there indoor plumbing at least?"

"It's not totally primitive, Simone."

Simone rolled her eyes skyward. She bit back the snarky comment that was on the tip of her tongue. In the past she would have picked an argument, but she really didn't want to fight. Things were good with them and she wanted to keep it that way, even if she wasn't happy about the potential conditions she was about to be tossed in. "So, no more luxury accommodations, like last night's motel?" she asked instead.

Paul chuckled. "I promise—it won't be that bad. In fact, I think you'll actually like the place."

"I was slightly surprised that I didn't know about it," she said, finally getting that off her chest.

He pondered the statement for a moment before responding. "We weren't in a good place with each other when my brother finalized my mother's estate. I wasn't trying to keep it from you, Simone, but we weren't talking. Not the way we should have been. And, I really wasn't interested in the house and just figured I'd eventually sign my half over to Oliver. But he convinced me to come up for a visit and I've been two or three times since. It's turned out to be a great getaway."

"And now it's a perfect hideout?"

Paul smiled, and nodded. "Until they find us," he said matter-of-factly.

Their light banter continued for the rest of the ride, both catching up with each other. Much time had passed since the big clash that had severed their ties. Despite the level of comfort they'd been able to reignite with each other, there was much they'd missed.

Paul discovered Simone was being courted by one of the top law firms in the state of Illinois, which offered a lucrative seven-figure salary, substantial perks and a potential partnership on the table. He knew it was the next step in what she hoped would eventually be a stellar political career.

Simone was surprised to learn that he had purchased a home in Morocco, the northwest African destination enabling him to do more mission work abroad while affording him a respite from the transcontinental travel. Learning he had considered making the move permanent felt like a punch to her gut.

"So, you're seriously thinking about moving?"

"I've left the option open, yes."

"What about your job at the hospital? You're highly regarded there. Enough that they accommodate your mission trips, so why leave?"

He nodded. "My mission trips help the hospital look good. The board appreciates being able to say that their doctors have international experience and exploiting our humanitarian endeavors. If I decide to leave, I'll be able to maintain my privileges when and if I come back to Chicago.

Simone paused, unsure how she felt or what to say. "I can't move to Morocco, Paul," she finally muttered.

Paul gave her the slightest smile. "I would never ask you to move, Simone," he said. "I did that once and you broke my heart. Remember?"

Before she could respond he pointed toward the exit, motioning for her to bear right toward the Detroit-Windsor Tunnel. She merged onto the toll road, her eyes skating back and forth between her mirrors and the road as she eased slowly forward with the line of traffic. When they reached the inspection plaza they were greeted by an Immigration and Customs official.

It was Simone's first time traveling to Canada and she hadn't expected the hustle and bustle of the big city that greeted them. Actually, she hadn't known what to expect but the tall buildings surprised her.

Paul seemed to read her mind. "Windsor is known as the 'Automotive Capital of Canada.' The town has a diverse industrial and manufacturing history. My father used to work for the Ford Motor Company engine plant which is here. Now it also has a well-established tourism industry and one of the largest casinos in Canada."

"It seems like a great city. I'd love to explore it some, one day," she said softly as she imagined the two of them exploring the city together. Hand in hand. A wave of sadness washed over her as she thought about all she had missed out on with him.

Something in her tone moved Paul to turn and stare. He pointed. "Pull into that parking lot up there. I'll take us the rest of the way. That way you can sightsee while I drive."

"Are we far from your house?"

He shook his head. "No, about another forty-five minutes if the traffic is good."

Pulling into the parking lot of a fast-food restaurant, they took a few minutes to stretch and change places. When they were back in the car, Paul settled behind the driver's seat, Simone drifted off in reflection. She was still reeling from his comment about never asking her to move to the other side of the world to be with him. She was suddenly heartbroken to think that he might not want to resume their relationship. That maybe he didn't see a future for the two of them, no matter where in the world he might find himself. The lyrics to Tina Turner's "What's Love Got to Do with It" suddenly came to mind. Her feelings were hurt but she couldn't muster up the wherewithal to tell him.

The silence was suddenly daunting, and an awkward tension filled the space like helium in an oversize balloon. Simone tried to focus on the city and the multitude of left and right turns Paul was making toward their destination. But her stomach was in knots and suddenly all she wanted to do was cry.

In the Black family, Simone was renowned for her emotional rants. Any slight could send her into overload and have her railing against every sin, real or imagined. Paul could feel the tension rising over her like a thick mist,

She was biting down on her bottom lip as she stared out the window, her brain surely spinning a mile per minute.

For reasons Paul couldn't begin to explain things between them suddenly felt like they did just before they had ended their relationship. Back then it had been easier to say nothing, to ask no questions and simply walk away from each fight. Communication had not been either of their strong suits.

But nothing they had done before had worked for them and he knew for things to be different this time, that they needed to make different choices. Changing their patterns of behavior was an absolute necessity if they hoped for a new outcome. So, this time, he asked.

"What's wrong, Simone? And, please, don't tell me it's nothing because I know there is something bothering you."

Simone shifted in her seat, turning slightly. She took a deep breath and held it briefly before she spoke. "Will you and I always be at odds over what we want in life? Is there ever going to be a time when we want the same thing?"

"I don't understand, Simone."

"I just…well…" she stammered, words failing her for the first time in a very long while. She couldn't begin to explain that it felt like everything was always stacked against them and nothing she could say or do would change that. The old Simone would have waged a verbal war to make that point, fear and anger clinging to every word. The new Simone was determined to not make the same mistakes.

"I'm sorry. Can we please shelve this conversation for now? I want to discuss it when I have a better handle on my feelings."

Paul's brows lifted slightly. "That's fine," he responded. "Whenever you're ready you let me know."

"Thank you," she whispered, still fighting not to break out into an ugly cry that would have her looking foolish.

Paul suddenly took a sharp right turn, pulling onto a dirt road lined with tall trees that quickly became an island of forest surrounding them. About two miles down the single-lane roadway a large log home loomed in the distance. It was a breathtaking sight to behold and not at all the simple cabin Simone had imagined from Paul's description.

The two brothers had expanded the original footprint of the home to add additional living space. With classic hand-hewn logs, a covered wraparound porch, the scenic setting and its familial history, Simone could understand the appeal. As Paul pulled the car into the parking area next to an old Dodge sedan, Oliver Reilly stepped out the front door to welcome them.

Simone stood back as the men greeted each other. The brothers hugged, hanging on like family do when they've been worried. Oliver was tapping Paul against his back and relief hit Simone like a tidal wave. She swiped at a tear that had rolled down her cheek.

"Simone, hey!" Oliver called out as he stepped toward her and pulled her into a big bear hug. "Am I glad to see you! Your brother told me what happened to the two of you."

"You talked to Mingus?"

"Yeah. He needed to get into Paul's place to get him some clothes. Told me you two were hiding out. That's when I figured it might be a good idea for me to come north until we can all figure out what's going on."

She smiled. "Well, it's good to see you, too, Oliver. And I'm really glad to be here. I'm also glad you got that electricity problem resolved," she said as she noted the lights radiating from every window.

Oliver laughed. "That was only a temporary problem! But we sometimes lose power still, depending on the weather. Come on inside. I was just about to put some dinner on. I wasn't sure if you were coming in today or tomorrow. Paul was concerned after seeing those guys at the hospital this morning."

Simone shot Paul a look. She pointed her index finger at him. "You and I really need to work on communicating better with each other!" she snapped.

Paul and his brother exchanged a look.

"Oops!" Oliver quipped. "I just figured…"

Paul chuckled. "I was looking for the right time to bring it up."

"I swear, Paul Reilly…" Simone muttered as she moved to the trunk of the car for her bags.

Chapter 7

Simone had needed some time to herself and she sensed the two brothers wanted their own moment. The home was divided into two separate wings that filtered off a central common area. There was a sizable kitchen and expansive back deck. Paul had led her down one wing to a spare bedroom. As he dropped her bag atop the mattress he pointed across the hallway.

"My room is there. Oliver is down at the other end of the house."

"Thank you," she'd said. "I just need to freshen up."

He had nodded, then he leaned and had pressed a kiss to her cheek.

Simone could still feel the warmth of his lips against her skin. Despite everything else between them, there was no denying their chemistry. Even when they had been at odds over something, their intimate connection always brought them back around, centered, focused and wanting to make things between them well.

Her fingers tapped gently at the spot, her eyes closed. Suddenly everything she had trusted and believed in shifted. She found herself reassessing what she wanted: most important, she realized she needed to be happy. She imagined herself following him to Morocco. Because being with Paul brought her the most immense joy. Falling asleep in his bed, waking to him beside her. Those intimate moments when it was just the two of them and they could shut the world out, nothing and no one intruding on those moments, that made her happy. And then she imagined if she didn't, the very thought of what would follow bringing her to tears. Minutes later, Simone was sleeping soundly.

Oliver moved inside from the rear patio. Smoke billowed from the freshly lit grill. Racks of spare ribs lay marinating in an oversize metal pan as he began to prep the evening meal. Paul looked up from the papers he was studying. The second package of samples had arrived safely, and Oliver had already begun to run the necessary tests.

"The drugs are contaminated," he said, locking gazes with his brother.

Oliver nodded. "It's the bacterium Burkholderia cepacia."

"How did they get this past the FDA?"

"That I can't answer, but I do know that all the samples you sent me tested positive for the same strain of B. cepacia."

"Unbelievable," Paul muttered.

"Look, you and I both know the multitude of ethical issues with the pharmaceutical industry, starting with questionable accountability. Between lack of healthcare reform, price gouging and greed, product contamination is just another blip on an already overloaded radar."

"They can't be doing this on purpose, can they?"

"Highly unlikely, but they are just as accountable for their negligence. But bottom line for them, is their bottom line. They're making money and that's all they care about. Now, it's highly possible this is a fluke. Maybe they aren't aware, but you asked questions that should have raised a red flag for them to do some testing. It doesn't look like they're interested in doing that."

Paul cussed, throwing the pages in his hand across the dining room table. He knew he wore his frustration like bad makeup, everything in his heart filled with horror and pain. He knew the system was broken but never imagined that he would be personally touched by the jagged edges. That patients he'd sworn to help heal would suffer instead because someone else didn't give a damn.

Oliver moved to his side and took a seat. "You been out to the barn yet?"

Paul shook his head. "No. Why?"

"I've been working on a few things that you might be interested in. Why don't you take a walk while I get our dinner ready?"

He blew a heavy sigh. "I should probably go check on Simone."

"How are things with you two?"

Paul shrugged, not sure he had an answer. "We have a lot to work through and this bull isn't helping," he said.

"Maybe the two of you working on a common goal is what you need to pull you back together."

"I actually don't know that we can ever resolve our issues. Simone is married to staying here in the United States with her family and I don't know if I can commit to that. My work is important to me."

"More important than Simone?"

The two locked gazes as Paul pondered his brother's question. Nothing was more important to him than her, not even the work he felt destined to do. He loved Simone. Loved Simone with everything he had in him. But he realized love might not be enough for either of them.

He pushed himself from the table, not bothering to

reply to his brother's question. "I think I'll take a walk and go check out the barn."

Oliver chuckled. "You do that. I'll call you when the food's ready."

Simone was startled out of a sound sleep. The room was dark, except for a small night-light plugged into a socket beneath the end table. She sat upright, clenched fists rubbing at her eyes, then rolled to the edge of the bed before she threw her legs off the side. She hadn't meant to fall asleep and she hadn't intended to sleep for almost three hours, she thought after she stole a quick glance at her watch.

She moved from the bed to the bathroom. Minutes later she felt refreshed, her teeth brushed, face washed and bladder emptied. She took one last look at her reflection in the mirror and pulled her hands through the short length of her hair.

Exiting the bathroom, she gathered her phone from the dresser and headed out the door down the length of hallway to the family room. Oliver stood at the counter in the kitchen. A small television rested in the corner, the station he was watching tuned to a repeat episode of *Family Feud*. He was laughing intently as he sliced vegetables into a bowl.

"Hey!" Simone said, tossing her hand up in a slight wave.

Oliver looked up and smiled. "Hi! You're just in time. I was just about to take the ribs off the grill. Everything else is ready, so we can eat. I hope you're hungry."

"I am and it smells really good."

"It'll taste even better. I promise!"

"Where's your brother?"

"Out in the barn. He needed to blow off some steam," he said as he gestured toward the dining room.

The table was littered from one end to the other with the documents that Liza had printed for him. Folders were piled together and a few pages were scattered across the floor. A notepad and pen sat at one seat, two-thirds of the page scribbled with notes. Clearly, Paul had been busy since she'd last seen him.

"I'd offer to neaten that up, but I wouldn't want to disturb anything. I know how your brother is about something he's working on."

"No, I wouldn't mess with it. We can eat here at the kitchen table. There's plenty of room and we can watch the snow come down while we eat."

"It's snowing?"

Oliver nodded. "We're supposed to get an inch or two. I think it'll just be a light dusting if anything at all. It just felt a little too warm out today, so I don't think the ground is cold enough for any precipitation to stick."

Simone moved to the back door to peer outside. It was pitch-dark out, only a spattering of stars and a quarter moon lighting the sky. Behind the house was a freestanding barn, a light from inside shining to the outside. And snowflakes were falling like dust from the sky.

"It's so pretty," she said, the comment more for herself than anyone else.

Behind her Oliver chuckled. "It's all right!"

Simone turned, her arms folded across her chest. "Can I help with anything?"

"Actually, I'm glad you asked. Would you mind setting the table for me?"

"Not at all," she answered.

He pointed to an upper cabinet. "Plates are up there,

and you'll find the silverware in the drawer below it. Glasses are in the top cabinet on the other side of the sink."

Simone moved into the kitchen and grabbed what she needed. There was a small breakfast table in the alcove that looked out the bay window. She grabbed three place-mats from the corner of the counter and began to set to the table. As she moved to gather three glasses, Oliver cleared his throat.

"It's not my business, but I'm putting my money on the two of you getting back together."

He moved to the table and filled two of those glasses with red wine, then gestured for her to take a seat with him. They both took a sip from their drinks before Oliver continued.

"And I say that not because I'm a gambling man, but because I see how Paul is without you. He's been missing you like crazy. You two are good for each other."

Oliver's comment was chilling, despite the warmth of his delivery. She and Paul were both close to their families and their siblings had a vested interest in what happened in their lives. Simone imagined the two brothers had discussed her more times than she could count. She knew how often she had cried on her sister's shoulder about Paul. That Oliver believed there was hope for them was endearing. She, however, wasn't as confident.

"I think your brother and I might be too broken to make things work."

"Apart, yeah. But you two are like two pieces of a larger puzzle. The last two pieces necessary to finish the perfect picture. You need each other, even when you think you don't."

Simone took another sip of her beverage. There was a moment of pause until she set her glass back onto the table. "So, how's your love life doing? The last time we saw each other you were dating that pastry chef? Right?"

"He owned a bakery. You know, that one down in Humboldt Park."

"The one that specializes in pies? That one?"

Oliver nodded. "They have the best pies! He would make me a different pie every Sunday morning. The chocolate velvet was to die for!"

"He's not making pies anymore?"

Oliver sighed. "Not on Sundays and not for me."

"I'm sorry. You were always so happy when I saw you together."

"He said I worked too much. He needed someone who wasn't always at the office."

"And you don't think you two can work things out?"

"I think when it's right, you know. With us, even when it felt good there was always a lot of doubt. Mostly because he was still very closeted. Being in public with me made him uncomfortable."

Simone pushed out her bottom lip in an exaggerated pout.

Oliver waved a dismissive hand. "It's all good. Haven't you heard? I'm a very eligible bachelor. Men are falling all over themselves to date me! Someone new will be making me pie in no time!"

"There's an attorney in my office who's single. I'd love to introduce you two. He's a really nice guy."

"Nope! Because if things go south, you'll be in the middle feeling bad about it."

"It can be a casual introduction. Like you both show up at the same cocktail party and just happen to cross paths as you're mingling. I'll point him out and you can take it from there. No pressure."

"And who'll be throwing this cocktail party?"

"I will, of course! You know I throw a mean party!"

"Maybe it'll be an engagement party?"

Simone laughed. "Now you're pushing it."

Oliver laughed with her. "I missed you."

"I missed you, too, my friend."

"You and my brother really need to figure it out. You can't keep playing with my heart the way you two do." He winked his eye, then chugged the rest of the wine. "Now, if you'll please grab one of my jackets there on that hook by the door and go to the barn and tell Paul Michael that his dinner is about to get cold, I would appreciate it."

She laughed. "This is serious. You used his full name."

"And I expect you to do the same. Otherwise he'll be out there for the rest of the night."

Her eyes narrowed. "What's so special about the barn?"

"That, my darling, you'll have to see for yourself," he said as he pointed her toward the door. "Now, hurry up. Two more minutes and I'll be taking the corn bread out of the oven."

"You made corn bread?"

"And your favorite macaroni and cheese!"

Simone jumped from her seat and threw her arms around the man's neck. She kissed his cheek. "Thank goodness someone still loves me!"

Oliver laughed. "Woman, no one could ever stop loving you!"

"Paul Michael and I will be right back," Simone said with a wide grin. "Even if I have to drag him kicking and screaming!"

"Tell him dinner is on the table," Oliver said as he rose from his seat to peer in the oven. "And I *will* start without you two!"

Simone stood in the doorway of the backyard structure, her eyes sweeping around the room. What had originally been a barn had been transformed into a laboratory. Oliver had clearly gone to great lengths and much expense to build a space that rivaled some medical facilities. The pristine space boasted fully equipped workstations and state-of-the-art laboratory equipment that included clean benches, biosafety cabinets, ductless enclosures and more. It was impressive and Simone didn't have a clue about most of it.

Paul sat at a table, staring into a microscope. He was completely engaged, his focus distracted from his surroundings. He didn't hear when Simone opened the door and let herself inside. It was only when he paused to jot down some notes that he seemed to realize she was there.

"Hey! You're awake!"

"Hi! I didn't mean to sleep so long."

"You needed the rest. I'm glad you were comfortable."

Simone moved to his side. "This is amazing," she said.

"Oliver's put in some serious work since I was last here. But he wants to move here to Canada and make this his home base. His job at the CDC will allow him plenty of leeway with this setup. Having the lab will enable him to continue his cancer research from home. He has full safety certification and all his Declarations of Conformity. He's ready to rock and roll."

"So, what are you working on out here?"

"Just trying to make sense of the data. I mailed a second box of samples here that made it, and Oliver's been running tests on them. We think that Halphedrone-B is contaminated with a bacterium called Burkholderia cepacia. It's an unscrupulous human pathogen that causes pneumonia in immunocompromised individuals with underlying lung disease."

Simone squinted, looking confused.

Paul continued. "Basically, it attacks systems in the

human body that are already compromised. Then it shuts down organs and eventually causes death."

"Does the drug company know?"

"I can't imagine them not knowing. Why else would they send people after us if they didn't know?"

"But we need to find out for certain, Paul. Right now, it's all just theory. We need to make sure the evidence is irrefutable."

Paul nodded. "I need to run some additional tests, but I also have to get my hands on more samples of the drug. What I sent to Oliver in Chicago originally is gone. Those samples were from a batch lot that had been shipped to my clinic in West Africa and tissue samples from infected patients. What we've been able to test thus far—the stuff that made it here—is a whole other drug lot. We just need to be sure that it's not just unique to one single production lot."

"We'll get it," Simone said. She pressed her fingers to his back and gently caressed the length of the broad area.

He suddenly looked exhausted, closing his eyes as he settled back against her touch. He took a deep breath, blowing it out slowly.

"I think you're the one who needs to get some rest now. Your brother said to tell you the food is ready. Why don't we go eat and get back to this with fresh eyes in the morning? Oliver made corn bread, and macaroni and cheese to go with the ribs!"

Paul laughed. "You're a little obsessed with the food, aren't you?"

"I like to eat, and your brother is a great cook. It's very easy to be obsessed."

"Just give me five more..." he started.

Simone shook her head. "Now, Paul Michael Reilly. Before Oliver comes out here to get us both."

He laughed again. "Damn! My full name? Really, Simone. That's some mess Oliver would pull!"

"He's a great influence," she answered. "So, let's go, 'cause I'm hungry!"

The laughter around the dinner table felt good. The food was delicious, and the company made everything feel right with the world. After filling their bellies, Paul and Simone relaxed, feeling completely at ease. They were safe, and in that moment, safe was home with family and each other. Nina Simone was playing out of the speakers, Oliver's comedic homage to his guest's name. But the soft tones of Nina's *Pastel Blues* album were appropriate for the mood, easing them all into a subtle trance.

Oliver rose from the table first, wishing them both a good night. "I'll let you two do the dishes," he said. "I have to fly to Atlanta in the morning for a meeting at the CDC. While I'm there I'll see if I can find out anything that might help you."

"Just please be careful," Paul admonished. "We don't know who you can trust."

"Not to worry."

"When will you be back?" Simone asked.

"I actually need to go back to Chicago after I leave Atlanta. It may be a few weeks before I get back up here. You two will have the house all to yourselves. I trust you'll take good care of each other." He rounded the table, hugged them both, and then he disappeared to his side of the home.

There was something calming about him and her doing dishes side by side. As Paul had cleared the table, Simone had loaded the dishwasher. Then he had washed the pots and pans as she dried them.

"Do you want to sit and talk?" Paul questioned, "Or are you ready to head to bed."

She smiled. "I had a long nap, remember? I'll probably be up for another few hours."

"More wine? Or my special hot chocolate?"

"That cinnamon hot chocolate you make would be very nice," she answered.

He moved to the cupboard and pulled two mugs from inside. "Hot chocolate coming right up."

Simone moved into the family room and settled herself down on the sofa. It was still snowing, and a fire burned in the fireplace. She watched him as he warmed milk on the stove and added cocoa powder, sugar, cinnamon and cloves. Every so often he would look up at her and smile, the gesture making her heart sing. Paul always knew what she needed, and he was diligent about taking care of her. Too often she hadn't shown him enough appreciation. She made a mental note to do better going forward.

When the cocoa mixture was just warm enough, he added a teaspoonful of vanilla extract and a shot of bourbon, then mixed it with an immersion blender until it was just the right amount of frothy. Nina was still singing softly in the background.

Paul joined her on the sofa, a hint of steam billowing off two oversize mugs. He had topped both with a swirl of whipped cream and a Pirouline dark-chocolate wafer cookie. Simone wrapped both hands around the mug to warm them.

"This smells divine!" Simone said as she inhaled the sweet aroma. "I've missed your hot chocolate."

"More than you missed me?"

Simone lifted her eyes to meet his. Amusement danced in his gaze as he stared at her. Her lips parted slightly and curled into the faintest smile. "I don't think I need to quantify how much I missed you, although it probably isn't nearly as much as you missed me."

Paul chuckled. "So, are you ready to tell me what was bothering you earlier?"

Simone sighed, a low gust of warm breath blowing past her lips. "Where do I start? The fact that so much has happened with you since we broke up that I feel like I've missed out? Or that if you decide to move to Morocco you wouldn't ask me to go with you? Because everything has had me in my feelings and despite my best efforts not to let it get to me, it got to me."

"I get it. I was feeling the same way. Here you are considering a major employment change and I haven't been there to help you make the decision and might not be there to celebrate with you when you do."

"Are we doomed to fail, Paul? Is our loving each other just not enough?"

"We are doomed to fail if neither of us is willing to compromise. I can't have everything I want if you don't get everything you want. It just won't work if we aren't each willing to give up as much as we give. If we're not willing to sacrifice as much as we gain."

"You make it sound so pragmatic."

"Not at all. I just know relationships don't work when they're one-sided."

"Are you saying I'm to blame for our not working? Because I wasn't willing to compromise?"

"I'm saying we're both to blame. Let's be honest, Simone…" He leaned forward and dropped his mug on the coffee table. "You are spoiled, sometimes mean, and convinced the sun should rise and set on your timetable."

She laughed. "I am not that bad!"

"Yes, you are! But I am equally as stubborn, occasionally self-absorbed, and too dismissive of the important things. Neither of us was willing to bend and it broke us. If we decide to try this again, we both have to make changes."

"So, you won't go to Morocco?"

"Or you'll go with me."

Simone shifted in her seat, adding her cup to the table with his. She turned her body until she was leaning against him, nuzzling her back to his chest, Paul wrapping his arms tightly around her torso. He kicked off his shoes and swung his legs up onto the sofa, reclining back against the pillows. The move pulled her alongside him, the duo stretching out until she lay comfortably in his arms. He pulled her closer with one hand and reached for a wool blanket with the other. They snuggled close together beneath the covering, staring into the fire to watch the flames dance.

Simone suddenly clutched the hem of his sweatshirt with a tight fist. She shifted and turned to nuzzle her face against his chest and took a deep breath to inhale his rugged scent.

"I want us to work," Simone whispered, tightening the grip she had on his shirt. "I *need* us to work, Paul."

Paul nodded. He slid a firm hand beneath her chin and lifted her face till she was staring up at him. There was a tear clinging to his eyelash and it rolled down his face, landing on his shirt. "So do I, Simone. Because I love you, and not that I need to quantify it, but I love you as much as I know you love me. Maybe even more!" His smile pulled full and wide across his face.

Simone's eyes skated back and forth across his face, as she felt her own smile become as magnanimous as his. She lifted herself up until her mouth met his in the sweetest kiss, flesh gliding like silk across satin. His hand slid into her hair, pressing against the back of her head.

Their connection deepened as the kiss became frenzied. Heat surged like a firestorm between them, tongues darting past parted lips. The moment was surreal as both allowed themselves to fall into the beauty of it. Outside, snow dusted the landscape, oblivious to the flames that continued to tango inside, embers doing a delicate two-step in raging shades of red and orange.

Chapter 8

Paul reached across the bed to pull Simone against him but came up empty-handed. He opened one eye and found her side of the bed vacant. A loud groan echoed around the room. His morning erection pressed against the mattress for attention then deflated rapidly. He turned and reached across the nightstand for his wristwatch. With no idea of the time, he jumped when he realized he'd slept past his eight-o'clock alarm.

They'd made love for hours, moving from the living room sofa to the bedroom. The fire had died down and the temperature in the room had cooled substantially. But neither had noticed, the heat between them so intense he thought they might combust. Her kiss had been like a lit match, igniting the fervor that had been simmering between them. His hands against her warm skin had been a fantasy come true and when she'd parted her legs and welcomed him home, he'd been no more good.

Pulling himself upright he threw his legs off the side of the bed, his feet brushing against the carpeted floor. He wiped a hand across his face, then stretched his arms upward. He called Simone's name, but she didn't answer. Rising from the bedside, he moved into the bathroom to relieve himself. After a quick shower and shave, he dressed, then went searching for her.

Simone sat at the dining room table, poring through the documents he'd piled against the hardwood top. She was re-sorting each pile, seeming determined to make sense of it all. The sight of her sent a shiver of energy coursing up the length of Paul's spine. Her determination gleamed across her face and he was happy to have her on his side. She looked up, greeting him warmly as he moved to her side and kissed her lips.

"Good morning! The muffins just came out of the oven and the coffee is still hot. Do you want eggs and bacon? Oliver left the kitchen fully stocked."

Paul shook his head. "Coffee's good for now. How long have you been up?"

"Since that darn alarm of yours went off. Then I couldn't get back to sleep. Figured I'd come work on our problem."

Paul moved to the kitchen to fill a mug with morning brew. "Have you found anything?" he asked as he stirred cream and sugar into his cup. He moved back to the formal dining room and sat down in the seat beside her. He took one sip and then another, allowing the first effects of caffeine to take hold.

"I have, actually. I had a very enlightening conversation with my soror."

"Which one?"

"Jillian Tanner."

"Isn't her father head of Tanner Insurance?"

"Yes, as a matter of fact, he is, and Jillian works for the FDA. What do you know about a drug called Phenylzeranol?"

Paul took another sip of his beverage as he paused in reflection. "I don't think I've ever heard of it."

"That might be because it was one of Lender's first products, but it was banned here in the United States by the FDA. Since then Lender has had twenty-seven other drugs banned by the government. According to what I discovered, the Food and Drug Administration had sent Lender numerous letters condemning their unsafe manufacturing protocols. They were warned that Phenylzeranol put patients at serious risk for harm."

"Do you know what it was prescribed for?"

"High blood pressure. But it was found to cause liver and blood cell damage, as well as damage to other internal organs."

"And this was how long ago?"

"Just over fifteen years ago. Apparently, a separate investigation found that there were significant violations at their manufacturing plants in India. Several drugs were found to be contaminated with cardboard and other multiple foreign particles. Lender was then taken to task for failing to respond appropriately to the incidents."

Simone took a sip from her own coffee cup, then continued. "They claimed they launched an investigation but then they closed the inquiry without fully reviewing the extent of the problem or taking any further action."

"So, they didn't do anything at all?"

"Well, evidently after a lot of pressure, they eventually recalled the entire lot of contaminated drugs, but that was almost eight months after receiving the initial complaint."

"So, did they destroy them?"

"No. They shipped them overseas and sold them through a distributor that's not bound by FDA regulations."

Paul stared at the document Simone handed him. "What's this?"

"Remember the three drugs you said never made it to sales and distribution?"

He shifted forward in his seat. "Yes. What about them?"

"All three failed FDA standards and were banned.

Their lab tests showed a blatant pattern of disregard, where technicians were regularly deleting any negative test results, then retesting them without bothering to identify how and why the original contamination occurred. There were even problems with drugs the FDA did approve, but because their inspectors don't do any additional tests for purity once those drugs come into the US, they weren't caught until a complaint had been lodged."

"So, Halphedrone-B slipped past the inspectors?"

"I think so. And between what I learned from Jillian and what I've been able to make sense from the documents Liza printed for you, I think Halphedrone-B may actually be one of the same drugs that was previously banned."

"How can that…"

"I don't know," Simone said, "but if I'm right, Lender has been purposely acting with malicious intent, with full knowledge of their wrongdoing. Jillian explained that the FDA is supposed to inspect all factories, foreign and domestic, that produce drugs for the US market. But there are literally thousands of documents, from inspection records to lawsuits, detailing the ways poorly manufactured or contaminated drugs reach consumers. How inspectors miss serious hazards, or drug makers fail to meet standards even after the FDA has taken enforcement action. She said there are hundreds of plants that haven't been inspected for years, if ever. And many inspections are stage-managed so that factories ensure they pass on the day of their review appointments but fall back into disarray the minute the inspectors leave."

"So, more times than not, any bacteria is detected *only* after an outbreak of disease."

"Or when people like you start asking questions and digging for answers."

"Medical sleuthing for dummies."

Simone laughed. "And Lender has a list of infractions that's miles long!"

"So, what now? Because I know I can make the case that their drug has poisoned patients."

"Which is a big question. Can you?"

Paul reached for a folder from inside the briefcase that rested on the floor. He passed it to Simone, who eyed it curiously. "That is a list of patients I've treated in the past five years who have died on my watch. The numbers abroad are almost triple that of the numbers here. More than seventy percent of my patients in Africa had been prescribed Halphedrone-B. I've only prescribed it to seven patients in the past year in Chicago. The last one died last week while I was still abroad. He had just turned seven years old. The autopsy shows he died from pneumonia. They've all died from pneumonia-related issues."

Paul took a deep breath and seemed to hold it as his comment settled between them. Simone could see the frustration in his gaze. He was conflicted at not having been able to do more and feeling whole-heartedly responsible. The hurt on his face fractured a sliver of her heart.

"Pneumonia caused by the bacteria in the medication that was supposed to make them better."

"I'd bet my life on it. I've been tracking the stats for a while now trying to make sense of what was happening and the only common denominator in all my cases was Halphedrone-B."

"So, we continue to connect the dots by detailing what we know and then we hit them where it's going to hurt the most. We go after their profits with a class-action lawsuit."

"That may take forever."

"The lawsuit, yes, but once we file, we also file a formal complaint with the FDA and go public with what we can prove and if nothing else, get the drugs off the market. We'll need to work out the details, but it's a start."

Paul leaned to kiss her again. "Did I tell you how much I love you?"

"Tell me again."

"I love you, Simone Black," he repeated, kissing her a second time.

"I love you, too. Now where can a girl find a computer around here?"

For the next three days, Paul lost hours of time, locked in the lab with the samples he'd been studying since he got there. He'd been running the same tests over, and over again, hoping against all odds that the results might be different, and he might be wrong. He didn't want to admit it, but he was having a hard time accepting that anyone would purposely hurt sick patients just for the sake of a profit.

When he thought of his patients in the rural communities where he volunteered, he became enraged. They were already facing enough challenges without adding distrust of the medical professionals who were supposed to help.

Before he'd gotten lost in the research, he had spent a few good hours on the phone with one of his colleagues in Ghana, telling her what to test for in the patients who were still suffering and prescribing alternate medications to treat them. He had also asked her to ship him samples of the drugs they had on hand and she'd promised to get them in the mail as promptly as possible. He hoped, against all odds, that they would make it to him.

When his stomach grumbled for attention he sat back in his chair. He hadn't heard a peep from Simone since their morning conversation over coffee. Morning coffee had become a ritual, a few quiet minutes before their focus shifted from each other to something else. She, too, had become obsessed with making his problem go away. He couldn't begin to express how much he appreciated her efforts. He had no doubts that if Simone wasn't there to fight the good fight with him, he'd be completely lost. She challenged him, helped him to take the emotion out of the facts and pushed him to consider every possible aspect of the case. She centered him and he whispered a prayer of thanks daily for her being in his life.

Rising, he put the equipment away and began to clean, making sure to maintain the integrity and safety of the lab environment. When he was finished, he tossed his rubber gloves, slid off his glasses, pulled on his jacket and headed back to the house. The temperature was starting to drop, the air chilling quickly. The sun had been lost behind a host of clouds for most of the day and the sky was just beginning to darken.

As he walked through the door, the home phone suddenly rang and he turned to stare at the device that hung on the kitchen wall. It was the ninth or tenth call that day. Simone had answered the first and the second and there had been no one on the other end. By calls four, five, and six, he had turned the ringer to low and they let them go to the answering machine, no one leaving a message. It was concerning and neither thought it accidental. It didn't leave them that they were there because someone had shot at them just a week or so earlier. In the back of their minds both were acutely aware that there was danger still very present in their lives. Whether or not it had found them was still debatable. What they agreed on was pushing past the fear and not allowing it to cripple them. He took a deep inhale and moved toward the dining room.

Inside, Simone was still working, having commandeered a corner of the dining room table and his laptop. There were pages of documents taped to one wall and the floor was littered with balls of crumbled paper. She was alternately typing and scrolling through her cell phone. There was a look of determination across her face and her cheeks were flushed. She bit down against her bottom lip as her eyes darted back and forth across her work. Watching her made him smile. She suddenly looked up, slightly surprised to see him standing there eyeing her.

"Hey! Everything okay?"

Paul smiled. "I was just thinking how beautiful you are."

Simone felt herself blush ever so slightly, her cheeks warming with color. "Thank you," she said, her voice dropping an octave.

"Why don't we take a break? I think we need a change of scenery and I'm tired of baloney sandwiches. I'm starving and I thought we could go get something to eat. There's a wonderful Italian restaurant not far from here that I think you'll like. They have the best Bolognese sauce that I've ever tasted."

Simone pursed her lips, her eyes widening. "You're talking my language now! You silver-tongued devil, you!"

Paul eased slowly to her side. "Rigatoni in vodka sauce, fettucine Alfredo, manicotti." His voice was a loud whisper, low and seductive, his words coming as if he was doing the voice-over for a commercial.

Simone gasped. "Yes! Oh, yes!" She began to pant in jest, her head rolling back as she clutched the front of her sweater. "Talk dirty to me, Daddy!"

Paul burst out laughing. "Really, Simone?"

She laughed with him. "Too much?"

"It's a bit over the top!" He nodded as he leaned to kiss her cheek. "Let's get ready and I'll talk dirty to you later."

Simone reached for him, pulling him to her as she captured his lips with her own. She kissed him passionately, her tongue darting past the line of his teeth. "Why don't we get ready together?" she said, her voice dropping seductively.

Paul kissed her again. "I like that idea! Last one in the shower gets to be on top."

Simone giggled. "I like being on top."

"I know," he said as he winked his eye at her, turned, then was heading for the bathroom and leaving a trail of clothes down the length of the hallway.

Simone watched Paul walk away, his self-assured swagger moving her to laugh heartily. He was a beautiful specimen of manhood, with perfectly sculpted butt cheeks that his briefs clung to like a second skin. He'd been immensely blessed, packing in the front and the back. As he turned once to face her, beckoning her to join him, his bulge strained against the fabric and then he pulled them off, and twirled the garment around his index finger as he did a little jig through the door of the master bedroom. He was such a tease, Simone thought as she giggled softly.

Taking a quick minute to save the file she'd been working on, Simone shut the laptop down, closed her notebook and silenced her phone. She moved swiftly to the master bath, entering just as Paul turned on the water and stepped inside. The room had begun to heat nicely, a gentle mist rising to fill the air. Paul leaned into the spray of water, tilting his face toward the showerhead as it rained over his back and down his chest. Simone marveled at the perfection, thinking she could stare at him all day. Everything about him took her breath away.

As he began to lather soap across his bare skin, she did

a slow strip tease out of her own clothes. She discarded her sweater, then unbuttoned her white blouse, pausing after each button until it blew open. Pushing the garment off one shoulder and then the other, she exposed inch after inch of bare skin to his hungry gaze, until she was standing in nothing but her bra and panties.

Simone pressed a palm to her abdomen, her breathing heavy as she continued to watch him, and he continued to eye her. Her other hand skated over her breasts, her fingertips grazing one nipple and then the other. He held himself in the palm of his hand, stroking the length of male flesh that had taken on a life of its own. It twitched and pulsed beneath his touch, seeming to beg for her attention.

She stepped out of her lace garments and into the glass enclosure, before reaching both hands out and pressing them against his broad chest. She felt his body quiver in appreciation and a surge of heat coursed up and down her spine.

"What took you so long?" he whispered, his breath catching in his chest.

"Better late than never," Simone answered, her own voice husky with desire.

Paul dropped his hands against the round of her shoulders and caressed her gently. His touch was iron strong and when he applied the barest amount of pressure she sank slowly to her knees in understanding. Simone worshipped his chiseled body slowly, damp kisses trailing against his skin as she made her way down to suck the very essence out of him.

No woman ever moved Paul the way Simone did. No one knew his idiosyncrasies or could manipulate him like her. And she was the only female who could leave him quaking with such pleasure that it brought tears to his eyes. After their shower, he lay sprawled atop the mattress, his hips pressing upward as Simone sat straddled over his lap.

She leaned over him for a kiss, the connection deep and hard and making him moan. When the contact broke, she nuzzled her cheek with his, then trailed her tongue along his jawline to his ear and nibbled at the lobe. That gesture always made him crazy and he felt his muscles spasm in response. He tightened the grip he had on her hips, pulling her body back to his. He muttered her name over and over again, each breathless utterance like a divine chant.

As she slid up and down his member, warm and very familiar sensations flooded his body. She worked herself into a frenzy and it had the effect on him that he needed. The pleasure was unbelievable as she slammed her pelvis hard against his, alternatingly hard and fast and slow and easy. He felt himself go deeper and deeper with each of her strokes, knowing that he wouldn't last much longer.

"Oh, sweet baby, I've missed you so much…" he groaned as he met her stroke for stroke.

"…so clo…close…" Simone murmured, and then her whole body exploded.

The moist, satin lining of her inner walls tightened around him like a vise, sending him skyrocketing over the edge. Paul spewed like a volcano, his orgasm blending beautifully with hers as they both dropped into a state of sheer bliss.

Simone collapsed on top of him. She laid her head down on his chest and shoulder, as he wrapped his arms around her. Completely satiated, he drifted off to sleep as she held tightly to him. They both woke up about an hour later.

"I'm starved," Simone said as she rolled down beside him. "And you promised me Italian."

Paul laughed. "You were the one who suggested dessert first."

"I like my goodies," she said as she lifted herself from the bed and headed back to the shower.

Paul propped himself up on his elbow to stare after her. "I like your goodies, too," he said, as she disappeared into the other room. He heard the shower running and Simone singing to herself, completely off-key. Lying back against the mattress, he took a couple of deep breaths and allowed himself the joy of feeling completely relaxed and happy.

Spago Trattoria E Pizzeria quickly became one of Simone's top-five favorite dinner spots. It was everything she loved about Italy, reminding her of the holiday excursion her father had taken her on for her twenty-first birthday.

They were greeted with bruschetta, a basket of warm focaccia bread, a bulb of roasted garlic and a bowl of fresh tomatoes tossed with garlic and olive oil. As she studied the menu, Paul ordered a bottle of Chianti and a traditional antipasto of mild *capicola*, salami, provolone cheese, roasted red peppers and eggplant for them to share.

For their entrées, Simone ordered the Italian risotto tossed with calamari and clams. Paul enjoyed the homemade manicotti filled with ricotta cheese and spinach, served with a meat sauce. They shared a slice of tiramisu for dessert. It was beyond decadent and by the time they finished both were stuffed.

"I just knew you'd need a take-home box," Paul said teasingly.

"No, you didn't."

He laughed. "I forgot just how much you love to eat."

She rolled her eyes, a slight smirk pulling at her lips.

"It really was good," she said. "Better than good! Thank you."

He leaned forward in his seat. "So, are you interested in a field trip?" he asked.

Simone leaned forward to meet him, the gesture feeling conspiratorial. "What did you have in mind?"

"I need to get my hands on samples of Halphedrone-B. Ideally from a different production lot than what we've already tested."

"How do you propose to do that?"

"I have a friend at Henry Ford Hospital in Detroit. I'm going to call him. I think he'll be willing to help if I ask."

"So, you want to go back over the border? And just hope your friend is just going to give you samples from their facility?"

Paul nodded. "Baby, I have a plan."

Chapter 9

It had been well over one month since they'd arrived in Canada. Most of their time was spent in their respective corners focused on their individual tasks. And when they weren't knee-deep in research, they were focused solidly on each other, reinvigorating their connection and rekindling the passion that had always been a cornerstone of their relationship. On this particular day, Paul had been on the phone most of the morning. International calls had occupied most of his time. He'd been hoping against all odds to convince the medical teams on the ground in the African countries to change the medication regime for patients he had treated who were still doing poorly. A few found his reasoning questionable and others wanted proof that he didn't have to give. Considering costs and availability, the alternative treatments he offered were met with trepidation and he felt as if he were banging his head against a brick wall. His frustration was palpable.

Simone had begun to outline the legal brief she intended to file. She'd been acting as her own law clerk, coordinating the data they knew with what they didn't as well as researching the legal precedents she would need to help make her case. Her frustration was equal to his, both challenged by the limitations and resources they had to work with.

Simone paced the floor, her mind racing. Every few moments she would pause to jot something down in the lengthy list of notes she'd been taking. With nothing else that he could do in the lab, Paul was cooking popcorn as he chatted on the phone with his brother. His tone was hushed, and she imagined whatever they were whispering about probably had more to do with her and him than their problem with the pharmaceutical company.

When her cell phone rang, she jumped, startled that anyone would be calling her. Her mother's face appeared on the screen, and Simone took a deep breath before answering. "Hi, Mom!" she said, sounding as cheery as she could manage.

"Where are you, Simone?" Judith Harmon Black asked, not bothering with hello.

Simone took another breath. "With Paul. Out of town."

"Out of town where, Simone?"

"What's wrong, Mom? Why are you interrogating me?"

"They've issued a warrant for Paul's arrest."

"For Paul's arrest?" she said, knowing she sounded like a parrot. "For what?"

"They want him to come in for questioning. Something about the three patients at the hospital and his involvement in their deaths."

"That's ridiculous! Paul would never hurt a soul. He's dedicated his entire life to helping others." A knot tightened through her abdomen and she suddenly felt sick to her stomach. She hadn't believed things could go from bad to worse, but clearly she'd underestimated karma.

"What's going on, Simone? Your father and I are worried sick about you."

"I'm fine. I'm safe," Simone said and then she explained to her mother what they were dealing with. "Now, with what you're telling me, we also need to prove Paul didn't murder anyone."

"You need to come home. Let Paul turn himself in and trust the judicial system to work."

"I can't, Mom. I'm sorry."

There was a thick pause that billowed heavily through the telephone lines. Simone imagined the look on her mother's face, the matriarch not at all happy with her, or with him. Paul had moved to her side, trailing a warm hand down the length of her back. His touch stalled the rise of anxiety that had threatened to consume her, and his presence was instantly calming. He'd been listening to her conversation after disconnecting his own.

Judith blew a gust of air into the phone line. "Let me speak to Paul," she commanded.

"Mom, don't…"

"Now," the older woman snapped.

Simone blew her own heavy sigh as she passed Paul the phone. "It's my mother," she said as she moved to the sofa and dropped down against the cushions.

Paul pulled the phone to his ear. "Yes, ma'am… No… I understand… Yes… Yes… I will… I promise."

There was another lengthy pause and Simone bristled at the lecture she imagined her mother was giving. Judge Black was a force to be reckoned with and she didn't take kindly to anyone messing with her kids or to her children disobeying a direct order. Simone and her siblings had been raised to be obedient and respectful and even as adults walked a fine line where their parents were concerned. Simone knew telling her mother no would not be taken lightly.

But if anyone understood why it was so important to Simone to be there for Paul, she knew her mother would. Her parents had the most solid relationship of any duo she'd ever known, and no one could ever say that Judith Harmon Black didn't always have her husband's back.

Most especially when it came to the law and seeking justice for those being exploited. As a power couple, they were undefeated and Simone wanted that for herself, no matter what it took.

"Would you like to speak to Simone again?" Paul was asking.

Simone shifted forward to the edge of the seat, expecting to hear her own lecture, but he disconnected the call instead, laying her phone onto the table.

"So, she told you about the arrest warrant?"

Simone nodded. "Yeah, but it doesn't make sense. Why would they blame you?"

"I had three patients at Northwestern Memorial that I personally treated with Halphedrone-B who've died. I stole their medical files from the hospital. Now they're saying they think someone purposely caused their deaths. I don't have all the details, so I don't know how they've come to that conclusion. Clearly, someone is trying to hem me up because they can't get to me. Oliver says they served a search warrant on my apartment this morning."

"Is that what you two were whispering about?"

He nodded. "I didn't want to upset you."

"Well, I'm not upset. I'm pissed! So, now we've got criminals trying to shoot at us, and the law looking to arrest us."

"They just want to arrest me."

"Trust and believe they'll handcuff and take me in too for aiding and abetting your criminal activity if they get the opportunity. And that's just the short list of the crimes I've committed." Simone tossed up her hands.

Paul shrugged. "My list is probably a little longer."

"I wouldn't brag about that if I were you."

"So, what do you want to do?" he asked, his eyes wide as he studied her intently.

"What did my mother say to you?" she said, answering his question with a question of her own.

"She told me to keep you safe."

"That's all?"

"Basically. She said she didn't think it was a good idea for us to try and deal with this on our own but that she would trust our judgment."

"She wasn't mad?" Simone asked, looking shocked.

"Oh, she was mad! She was fuming!"

Simone dropped her face into the palms of her hands, swiping at her eyes. She pulled her knees to her chest and wrapped her arms around her legs. She suddenly felt like they had the weight of the world bearing down on their shoulders. She thought they'd been steadily digging their way out and now it felt as if the sides of the hole had caved in, burying them back under. She couldn't help but wonder if they were ever going to catch a break.

Paul dropped down onto the seat beside her. He slid an arm around her torso and pulled her against him, kissing the top of her head.

"Do you want the good news?" he asked.

"There's good news?"

He nodded. "Tomorrow morning the sales rep for Lender will be meeting with my doctor friend. He'll get the samples we need."

"I'd like to ask her a few questions."

"I'd rather we stay as inconspicuous as possible."

"You realize if we don't get stopped at the border going back into the United States, depending on how far that arrest warrant has already extended, that we probably won't be able to cross back into Canada, right?"

"That is very possible," he answered. "But it's a risk we're going to have to take."

"Okay," Simone said, reaching for the bowl of freshly

popped popcorn that he'd drizzled with truffle butter, and sprinkled with cracked pepper and Parmesan cheese. "As long as we're on the same page."

The customs agent who welcomed them back into the United States barely gave them a second look. Once the car was inspected and their documents verified, he waved them on through. They arrived at Henry Ford Hospital some thirty minutes before the scheduled appointment with Paul's friend, Dr. Stephen Alexander, a pediatric resident who'd gone to medical school with him. For ten of those thirty minutes they strategized where to park in case they needed to make a quick run for it.

"Are you sure about this?" Simone questioned, her nerves beginning to get to her.

Paul shot her a quick look. "Right now, no one knows I'm a wanted man. At least I don't think so. So as far as anyone is concerned, I'm just meeting my friend the doctor who's helping me with a problem. I'll go in, make nice and come right back out. But you do not have to do this with me, Simone. I don't want you to be uneasy."

"I don't want you to get arrested. I just want to make sure you're sure about this! So just say you're sure!"

He gave her smile and nodded. "I have to do this, Simone."

"Then I have to do it with you. We're in this together."

The light in his eyes dimmed ever so slightly. He turned in his seat to face her. "Before we go in, there's something I need to tell you."

Simone's nerves suddenly shifted into another gear. Her palms began to sweat and she swiped them against the leg of her black pants. "Why are you giving me anxiety?"

"I don't mean to, baby, but it's important I'm totally honest with you."

"About what?"

"The sales rep for Lender is a woman named Vivian Lincoln."

Simone bristled, crossing her arms over her chest, her jaw tightening. "And?"

"Vivian and I dated for a minute after you and I broke up. It wasn't serious and didn't go anywhere but I wanted you to know."

"Define 'dated.'"

"We went out a time or two. Dinner mostly and to the theater once."

"The theater? What show?" The question came with significant attitude. Simone was simmering on a low burn, Paul's admission hitting her broadside. Despite the length of time they'd been apart she had never considered he might date someone else. She was squarely in her feelings and unable to contain her displeasure. Jealousy grabbed her by the seat of her pants and was hanging on with all fangs.

"Why does it matter what show?"

"What show, Paul?"

"*Hamilton*. We went to see *Hamilton*."

"*Hamilton*? On Broadway? In New York?"

He nodded. "Yes."

"And you slept with her?"

He shook his head vehemently. "No, we've never slept together."

"You went to New York with her to see *Hamilton* and you didn't stay in a hotel room together?" Simone found herself imagining the worst and it broke her heart to even think that Paul had been able to spend time with any woman that wasn't her. She knew she was being irrational, but she didn't care.

"I flew into New York and met her on one of my layovers to Europe. We had time for dinner and the show, then I went back to the airport to catch my plane. I don't know where she went after that."

"Do you like her?"

"I enjoy talking with her, but she's not a woman I would be romantically interested in."

"But you took her to see *Hamilton*?"

"Actually, she invited me."

"What's wrong with her?"

"She's not you," Paul said matter-of-factly.

Simone sat for a moment, pondering his comment. "For the record," she finally said. "I never dated anyone when we were apart. Not even a date for coffee."

He smiled. "I appreciate that."

"Absolutely no one! And trust me, I had more than my fair share of invitations."

Paul laughed. "You're mad."

"I am not mad."

"Yes, you are. But I swear, it was nothing!" He stole a quick glance down to his wristwatch. "We should probably get inside," he concluded.

She rolled her eyes. "You know we're not done with this conversation, right? I have more questions."

Paul shook his head. "No, we're done. There's nothing else to discuss and you are not going to drive me crazy being jealous over a woman who is irrelevant in the scheme of our future. That's not going to happen."

"Who said anything about being jealous?"

He shrugged, eyeing her with a raised brow.

Simone narrowed her gaze slightly. There was a lengthy pause as they sat studying each other. "Okay," she said finally.

"I mean it, Simone."

"I said okay!" There was still a hint of attitude in her tone.

Paul continued to consider her, apparently trying to read the expression on her face. He leaned forward and gave her a kiss on her lips. "I love you, Simone. I don't love anyone else."

Simone smiled, then she pushed open the door and exited the car. The tidal wave of emotion was passing slowly and she was determined not to let it get the best of her. She believed Paul. And she trusted him, having no doubts about any other woman in his life. But Old Simone was trying to rear her ugly head and make his admission more than it needed to be. It was taking everything in her for New Simone to put those feelings in a headlock and send them away.

Paul jumped out of the driver's side as she moved to the sidewalk, turning as she waited for him to join her. She extended her hand, reaching to hold his hand. Their fingers intertwined and he gave her a slight squeeze.

"We good?" Paul questioned as they headed for the hospital's entrance.

"She better be ugly, that's all I'm going to say," Simone answered. "And I mean butt-ugly."

Paul laughed. "There's not a woman around that can hold a candle to you, Simone Black!"

"And don't you forget it!"

Dr. Stephen Alexander reminded Simone of a young Jeff Goldblum. Before Jeff Goldblum had matured into the sexy version of himself that he was now, she thought. He had a beautiful smile that gleamed from his eyes and Spock-like ears that didn't go unnoticed. His chestnut-blond hair was cut a half inch too short and his glasses were too large for his face.

She stood back as the two men greeted each other

with a weird fist-bump-and-hand-tap thing and a deep bear hug.

Paul grabbed her hand and pulled her forward. "Stephen, this is Simone Black. Simone, this is Dr. Stephen Alexander. Stephen and I go way back."

"It's nice to meet you, Dr. Alexander. I've heard a lot about you," she said, as he took her hand and kissed the backs of her fingers.

"The pleasure is all mine. But Paul didn't tell me anything about you!"

Paul laughed as the two shot him a look. "I'm no fool. Stephen's quite the ladies' man and back in the day the women wouldn't even look in my direction if he was around. I couldn't risk the chance of him stealing you from me."

Stephen laughed. "I definitely would have tried," he said as he winked an eye at Simone.

Paul smirked as he wrapped his arm around her shoulder protectively and hugged her to him. "We really appreciate your help."

"I wish I could do more. You know how I feel about Big Pharma. I don't trust the whole lot of 'em."

"Stephen believes in a more holistic approach to patient care," Paul said, directing his comment toward Simone.

"I don't believe physicians serve their patients well when all they're doing is prescribing meds unnecessarily. Unfortunately, the pharmaceutical business has played on people's greed. Incentivizing doctors to market their products and prescribe medications in exchange for payments is just wrong on many levels."

"Criminal enterprise happens in all forms," Simone said.

Stephen smiled. "So, Ms. Lincoln is actually here. She's

down in our cafeteria, waiting for me to join her for a cup of coffee. You didn't tell me she was so attractive."

"If you like that type," Paul muttered. He shot Simone a look, noting the look she gave him back. Her jaw had tightened, and she clenched her teeth. He changed the subject. "Did she leave you any product?" Paul questioned.

Stephen nodded, pointing to a clear cellophane bag filled with samples that rested on his desk. "She's pushing a new blood pressure medication, but I did ask for the Halphedrone-B. She said she only had a few samples left but she tossed them in there, too. Take all of it."

"Thank you. I owe you," Paul said.

"If it will save lives, my friend, you can always rely on me. But I need to run right now. I have a patient I need to check on and then I have a coffee date to discuss homeopathic medicine with Ms. Lincoln. You two be safe out there."

The two men bumped shoulders one last time and Simone gave the man a warm hug. Paul didn't miss the squeeze the good doctor gave her, or that his hands rested just shy of her backside. He bit back his comment, knowing it would only escalate an unnecessary argument and expose the tinge of jealousy that had teased his spirit.

Simone grabbed the samples bag and shoved it into the leather tote over her shoulder. "What now?" she asked.

"We can try to cross back into Canada, or we head back to Chicago. Your choice."

"No, it's your choice. I can't make that decision, Paul."

"I really want to test these samples and Oliver is flying back tomorrow."

"Then we take our chances and hope they haven't put you in the system yet. But I'm thinking the sooner we go, the better."

Paul nodded. "Let's get on the road!"

Exiting the office, they headed in the direction of the elevator. Simone spied a rest room just as Paul pushed the button to go down to the main lobby.

"Wait for me. I need to use the bathroom," she said as she hurried toward the women's room door.

"I'll be right here," Paul replied.

He stepped back out of the walkway and leaned against the wall to wait for her. Surprise flowed through him when the elevator door opened and Lender's drug representative, Vivian Lincoln, stepped out.

"Vivian!"

"Paul! Oh, my goodness! What are you doing here?"

"Visiting a friend," he said. "What are you up to?"

"Business." She gestured to the leather carry bag she was rolling behind her.

"I didn't realize your territory extended this far east."

She smiled. "It does." She changed the subject. "You never called me."

"I was in Ghana longer than I anticipated. I've only been back for a few days."

The woman named Vivian nodded. She took a step forward, pressing a hand against his chest. "If you're not busy, maybe we can grab lunch after I'm finished with my appointment. I think we need to talk."

"About?"

"I heard you might be having some issues with one of our products. I was hoping to alleviate your concerns and maybe answer any questions you might have. I also want to catch up. I've missed you." She gave him a bright smile, her lashes batting at him as she tapped her manicured fingertips against the buttons of his shirt.

Paul hesitated for a split second and then he returned her smile. "I'd love to. I can meet you downstairs?"

"Wonderful! Let me swing by and let the doctor know I can't wait and then we can get out of here."

Paul gave her another bend of his lips, showcasing his picture-perfect teeth. "I'll be in the lobby waiting," he said as he pushed the down button for the elevator to return.

Vivian headed down the hallway, tossing one last look over her shoulder. As Paul stepped into the conveyor, he pulled his phone into his hands to send Simone a text.

Simone was washing her hands when the other woman walked into the bathroom. Waif thin, she was supermodel tall with hair the color of corn silk cascading down her back. Her features were delicate, like fine porcelain. The suit she wore was perfectly tailored and expensive, as were her red-bottomed high-heeled shoes.

She was dialing her phone and she looked slightly discombobulated. She gave Simone a dismissive glance, then turned her back as she waited for the party she called to answer on the other end.

Simone reached for a paper towel to dry her hands. She turned back to the mirror, leaning forward to inspect her face. She was as dismissive of the stranger as the stranger was of her. Until the woman began speaking and recognition settled over her. The stranger had to be Vivian Lincoln!

Simone struggled not to stare. And not to stare so that the other woman noticed. Eyeing her own reflection in the mirror, she suddenly felt frumpish, having thrown on a pair of jeans, running shoe, and her favorite sweatshirt. Her makeup was sparse, just a hint of eyeliner and some lip gloss. She pulled her hands through her hair, hoping to give the curly strands a hint of volume. She didn't look bad, but she didn't look like she'd just stepped off the cover of *Glamour* magazine. Simone suddenly understood why Paul had even considered dating the woman. She was overly attractive and clearly confident. Simone's insecurities suddenly tied a knot in her midsection. She swallowed hard, biting back the feelings that had snuck in to ambush her.

The other woman was tapping her foot anxiously before whispering loudly into her phone. "He's here… I don't know why… I just ran into him in the hallway… What do you want me to do?" There was a lengthy pause as she seemed to be listening to instructions.

She still had her back to Simone as she began to speak again. "We just made plans for lunch… Okay… Okay… I'll do that… I'm staying at the Hyatt, room twenty twelve… Trust me. I'll get him there… Just tell them to hurry… We can't afford for them to miss this time… If I have to, I'll call the police and scream bloody murder as a last resort… I won't… I said I won't…"

When she disconnected the call, inhaling a deep breath of air, Simone was pulling a brush through her hair. She didn't bother to look in Simone's direction as she stepped to the sink to rinse her hands.

Simone smiled as they exchanged tentative gazes in the mirror. "Love those shoes," she said, her eyes dropping to the woman's feet.

The blonde looked where she stared. "Thank you," she said, her tone indifferent.

"Are you a doctor?" Simone asked. "You look like you might be a doctor."

The woman shot her another quick look. "No, I'm a sales rep. I represent a drug company."

"Interesting. It must pay well for you to afford those shoes. Or are they knockoffs?"

"They are very real," the woman said, clearly offended

by the insinuation. She turned toward an empty stall, dragging her medical case behind her.

Simone shrugged. "Good luck with that sales job," she said as she moved to the door and exited the space. She hurried to the elevator. As she waited for it to return to the floor, she read the text message Paul had sent her. Car. Now! Hurry!

Chapter 10

"I can't believe you dated that woman. How did you know she was trying to set you up?" Simone asked Paul once she returned to the car.

"She's a sales rep. There was no reason for anyone in Africa to call a US sales rep about me questioning their international representative. And I haven't spoken to her since before my last mission trip."

"Why did she think she'd be able to get you to her hotel room?" There was something accusing in her tone, her words laced with attitude. Clearly, Vivian Lincoln had reason to think Paul would actually have lunch with her, Simone thought. She was suddenly curious about the time they'd spent together. What else had they shared? How much did Vivian know about her? Did Vivian know anything at all about her? About them and their relationship? And what about Paul? Had seeing her again reawakened feelings he hadn't yet shared with her?

Paul cut his gaze in her direction. "Simone, please, don't do that. You know me better than that."

Simone shrugged. "It was just a question. Don't get an attitude with me."

Paul reached for her hand and kissed the back of it. He'd been sitting in the car with the engine running when Simone came racing back. She'd been beside herself with rage, detailing her encounter with Vivian. Then her emotions had gotten the best of her, her frustrations becoming irrational. Jealousy had always been a character flaw with Simone, even as she asserted with much conviction that she wasn't jealous. It was equally frustrating for him to argue about things that were not relevant in their lives and gut-wrenching to see her put herself through such turmoil. It also annoyed the hell out of him that Simone continually insisted it wasn't him she didn't trust, but the other women who sometimes set their sights on his attention. Vivian was now her latest source of outrage. Her ranting had taken on a life of its own as they navigated back to the Detroit-Windsor Tunnel.

"What happens if they run your information and the warrant comes up?" Simone questioned, changing the subject.

Paul took a deep breath and exhaled. "I'll need you to take the samples back to the house for Oliver. Then I want you to go back home to Chicago. I'm going to need an attorney and you can't represent me from Canada."

"I still work for the prosecutor's office. I can't represent you at all."

"Have you decided against the job offer?"

"No. Not really. In fact, I was thinking that my bringing the case against Lender to the table would probably score me some points."

"So, you'll have two cases to bring to them, because I didn't kill anyone. Not through any fault of my own," he said, his voice dropping an octave.

Simone squeezed his hand as he pulled up to the toll station. The customs inspector asked for their passports and the car's registration. Neither wanted to admit it, but they were both scared. Simone closed her eyes, sending a prayer skyward. A few minutes passed before the agent returned their documents.

"Welcome to Canada," the man said, giving them both a nod. He gestured for them to proceed forward.

The couple held their breath until they passed the toll station on the Canadian side and were five miles away from the border.

Simone suddenly burst out laughing, tears streaming down her cheeks. "Boy, did we get lucky." She held her hand out, palm side down, the appendage still shaking.

Paul exhaled the breath he'd been holding. He'd been scared and couldn't begin to tell Simone just how frightened he'd been. Jail definitely wasn't on his bucket list of things to experience. He also wasn't prepared to be derailed when there was still so much they needed to do to prove their case. He blew out another deep breath. "God was definitely on our side!"

Simone nodded. "I've lost count of the laws we've broken. It'll be a miracle if I can keep my law license after all of this." She swiped at her face with the backs of her hands.

Paul bristled, her expression pulling at his heartstrings. She hadn't asked for any of this and he couldn't begin to know how to make things right and get her out of the mess he'd managed to drag her into. "I'm really sorry, Simone," Paul said. "I never meant for you to get caught up in any of this mess."

"I know. I'm here because I chose to be. I could have walked away before we left Chicago and I didn't. I didn't know what might happen and I didn't want you to be alone. I wanted to be here if you needed me. I failed you once. I couldn't live with myself if I failed you again."

"But Simone, baby, you've never failed me. You had a right to feel the way you did. I never held that against you. I've always just wanted you to be happy."

"I'll be really happy when I can put my foot up Vivian's…"

Paul laughed. "Dial it back a notch," he said stalling the expletive he knew was coming. "She'll get hers. But we need to stay focused."

"I am focused. Clearly, she's knee-deep in this and the fact that she was willing to throw you under a bus doesn't sit well with me. She's not going to get away with it."

"Let it go, Simone. Please!"

"Do not tell me you're going to give that woman a pass?"

"Of course not! She'll get what's coming to her, I'm sure. But since we don't know how she's involved we can't jump to any conclusions."

"You're actually going to defend that witch?"

"That's not what I'm doing. Why are you getting so heated over this?"

The look she was giving him was classic Simone, attitude-filled and unhappy about something. The mood between them suddenly did a nosedive. His frustration level increased tenfold. It was moments like this, going back and forth with her, that made him question what they were doing with each other. Doubt trickled like water from a leaky faucet and suddenly he found himself questioning if they'd ever get past the issues that had torn them apart previously.

Paul's defenses kicked into second gear. "I am not going to fight with you, Simone. I do not have the energy to do that song and dance you like to do when you're feeling insecure about something."

"Insecure?" Her voice had risen a few octaves.

Paul's voice rose to match hers. "Yes, insecure. You get in your feelings and then you lash out. It's Simone 101— if you can't control it, it's a fight. If you feel threatened, it's a fight. Hell, even when it should make you happy, you make it a fight! And I don't want to fight with you!"

Simone sat with clenched fists, every muscle in her body hardened with ire. Her breathing grew labored. "You need to get back into the lab," Simone snapped, her mind clearly spinning in a hundred different directions.

There was an awkward pause that rose like a morning mist. Paul pulled onto the lengthy driveway, stopping when they reached the house. He shifted the car into Park and cut off the engine. Simone was staring out the window, her eyes narrowed, her jaw tight.

"Simone? What are you thinking?" Paul questioned, reading her mood.

"Nothing," she muttered.

"Simone?"

"What?" She met the look he was giving her with one of her own, something like defiance spinning in her gaze.

"Tell me what's going through your head, Simone. You need to talk to me."

"Nothing! Why are you badgering me?"

"Badgering? Really? I'm trying to figure out why you suddenly have attitude."

Simone rolled her eyes skyward. "I need to get back to work," she snapped as she opened the car door and exited the vehicle.

Paul watched her stomp to the door, her arms folded across her chest as she waited for him to come unlock it. Despite his own annoyance, a slight smile pulled across his face. Some things clearly hadn't changed, and Simone's short fuse was still short.

Hours later Simone poured salt-and-vinegar potato chips into a large glass bowl and white wine into a glass. The light was still on in the barn and she knew Paul had thrown himself into his research. She had pushed his buttons and then she had shut down, leaving him annoyed and anxious. It was a typical play out of their relationship handbook and once again Simone felt like she was dooming them both to fail. She stuffed a chip into her mouth as she headed down the hallway to lock herself back in the bedroom.

Simone was feeling slightly foolish and she wasn't quite ready to face Paul and apologize. She didn't have any reason to be angry at him, yet she'd thrown every ounce of her frustration in his direction. It never made any sense before and it didn't now. She needed to do better, yet she seemed unable to get past the bad behavior that had always been her downfall.

The only time emotion didn't rule her life was when she was in a courtroom. In front of a judge, Simone was always calm and collected, the epitome of professionalism. But once she stepped out the courthouse doors she was a simmering volcano and it took little for her to erupt. In her head, being quick to put others in their place, rage against the status quo, and just being a general pain in the ass masked what she was truly going on in her head. Being brash, aggressive, and keeping others an arm's length away kept them from seeing her vulnerabilities and her weaknesses.

She couldn't begin to explain to Paul or anyone else how she sometimes felt inadequate and unworthy. Everyone loved to tell her what a great guy Paul Reilly was, and she was always questioning why someone like him would want her. She could be a handful most days: snarky, ill-tempered and contentious. She wasn't sugar and spice and all the nice things the fairy tales said little girls were made of. She always felt like she wasn't doing enough or being great enough, always falling short on an imaginary scale of her own making. Despite a public perception of her being attractive, intelligent and accomplished, and her parents constantly hammering how wonderful she was, she felt like an imposter in her own body.

Living up to her parent's expectations left little room for failure. She had big shoes to fill and with siblings who'd made it successfully to the finish line with few missteps, she couldn't afford to be a disappointment. To them, or the man willing to take her on and love her. No amount of rationalizing every good thing she brought to their relationship stopped her from doubting her worth and when doubt set in, Simone lashed out and usually at Paul.

After resting her popcorn and wine on the nightstand, she threw her body across the bed and reached for her cell phone. She dialed her sister's number, taking a quick sip of her drink as she waited for the woman to answer her phone.

"Hello?"

"Vaughan, hey!"

"My little sister the fugitive! How are you?"

"That's not funny, Vaughan."

"Actually, it's hilarious! What's not funny is that our parents are on the verge of divorce, arguing about what to do about you. Our father is ready to call in the cavalry."

"Would you please tell them I'm fine?"

"Did Mom tell you there's a warrant out for Paul's arrest?"

"Yes. She said they think he may have killed three of his patients."

"She exaggerated that a bit. A lot, actually. The hospital filed a report that they suspected he was in possession of files for three of his patients and they've not been able to reach him to question why. Plus, they're concerned, because some FBI types in suits with badges have been there asking questions about him. But Parker did a little digging and the suits aren't associated with law enforcement and their badges are fake. Then, when Daddy found out someone took a shot at you both, he issued a city-wide alert to bring Paul in for his own protection and to get you home."

"Does he always have to manipulate everything?"

"Do you not remember who your father is? The superintendent for the entire Chicago Police Department, appointed by His Honor, the mayor, thinks his baby daughter might be in serious trouble. He's going to manipulate everything he can personally control and some things he can't. He's even threatening to issue a warrant for *your* arrest. We've all been given explicit instructions to call him if you reach out to any of us. He tore Mingus a new orifice when he found out our brother helped you go off the grid."

Simone's heavy sigh was tempered with a sudden case of the hiccups as she choked back tears. She was suddenly feeling very emotional and she couldn't begin to explain why. Her family was worried about her, Paul loved her, and she was kicking herself for being ugly about a woman who didn't matter one iota in the grand scheme of things. Everything that had happened since Paul had called her suddenly flooded her spirit and twisted her insides into tight knots. The deluge of emotion was overwhelming.

"What's wrong?" Vaughan asked, as if sensing her sister's distress.

"Mom and Dad really just need to chill," Simone muttered. "I'm fine."

"Are you sure? Because you don't sound like you're fine."

"I picked a fight with Paul for no reason."

"That's sounds like par for the course with you, Simone. Self-sabotage has always been your specialty."

"I didn't call for you to be mean to me, Vaughan."

"Honesty is not mean, little sister."

"Whatever! He told me the other day that I was spoiled. And mean. And he dated this other woman while we were separated."

"Ohhh, so now we're getting to the real reason for your call. Give me all the juicy details. But wait, let me pour myself a glass of wine first because this sounds like it's going to be good."

Simone listened as her sister dropped her phone, still talking as she moved around her kitchen.

"I'm coming… Hold on… Do not hang up… Okay, I'm back. Who is this woman Paul dated? Are they still together?"

"Her name is Vivian Lincoln and she's a medical sales rep for the drug company we're investigating."

"Was it serious? Or just a casual fling?"

"They went to see *Hamilton* together."

"*Hamilton*?"

"Yes!"

"The musical? In New York?"

"Yes! And I met her and she's this horrible person and just because I had a little attitude about it, Paul had the audacity to call me insecure." Simone's voice rose an octave. "There is nothing *insecure* about me!" she insisted.

Vaughan didn't bother to respond, complete silence coming from her end of the telephone line. The quiet was suddenly deafening, and for the briefest moment, Simone thought the cell service had dropped the call.

"Hello? Vaughan? Hello?"

"I'm still here."

"Why didn't you say anything?"

"Oh, I'm sorry. I was waiting for you to say something I could agree with."

"I am *not* insecure!"

"You have moments, Simone. Especially when it comes to Paul! So, why did you get all in your feelings about him dating this woman? You did dump him, remember?"

Simone blew the faintest sigh, her voice dropping to a loud whisper. "You didn't see her."

"Paul loves you, Simone. I can't for the life of me figure out why you have never trusted that."

"He said the same thing."

"Well, you really need to think about it. And you need to think about why you're always so bitchy toward him. Because most men would have been done with you by now. In fact, I'm starting to question why he puts up with you and your bad behavior."

"Paul Reilly loves me."

"Ding, ding, ding!"

Simone laughed. "Okay! I get it."

"He deserves better from you, Simone. He's one of the good guys and there is a long line of women who are chomping at the bit to take your place so stop playing games with him."

"I just can't seem to get out of my own head."

"Well, only you can figure out what is holding you back. We can all tell you how great you are. How great Paul is. Paul can tell you over and over again what you mean to him. But ultimately, if you don't believe it, then why should anyone else care?"

Simone paused to reflect on her sister's comment. Since they'd been little girls, her big sister had been her voice of reason. Vaughan had never hesitated to point out the error of Simone's ways or to turn her around when she was headed off track. When Simone felt like a dim light in a room full of bright bulbs, Vaughan would push her to shine. The bond between them was irrefutable and even when Simone felt off-balance or completely lost, just talking to her sister brought her back to an even keel.

"I need you to do me a favor," Simone said.

"Anything. You know that."

"Ask Mingus to find out everything he can on Vivian Lincoln. She works for Lender Pharmaceuticals but I'm not sure where she's based out of."

"Will this help with the problem you two are trying to resolve? Or is this for your own personal vendetta?"

"It's not personal," Simone said, sharing the details of her bathroom encounter with the woman. "I need to figure out who she's connected to and why she's gunning for Paul."

"What do you want me to tell Mom and Dad?"

"I'll call Dad when we're headed back that way but until then, ask them to please call off the dogs."

"I'll see what I can do. Just stay safe, please."

"I love you, sissy!"

"I love you, too!"

Disconnecting the call, Simone tossed the phone onto the nightstand and fell back against the pillows, debating whether she wanted to analyze her own shortcomings or ponder dryer lint while she waited for Paul to finish what he was working on and come back inside.

Paul paused in the back door that same night, listening to a playlist of love songs Simone had programmed into the sound system. He knew her better than she knew herself sometimes, and he knew she was feeling contrite about her mood swing and the tension that had bloomed like a brick wall between them.

Her tantrums remained a bone of contention between

them and he had come to acquiesce that he'd have to accept her moodiness if they were going to move forward. If he weighed her positive attributes against the negatives, her moments were well worth the heated arguments that always led them back to what was most important to them. Each other.

Simone was a powerhouse and highly accomplished. She'd graduated magna cum laude from Western Illinois University and then summa cum laude from Harvard Law School. As a state prosecutor she was known to be a shark in Jimmy Choo stilettos and pristinely tailored designer suits. She served on multiple corporate boards, volunteered at the Boys and Girls Clubs of Chicago and was well-known in the community for her philanthropy, most especially where it served the issues and rights for women and girls. She was bold, sometimes brash and always brilliant.

Success oozed from Simone's fingertips. Everything she touched was gold. So, it completely baffled him that she was sometimes so doubtful about their relationship and her own self-worth. She could frequently be jealous and too often quick to try to blow them up. They had argued about it often and Paul was willing to wager that her problems had nothing at all to do with Simone fearing failure and everything to do with her fear of being a disappointment to everyone she loved, particularly her parents.

Simone came from a family of high achievers and her parents' expectations were monumental. When the two of them had discussed marriage, Simone had held her mother and father's union up as the example she intended to emulate. They were ride or die for each other, but neither had ever given up on their own dreams. She and her siblings had been raised that relationships weren't to be taken lightly and marriage was sacred. She wasn't willing to take the risk if she believed the union could have major problems. She only intended to be married once and divorce wasn't an option she ever wanted to consider if things went left. Road bumps in the dating stage were red flags she wasn't willing to ignore. Her theories about relationships in general, and theirs in particular, had driven him crazy. Because their biggest challenge had always been getting Simone to simply trust the process, his intentions, and to let their love be what fate intended for it to be. And Simone could never trust what she could not control and manipulate.

He moved to the kitchen. A plate sat table center covered in aluminum foil. A sticky note rested against an empty glass. Simone had drawn a simple heart and signed it with a lipstick kiss. Again, classic Simone, an apology that was everything but an actual apology. But it was heartfelt, and he knew she truly was remorseful about their fight.

Paul pushed the foil aside to expose a baked chicken breast, canned string beans and cheesy potatoes au gratin. He had to smile because Simone didn't typically cook, so the effort must be genuine. He moved to the microwave, set the timer for two minutes and poured himself a glass of wine as he waited for the food to warm.

Minutes later he realized how hungry he was as he wolfed the meal down, barely chewing before he swallowed. It was tasty and quickly stalled the pangs of discomfort that had cramped his stomach. He only wished she had been there to share dinner with him, but he realized it was well after midnight and Simone was probably sound asleep.

After washing the dirty dishes and straightening the kitchen Paul poured himself a glass of bourbon and moved to the living room sofa. Sam Smith echoed out of the speakers, singing some sad, slow song questioning why he was so emotional. Paul sat sipping his drink as the last embers of a fire died down in the fireplace. With everything Paul had on his mind he couldn't focus. All he could think of was Simone, wondering if a time would come when all he needed to worry about was making her happy.

Simone thought she was still in a dream as she rolled onto her back. It was warm and she was comfortable, her body temperature rising sweetly. Feathers, she thought, as the gentlest touch passed against her bare skin. It felt like feathers doing an erotic dance around her knees and up her inner thighs. It tickled, but it didn't, just feeling heated and teasing. She heard someone moan and the slightest smile pulled across her face. And then that touch became a nibble and she gasped loudly, realizing that it was her who was moaning.

Simone took a deep inhale of air and her eyes fluttered open and then closed and then open. The room was dark, just the faintest rays of moonlight shining through the windows. She didn't know what time it was, only that Paul had finally come to bed.

She felt Paul's hands trailing a lazy path down the length of her legs, his mouth fluttering damp kisses against her flesh. He had her body on fire, all her synapses firing with electricity. It felt like the Fourth of July fireworks from her head down to her toes. She murmured his name, a soft chant blowing through the air like a prayer. Then she parted her legs in invitation.

Simone was in agony with desire, the pain like a deep craving that was intoxicating and addictive. When he blew warm breath against her most private space, she pushed herself toward him, the need having grown more than she had ever imagined. She pushed forward again, wanting his touch to quell the rising heat. But he teased again, in no hurry to rush his ministrations. He blew softly against her again, then gently nipped at her inner thigh until he reached the apex of her parting.

He tugged first at her outer lips, then the inner, using his mouth to send waves of pleasure through her, and then his tongue prodded her clitoris and his fingers slipped into her damp, moist cavity. Simone grabbed the bedclothes with both hands and her back arched. She bit down against her bottom lip, fighting not to scream.

Giving in to the frenzy of feelings, Simone felt her body swirl and spin. It was a rollercoaster ride of sheer gratification and she savored the decadent sensations that were suddenly consuming. Her eyes rolled and her muscles clenched and then just like that her world exploded, the sensation like a tsunami rushing through space. It was a staggering tide of pleasure, with rolling waves convulsing through her body. She rode the crest for what seemed like an eternity, slowly slipping back to the sound of Paul's voice murmuring endearments as he kissed a slow trail up the length of her torso, until he was nuzzling his face into her neck. She opened her eyes and he was smiling down at her.

"You good?" he asked, kissing her neck, along her jawline and then her cheeks.

Simone nodded. "Better than good," she whispered back. "Do you forgive me?"

Paul nodded. "I always do. I love you."

Simone nodded her own head a second time and then she widened her parted legs even more as he nestled the entirety of his body against her. As he slid himself into her, she wrapped one leg and then the other around his back, her arms tightening around his torso as she clung to him with complete abandon. He loved her, and he whispered it repeatedly like the sweetest mantra, and Simone loved him back as fiercely.

Chapter 11

The next morning, Paul was already back in the lab when Simone finally crawled out of bed and made it to the kitchen. He'd left freshly cooked bacon and croissants on the table. A clean frying pan rested on the stove and eggs sat in a bowl on the counter beside a softened stick of butter.

Simone wasn't feeling one-hundred-percent and hoped the coffee would give her the push she needed to get her day started. Despite what had turned out to be an incredible night, she was feeling like her body was failing her. She had her fingers crossed that she wasn't coming down with a cold, or worse, the flu.

With her coffee mug in one hand and a croissant in the other she moved into the dining room. Standing before the notes she'd pasted to the wall, she studied the line of data that was known to them with the data that wasn't.

Paul and Oliver had identified the contaminant and had established a pattern of exposure. How the contaminant had been created was still questionable, although Paul had a few theories that he hoped the additional testing would help answer. Nor did they know for certain that Lender even knew about the contaminant and if they did, why they were ignoring it. Simone was discovering that drug manufacturing was far more complicated than she originally realized and companies that routinely outsourced their manufacturing processes and acquired their active ingredients from global marketplaces were subject to all manner of catastrophes.

The hard facts they could prove, they planned to present to the FDA and demand further investigation and a recall of the product. She also planned to file a civil lawsuit, hopeful that litigation would motivate Lender to remove the drug voluntarily and do what was right by the patients affected by their flawed business practices. It wasn't going to be a cheap endeavor and neither one of them necessarily had the personal resources to fight Lender on their own and that meant finding additional legal help, preferably a law firm with deep pockets and a solid reputation. In theory, it all sounded like a solid plan. In reality, Simone knew there was a lot of hard work ahead of them and no guarantee there would be any return on their investment.

She dropped down onto one of the cushioned seats and took a sip of her coffee to wash down the bite of pastry that seemed stuck in her chest, feeling too heavy to swallow. Her stomach flipped and for the briefest second, she thought her breakfast might not stay with her through lunch. The sensation passed just as quickly as it had bubbled her tummy.

She suddenly felt overwhelmed and she knew it might take making a decision Paul would not agree with to get the job done. She closed her eyes and let herself sit in the quiet, her mind racing as she pondered what her next steps would be and if her steps and his led them in the same direction.

"Simone? You okay?"

Paul was standing before her, eyeing her with concern. He was wearing her favorite gray sweatshirt, the one she'd given him for his last birthday. They had gone skiing in

Aspen for an extended weekend and had spent most of their time in their cabin, snuggled against each other. It had been his birthday, but he had made that whole weekend about her, making her feel like the luckiest woman in the world. The memory still made her tingle with joy.

She reached out her hand to press it against his abdomen, relishing the feel of the soft cotton blend. She tugged at him gently, pulling him toward her until his lips met hers in the sweetest kiss.

"I'm good. Good morning."

"Good morning. How long have you been up?"

Her eyes skated from side to side. "What time is it?"

"Just after twelve."

"After twelve? It wasn't quite ten o'clock when I sat down!"

Paul laughed. "You didn't get a whole lot of rest last night."

"I got enough that I shouldn't be falling asleep in a chair!"

His smile was consoling. "It happens."

"Not to me it doesn't. I think I'm catching something. I didn't feel well when I got up."

Paul pressed his palm to her forehead. "You don't feel like you're running a fever, but we don't want to take any chances. Any other symptoms I should be aware of?"

She shook her head. "I was slightly nauseous this morning, but I think it was just because I drank coffee on an empty stomach and got a slight caffeine rush."

"But you always drink coffee on an empty stomach, don't you?"

"Usually. I can't think of anything else it might be."

"Well, just to be on the safe side, I'm going to make you a cup of tea and some chicken noodle soup for lunch.

And I want you to take a dose of vitamin C for me. I think you might just need to take a break today."

"I have way too much work to do. And I'm sure it's not that serious," she said.

"Well, we're going to relax together. I've done all I can do, and Oliver doesn't get in until later tonight. So, we can watch Netflix movies and chill all afternoon."

Simone pursed her lips. She started to balk but changed her mind. She still felt funky and lying around watching movies with Paul wouldn't be that bad. She nodded. "If you insist."

Paul gave her a wink of his eye. "I do. And even though you don't feel warm, I want to get your temperature. Let me grab the thermometer."

That day, they felt like they were on vacation and not trying to save the world, Simone thought as she snuggled against Paul. His idea of chilling was to alternate between watching a documentary and reading some scientific study on his iPad. Simone had been dozing off and on for most of the afternoon, convinced the cold weather was trying to throw her off-balance. She couldn't afford to be sick, as every time she thought about the case her to-do list lengthened substantially.

The sounds of the door opening and closing pulled them both from the reverie. Oliver's booming voice filled the space and lifted the mood from serene to serendipitous. He was in rowdy spirits, delighted to be home and fretful about a storm purported to be racing toward them. He rushed in, greeted them both with hugs and then disappeared down to his side of the home.

Paul laughed. "Well, so much for peace and quiet."

"Your brother's exuberance is in a league of its own."

"I just hope he plans to use some of that energy to cook."

Simone laughed with him. "Me, too!"

As if on cue Oliver barreled back into the room. "I stopped by the market before I came in. Wasn't sure what you two had left in the fridge and I picked up the most stunning red salmon. It's so gorgeous I had to get it for dinner. One of you come help me with the grocery bags. I hope you two are hungry. I thought we'd have Thai black rice salad with honey-glazed salmon, and I picked up a wonderful sponge cake from the bakery for dessert."

Simone and Paul gave each other a look. "Thai black rice salad," they both mouthed in unison before bursting out laughing again.

Oliver halted in the doorway, turning to give them a narrowed look. "Peel yourself off that beautiful woman, little brother, and come help me please!"

"I swear, Oliver," Simone said as she spooned the last of her dinner into her mouth. "You are in the wrong profession."

She slid a finger across her empty plate and into her mouth, licking the last taste of the meal away. It was the first full meal she'd been able to eat since being nauseous earlier that morning. She was feeling much better and she was grateful she hadn't had to cook it. That salad had been a delectable melding of black rice, mango and bell pepper tossed in a vinaigrette of soy sauce, vinegar, honey, sriracha and mint. Combined with the glazed salmon that had been cooked to sheer perfection, it was almost orgasmic.

Paul nodded in agreement. "You should seriously consider opening a restaurant. Everything you cook is good, but this is amazing!" he added.

Oliver laughed. "Y'all can butter me up all you want, you're still washing dishes," he said.

"We will gladly do dishes if you promise to make this at least once per month for us," Simone said. "It was excellent!"

"For you, doll, I'd make it twice per month."

Simone grinned foolishly. She held up her plate. "Can we taste the dessert now?"

Oliver had risen from the table and stood at the counter. He turned back toward her holding a slice of layered orange sponge cake with a decadent cream icing sprinkled with pecans. Simone's eyes widened with joy and she started bobbing up and down in her seat with glee.

Paul shook his head. "You're killing me, Simone! Your sweet tooth is ridiculous. Just go slow though, in case it upsets your stomach, please!"

"My sweet tooth ensures my sanity," she replied as she took her first bite and swooned. "Oh, my goodness! This is pure..." she started, then she purred, her whole body shivering with excitement.

"Okay," Paul muttered. "This is really some delicious stuff!"

Oliver nodded excitedly. "And the bakery is owned by this little cutie from Ireland. His name's Dermot." He grinned widely.

Paul laughed as he swallowed his second bite. "What's with you and bakers?"

Oliver shrugged and rolled his eyes skyward. "Just can't help myself!"

Two slices of cake later and the trio sat planning what they wanted to do next.

"I need a good night's sleep," Oliver said, "but I'll be in the lab first thing in the morning. I'm anxious to get my hands on the new samples."

"Preliminary tests don't look promising."

"That's not good."

"No, it isn't," Paul said, shaking his head.

Simone pushed her dessert plate to the center of the table. "Since we're on the subject, I think we need to go public sooner than later."

Paul leaned back in his chair, crossing his arms over his chest. "What are you proposing?"

"A news conference to announce the pending lawsuit. I think if we call them out publicly, and focus a national spotlight on their practices, it might force their hand."

"That, or they'll tie us up in litigation so quick, neither one of us will ever work in our selected fields again."

"There's always that restaurant," Oliver muttered as he swept the dirty dishes from the table. "You two would look good bussing tables."

Paul gave his brother a smirk, his eyes rolling skyward.

Simone shrugged. "We still have more questions than we do answers. We're never going to be able to fix this by ourselves, and to get the help we require and stop children from dying we really need to do something drastic."

"What kind of danger does that put you two in, though?" Oliver asked. "If Lender sent people to shoot at you, I doubt they're going to sit by and let you just tell the world how bad they are."

"That's what I'm worried about," Paul said.

"Well, we have to do something. We can't just sit up here playing with the data and running tests. We also can't be the only ones looking at these meds. We need to involve the FDA, maybe the FBI, and we haven't even begun to consider the international implications. Do we need to reach out to the World Health Organization as well?"

"She makes a good point," Oliver interjected.

Paul nodded.

"We're in over our heads," Simone observed. "Now we need to figure out how to get out from under and then get ahead of this. It's been almost six, seven weeks now since we left Chicago. We need to think about going home."

"But we don't have any guarantee going public or trying to go public isn't going to get us killed."

"No, we don't, but we knew we were putting ourselves at risk the minute we ran."

Paul took a deep breath. He stood, moving to the sink to rinse the dirty dishes and rest them in the dishwasher.

"I think I'm going to bed," Oliver said. "Let me know what you decide in the morning."

"Thank you for a wonderful meal," Simone said, her smile shining in her eyes.

Oliver winked his eye at her. "I left you another piece of cake on the counter."

She blew him a kiss and giggled like a five-year-old.

Paul shook his head, his own smile pulling across his face. She looked happy and he didn't want to risk anything sweeping that joy from her. "Let's table the conversation until tomorrow. Let me think about it and we can decide what we want to do after Oliver and I finish testing these last samples."

Simone nodded. "That's fine, but we need to make a decision, Paul." She had moved to his side and stood with a dish towel in her hand.

Paul leaned to kiss her cheek. "Are you feeling any better?" he asked.

She shrugged. "I think I ate too much cake."

He laughed. "Why don't you head to bed? If you are trying to catch something your body needs to get as much rest as it can. I'll finish up the dishes and be there in a few minutes."

Simone leaned her head on his shoulder. "I am tired," she said. "Thank you."

Paul wrapped his arms around Simone's torso and hugged her close. He kissed her forehead and then her lips. As she ambled across the family room, he found himself suddenly feeling panicked. What if he couldn't keep her safe?

Concern twisted his insides and the stress tightened the muscles across his shoulders and back. Paul couldn't help but think about what could happen if things went wrong, despite their best efforts. What impact their actions would have on both their careers, most especially Simone. She was only there because she believed in him. What if they went through all of this and found themselves still at odds over their future? The uncertainty was stifling, a lengthy list of questions he had no answers to. No scenario that was playing out in his head guaranteed a successful outcome or that he and Simone would get their happily ever after. That fact haunted him the most.

When Simone woke the next morning, she was feeling shaky again. Not worse than the day before, but not better. Just not one-hundred-percent yet. After a quick shower and change she headed to the kitchen. A note rested on the table. Paul and his brother had gone out to run an errand. She'd been left to fend for herself and she had no interest in the bacon and eggs in the refrigerator. Instead, she made herself a cup of coffee and settled on a bowl of fruit salad Oliver had left for her.

Paul hadn't come to bed, instead sleeping in the room across from hers. She knew it had everything to do with her suggestion about going public. He had doubts and was worried, although he would never say so out loud. But she had seen the concern on his face when she'd left him finishing the dishes. He had probably tossed and turned most of the night, not wanting to disturb her rest. She knew he was still on the fence about what their next step should be and though she understood why, she also knew it was time to do more than just rewrite their plan to do something. She stood by her suggestion to press forward and expose what they knew.

As the coffee kicked in, she felt much better, the fog seeming to lift from her skull. She moved to the dining room and the beginnings of the legal brief she intended to file. It was a good start. Not great, and nowhere close to being the perfection she needed it to be. She needed access to a law library and a paralegal team to help her research legal precedents. She needed more than being there could afford her. She took another quick sip of her coffee. Reaching for her cell phone, she dialed.

Mingus answered on the third ring. "You okay?"

"Yeah. Did you find out anything about that woman?"

"Give me a sec," Mingus said, the sound of papers being shuffled in the background.

He continued. "Vivian Lincoln, age twenty-nine, born in Michigan, was the wife of the late John Thomas Lender, the son of CEO and founder John *Mitchell* Lender. She's been with the company since before her marriage to John Thomas. After his death in an automobile accident two years ago, she inherited thirty-five percent of the company. Rumor has it, she and her father-in-law have been consoling each other in a nonfamilial manner over the past year. Some refer to her as John Mitchell's beck-and-call girl."

"Eww! Her dead husband's father? That's just nasty!"

"Hey, you can't make this stuff up!"

"So, why is she still doing sales if she owns stock in the business?"

"Why does anyone do what they do? From what I could learn, it looks like Daddy-in-Law is grooming her to take over all the business. She spent a month overseas recently learning their distribution business."

"Overseas?"

"Yeah, she was in Africa for a few weeks. Morocco, I think. Then she went to Thailand and China before returning here to the US."

A sudden shiver went up Simone's spine, and questions had her pacing the floor. Questions she couldn't ask her brother.

"So, it's reasonable to think she was talking to her father-in-law when I ran into her in the restroom the other day?"

"Liza hacked her cell records and she did indeed place a number of calls to his corporate office after seeing you two."

Simone nodded into the receiver. "Okay. I appreciate the info."

"And because I know you so well, little sister. She's only called Paul twice. On the day he returned from Africa and on the day you two saw her at the hospital. He has never called her. So, I doubt highly they're having some illicit affair you need to be concerned about."

Simone didn't know if she should thank her brother or cuss him out. She wanted to be angry, but he knew her too well. He knew she wanted to know but would never have asked him outright. Mingus was good like that and she loved him immensely for it."

"You need anything else?" he asked.

"I don't think so."

"What are you two planning?"

"Not sure yet."

"Just be safe, Simone. Please."

Simone disconnected the call, not bothering to respond. She was still trying to make sense of Vivian being in Morocco the same time Paul had been, and her possible connection to his sudden interest in moving there. Had he not been totally forthcoming with Simone? Was there something he was hiding? Had he lied outright? Did he even know she'd been there?

She shook her head, all of it suddenly unsettling. Before she could catch her breath and figure out what added up and what didn't, her stomach pitched, a demon sweeping through her insides. Tossing the phone to the table Simone rushed toward the bathroom, making it just in time to spew her breakfast into the commode.

Paul was surprised to find Simone on the bathroom floor, a damp towel pressed to her forehead. Her knees were pulled up to her chest as she leaned against the tub, her complexion two shades of green.

"I've caught some crud," she said, meeting his stare.

"Yeah, you're not looking good," he said. He instinctively shifted into doctor mode, his mind considering a potential diagnosis as he moved into the space and leaned down to swoop her up in his arms.

"What are you doing?" Simone questioned, starting to protest.

"Putting you to bed. Then I'm going to examine you."

"I'm fine. I'll be fine."

"Is that why you had your head in the commode?"

"Did you know Vivian was in Morocco when you were there?"

Paul's eyes widened. "No, I didn't. Who told you that? And I wasn't in Morocco on my last visit."

"But you want to move there? Isn't that why you bought a house there?"

"It's one of a few places I'm considering, and the house was an investment. It may just turn out to be a vacation spot. I'm not sure yet. What's your point, Simone?"

Simone shook her head. "I was just asking."

"Well, it sounds like you were about to go off on a jealous tirade and I'm not sure why."

Simone didn't bother to answer as he laid her on the bed. He pressed his palm to her forehead and then to her cheeks. He also gazed into one eye and then the other, gently lifting the lids with the pad of his thumb.

"What did you eat?" he questioned.

"Coffee. And a spoonful of fruit."

Paul pressed two fingers to her wrist to feel her pulse. "Have you been feeling bad all morning?"

"I was sluggish when I first got up. It's like my usual energy levels aren't there but I thought I was doing better until I suddenly wasn't."

Oliver suddenly interjected from the doorway. "You're flushed, too. It's not that time of the month, is it?"

Simone shot the man a glare. "Really?" She suddenly paused, counting days in her head as she thought about her cycle.

"You couldn't possibly be pregnant, could you?" Oliver asked, his brows raised.

"That's ridiculous! You need to focus on your culinary skills and leave the doctoring to your brother." Annoyance washed over her face.

Paul was staring at her intently. "Simone, are you still on your birth control?"

"Now you? Paul, I am not pregnant."

"What are you using for birth control, Simone, because we haven't been very responsible since we've been back together."

"I…well…it's…" She was suddenly stammering. "Damn

it," she finally cussed, because with everything that had been going on, she hadn't thought about protection. And she had stopped taking her birth control pills the week she and Paul had called it quits. Panic suddenly swept in and consumed her. She was suddenly petrified because a baby had not been on her short list. She hadn't even considered motherhood! But there was no way possible she could be pregnant and definitely no way she'd be feeling the symptoms of it so soon!

Paul tossed his brother a look. "Will you please run to the lab and grab a venipuncture kit? I need to get a blood sample."

"For what?" Simone asked, eyeing him curiously as Oliver dashed out of the room.

"A pregnancy test, why else?"

"But it's barely been seven weeks since we've been back together. If I am pregnant, which I'm *not*," she emphasized, "it's too soon for any test."

"It's been more than ten days since the first time we were together. If you conceived then, a blood pregnancy test will let us know."

"We can go to the pharmacy and get one of the sticks I can pee on, but it's going to be negative."

"A blood pregnancy test will be more accurate. It can detect the presence of HCG as early as six days after the egg implants."

"HCG? What's that?"

"It's a hormone produced by the placenta in pregnancy. We'll take a sample of your blood and then get a measurement of the hormone in your body."

"And if there isn't any?"

"Then you're probably not pregnant."

Oliver raced back into the room, passing his brother

the medical supplies he needed. "This is so exciting!" he gushed, his excitement palpable.

The duo shot him chilly glares in reply.

"I'll just give you two some privacy," Oliver said as he backed his way out of the room, still grinning like a Cheshire cat.

"I'm not doing this. It's a waste of time," Simone snapped. "Just because I'm a little nauseous doesn't mean I'm pregnant. Besides, don't you get morning sickness, like, in the second trimester?"

"Most women experience morning sickness in their first trimester and it typically starts around week six and stops around week twelve. It's caused by the increased hormones in a woman's body and it might be the first indication of pregnancy. But you know women who have had morning sickness throughout their entire pregnancy and women who never had morning sickness. Every woman is different. Your body is unique, and you may be one of the lucky few who don't follow what others consider to be medical norms."

Simone's jaw tightened. "I still think this is crazy and I'm not doing it," she muttered.

"Yes, you are," Paul replied firmly. He moved to the bathroom and washed his hands. When he returned, he laid out the supplies he needed on the nightstand and slipped on a pair of white rubber gloves. "Extend your arm for me," he said, laying a white towel down for her to rest her arm against.

"You can't make me." She snatched her arm from his reach.

"Take the test, Simone!" Paul's voice had risen slightly as he held up a cotton swab saturated with alcohol.

"I'm not taking that test."

"Take the damn test, Simone," he said, louder.

She flung her arm toward him. "Fine! But you're going to feel really stupid when you find out it's just a stomach bug or some bronchial infection thing." Because she couldn't be pregnant, she thought. There was no way in hell life would play such a cruel trick on her. She wasn't ready and the mere thought left her panic-stricken.

Paul inspected her arm with the pads of his fingers, looking for a sizable vein to draw blood from. He disinfected the site, swabbing her inner elbow. He tied a tourniquet on the upper part of her arm to apply some pressure to make the vein enlarge with blood.

"Make a fist for me," he said. "Now open and close your hand a few times." He pushed against her skin with his finger then inserted a needle gently into her vein. He attached a small vial for the venipuncture and as it began to fill, he untied the tourniquet. The process took a few quick minutes and then it was over.

"Now what?" Simone snapped as she folded her arm upright, her finger pressing down on a gauze pad to stop the bleeding.

Paul leaned in and pressed his face to hers, his cheek gently settling against her cheek. He whispered into her ear, his breath warm against her skin, "No matter what happens, Simone, it's all going to be okay. I promise." He gently kissed the side of her face. Gathering the vial and the remnants from the medical supplies, he headed out of the room.

Despite the gesture, Simone knew that for all his calm, this had thrown Paul for a loop even more so than it had thrown her. And truth be told she couldn't begin to fathom what would come next if the test came back positive. They had once talked about marriage and children, both deciding that such was light years down the road for them. Then they broke up, their relationship disintegrating, and they'd been grateful there was nothing for them to divvy up or fight over for custody. Neither she nor Paul were prepared for parenthood. They could barely hold their relationship together. Tossing a child into the mix would be like throwing lighter fluid onto a raging fire. No kid deserved that.

Simone took a deep breath. She felt a thousand times better. Her stomach no longer seemed like a rollercoaster gone awry and she felt halfway whole again. There was simply no way she could be pregnant. Not when everything seemed to finally be falling into step for her and Paul.

Rising from the bed she moved to the bathroom to brush her teeth and wash her face. When she felt completely refreshed, she headed to the kitchen for that last slice of orange sponge cake.

Oliver had changed into a lab coat and had taken the blood sample. Paul stood off to the side and watched as his brother prepped the specimen.

"Do you want to know my methodology?" Oliver questioned.

"I know the process," Paul answered. And he did. He could recite verbatim the technical steps from start to finish. The science spun in his head because that was all he wanted to focus on and it would be a few hours before they knew for certain. But he wasn't prepared to think about what he would do if Simone were pregnant. Just the prospect of such a thing being possible had him in knots, fear settling in too comfortably. One more concern to add to his worry list.

"What are you going to do if the test is positive?"

"I'll do whatever I need to do."

"My little brother is going to be a father!"

"Foreshadowing, are you?"

"Wishful thinking. You and Simone will make beautiful babies and I can't wait to be an uncle."

"I don't know if I'm ready for fatherhood." He began to pace the floor, then sat back down staring as his brother worked. His nerves were frayed and he was anxious. He was also conflicted, not quite sure how he honestly felt about the situation. But mostly he was terrified that Simone would break under the pressure, almost guaranteed to not take the news well. Deep down he knew it would break his heart if Simone didn't want to mother his children.

"Hell, I don't think anybody is *ready* for it until it happens."

Paul shrugged. "Probably not. How long before we know?"

"You know how this goes. I'm going to test, retest, then retest again. You'll know before the day is done. So, why don't you go check on Simone. Make yourself some lunch. Take a walk. When I know, you will." Oliver tossed him a look over his shoulder, his expression smug. "Maybe even go buy you some cigars to celebrate."

"You already think you know, don't you? You are so not funny!"

Oliver grinned. "Congratulations, Dad!"

Chapter 12

When Paul entered the kitchen, he looked like death warmed over. They had successfully avoided each other for most of the day, and outside the sun was beginning to set. Simone stopped eating in midbite, her fork hovering above the last of her cake, finally getting around to that sliver Oliver had saved for her. She knew before he could begin to tell her. That cake was suddenly doing flips in her midsection and something like genuine fear pierced her spirit.

Paul slid his fingers into the short length of her hair as he leaned to press a kiss to the top of her head. "As soon as we get back to Chicago, you need to make an appointment with your ob-gyn. They may want to run the test again, as well as give you an ultrasound. It's still very early. I'm thinking we probably conceived that first night we were back together."

Simone dropped her fork to the plate, the silver rattling awkwardly against the china. "This can't be happening! There has to be some kind of mistake. There's no way I'm pregnant. We haven't been back together long enough! I remember sex education," she quipped.

"Then you remember it only takes one time!" Paul snapped back.

"But it takes weeks for that damn egg to implant. It has to! So the test is wrong," she said, pouting profusely.

Paul sighed. "Clearly, you *failed* sex ed. Implantation

doesn't take weeks." He shook his head as he continued. "Oliver will run the test again, but he's very thorough."

Simone pulled her knees to her chest, wrapping her arms around her legs. She dropped her forehead against her thighs. She felt like she'd been slapped with a sledgehammer. This was not supposed to happen. She had always imagined the point in her life when she would share with a partner that they were expecting a baby, romanticizing the moment. But there was nothing romantic about her current situation. It actually felt instead like the two of them were being punished for something horrific they had done. Because a baby clearly wasn't what either needed. They weren't at that place in their personal relationship, barely holding what they shared together by a thin thread. They had made mistakes they were still trying to atone for. Were still struggling to get it right. Tossing a baby into the fray was just wrong on many fronts.

She suddenly thought about the adage her father often invoked. That if you wanted to make God laugh, tell Him your plans. She imagined the good Lord was having Himself quite a snicker.

Paul dropped to his knees beside her, reaching to wrap his arms around her body. He hugged her tightly, then slid his hand beneath her chin and lifted her head so that he could stare into her eyes.

"I know it's a shock, and not at all what we were expecting, but I don't want you to have any doubts about how much I love you. We have plenty of time to think about this and decide what we want to do. I'm sure you need to get used to the idea, just like I do. But no matter what, Simone, you and I are going to be fine. I hope that you trust that."

Simone leaned forward and pressed her lips to his. In that moment, she wished she had half of his confidence.

But truth be told, she was scared, and she didn't know if she even wanted to proceed with this pregnancy.

"So, you want this baby?" she questioned, the words coming before she could stall them.

"Why wouldn't I, Simone? This baby was conceived in love. Our love. Of course, I do!"

She nodded her head slowly. Uncertainty and doubt rushed through her like a tidal wave through a calm ocean. Her confidence had taken a hit and she was feeling so completely lost, most especially when Paul was standing rock solid in support. Because she wasn't feeling as convinced about this pregnancy as he was.

She kissed him again. "Why don't we table this conversation until later? I need to make a few phone calls and get some work accomplished before the day's done."

Paul stared at her intently. A moment passed between them and both knew the dynamics of their relationship had taken another shift. He nodded. "Whenever you're ready," he said. "Oliver and I still have some work to do in the lab, so I'm going to run back to the barn and see what I can get accomplished, as well. And I would really like it if you took it easy. You need to put your feet up and relax." He kissed her one last time, then disappeared out the back door.

Everything about the rest of the evening felt awkward at best. Simone was grateful that most of the work Paul needed to do kept him out of the house and that most of the work she needed to do kept her focused on everything except her situation.

She was pregnant and having Paul's baby. And wasn't having Paul's baby ultimately what she wanted more than anything else in the world? Wasn't that part of her ten-year plan? She had already determined that Paul was her future, so having his children was a part of that plan, as well. Right? So why was she feeling like her whole world was coming to an end? And why was she feeling like Paul felt the same way but was desperately trying to put on a positive face to keep her from having a nervous breakdown? She knew she needed to talk to him, but she was afraid of saying the wrong thing and making a bad situation worse. Why couldn't she find the words to say what she was feeling? And why wasn't she happy? She suddenly had more questions than answers.

By the time the men finally made their way back into the home, Simone was in bed, pretending to be asleep. She didn't want to face Oliver's excitement or have Paul look at her with any reservation of his own. And she didn't want to let her mood sour the evening. She was grateful that neither man tried to engage her. They let her be, understanding that she just really needed time alone.

It was hours later when Paul crawled into bed beside her, curling his body around hers, his hand pressing warmly against her stomach. He placed a damp kiss against the back of her neck and minutes later began to snore softly. In that moment, Simone knew only one thing with certainty: she wouldn't be there when he awoke.

The next day, the sun outside was shining brightly. Paul woke slowly, reaching out an arm to pull Simone to him. He was only half-surprised to find the bed empty, his hands brushing against a sheet of paper instead. He lifted himself up enough to read the note she'd written. The words *I'm sorry, I love you* had been printed in dark ink against the stark white paper.

Paul crumpled the paper in his hand and rolled onto his back pulling both arms up and over his head. He didn't need to check to know that Simone was gone. The last time he woke to a note on the pillow had been when Simone had broken off their relationship, only saying she was sorry. Those two words to apologize for not following him on his mission journey had been all she'd left him with. Two words to say she didn't love him enough to want to stay in the fight. Two words that had haunted him for months. In that note she hadn't even bothered to say she loved him. Now, once again, Simone was apologizing, and he didn't know if it was for a pregnancy neither had expected or leaving him high and dry without the courtesy of a conversation.

He stared at the ceiling. He wanted to be angry, but he didn't have the energy to invest in being mad. His heart hurt, a physical ache that made him want to yank the organ from his chest. He felt abandoned and hated that his adult self was even remotely considering that Simone might be gone for good. But he had more questions than answers and once again, she had left him hanging.

Oliver was sitting in the kitchen savoring his morning cup of coffee when Paul finally made his way there. The two men locked gazes before he rose from his seat and poured his brother a cup of brew. "I'd say good morning, but you don't look like there's anything good about it."

Paul shrugged his shoulders. "Were you awake when she left?"

Oliver nodded. "I tried to get her to stay, but she said she really needed to go back to Chicago. She said she left you a note."

"Well, you know Simone. She's not one for a lot of conversation."

"She said to tell you she'll call once she's home and settled and that she'll see us in a few days when we get back. She also took all of the data with her."

Paul shifted forward in his seat, his coffee mug locked tight between his palms. "What do you mean, she took *all* of the data?"

His anxiety level suddenly quadrupled. That data made Simone a target and he couldn't begin to reason why she would put herself at risk, especially now that she was pregnant. Had she not even considered her own safety? Their child's? He had no doubts that the men who'd been after him would go after her so he couldn't begin to imagine what she had to have been thinking.

Distress flooded his eyes with tears, his gaze shifting frantically back and forth as he considered everything that could possibly go wrong. Trying to decide the best course of action to insure she was safe and well. Deciding if he should go after her and if he did, if she would want him there.

"She took everything she was working on as well as the test results that we had finished."

"Did she say anything else?"

Oliver shook his head. "No, just that she needed to do this. And that everything would be okay."

The drive back to Chicago took Simone three hours longer than the first trip to Windsor had. And only because Simone had taken her time debating whether or not she should turn around and go back. Because she had wanted to go back to Paul. Just like she hadn't wanted to leave him, even though she knew it was for the best.

This pregnancy had thrown them off course, becoming a distraction from what they should have been focused on. She heard it in Paul's voice. From the moment he confirmed her pregnancy, he'd become concerned only with protecting her. They'd lost a whole day and would have lost many more had she stayed. Days overthinking and overanalyzing their relationship and her condition. Days concentrating on everything but what they needed to focus on. It was way too much for her to handle and if she had stayed it would have been a battle of wills that neither would have won.

Her cell phone rang again for the umpteenth time, and again, Simone pushed the button to cancel the call. She wasn't ready to speak to Paul yet. He'd be mad for a few days, she thought. But eventually, he'd get over it.

As she pulled into the assigned parking space, Mingus exited his car. Her brother was like clockwork, coming whenever she called. He opened the driver's door and greeted her.

"Please don't tell me you two had a fight?"

"No, nothing like that. And hello to you, too!"

"Your boyfriend has called me a half-dozen times wanting to know if you'd made it back. He said you're not answering his calls."

"I will. I just needed some time to think and I couldn't focus."

Her phone suddenly rang again. She and her brother both stared as she turned it over in the palm of her hand, looking at Paul's reflection on the screen. Mingus snatched it from her and answered the call.

"Paul, hey… Yeah, she just pulled in… She's fine… I know… I'll tell her… Later…"

Mingus disconnected the call. "He said to tell you he loves you."

Simone nodded. "Thanks." She blew a soft sigh as she and Mingus exchanged a look.

The loud screech of car tires at the end of the road suddenly pulled at their attention and shifted the mood. A car was careening in their direction, seeming out of place for the evening hour. Simone could feel her brother tense as he suddenly drew his weapon and stepped gruffly in front of her. With a soft shove he pushed her back into the vehicle and as she fell back onto the seat, her own anxiety rose substantially.

The car sped past, the driver seemingly oblivious to the two of them standing there. As he lurched through the stop sign at the other end of the road, rounding the corner out of sight, Mingus secured his weapon, putting it back into the holster beneath his jacket.

It wasn't until the vehicle was out of sight that Simone realized she'd been holding her breath. She took a swift inhale of air, her pulse racing, and then she cussed, profanity spewing out of her mouth.

"You okay?" Mingus asked as he extended his hand in her direction.

Simone nodded. "Only slightly bruised."

"I didn't push you that hard."

"Like when I was five and you didn't give me a concussion?"

"That was not my fault."

"Says you!" She wrapped her arms around his waist and gave him a tight hug.

"I'm not comfortable with you being out in the open like this. Let's get you inside," Mingus said, his gaze sweeping back and forth over the landscape.

Simone nodded, her own comfort level suddenly diminished. It had taken a split second to be reminded that home might not be safe and running from one problem had probably landed her squarely in the center of another.

She reached into the back seat of her car and passed a large box into her brother's hands. "Can you get this for me?"

As he took the container, his gaze narrowed. "You

okay? You seriously don't look good. You actually look a little green!"

Simone shook her head. For a split second she thought about telling him the truth, but she wasn't quite ready for that conversation. Of all her siblings she knew Mingus would understand and forgive her for a little white lie. "I think I might be coming down with something. It's all good, though."

"So, do you want to tell me what's going on with you and Paul?"

She engaged the lock on her car and headed in the direction of her home. "No. I'm tired and I need to get some rest. I have an appointment tomorrow."

"What kind of an appointment?"

"A job interview, of sorts. Two actually."

Her brother's brows lifted curiously. "You're thinking about leaving the prosecutor's office?"

She nodded as she pushed her key into the lock and opened the door of her home. It was a stunning property in the heart of Bronzeville, one of Chicago's most sought-after neighborhoods. The luxury, two-story residence was nestled amid historic architecture. As she'd moved into the space, Simone was reminded why she loved the place as much as she did. The spacious rooms with distinctive, massive windows, ten-foot ceilings, and contemporary finishes epitomized the lifestyle she enjoyed. And she had really missed her stuff!

For just a second Simone suddenly imagined a baby crawling across those polished, hardwood floors and her breath caught in her chest. Imagining all she would have to do to baby proof the structure suddenly had her heart racing. Her eyes swept from the glass-topped tables to the bookshelves lined with books and knickknacks from her travels. It all felt very daunting. Her stomach flipped as she pressed her palm to her belly. Shaking the sensation that suddenly had her feeling ill at ease, she turned her attention back to her brother.

"What about Paul's problem?" Mingus was asking, eyeing her curiously.

"It's why I'm leaving the prosecutor's office. Private practice will afford me a better opportunity to help him fight this."

"Cool! Make yourself a target, why don't you!"

"I can't *not* do this, Mingus."

"Have you even considered the danger you might be putting yourself in? Corporations like Lender, with deep political connections and ties to dirty money, don't necessarily play nice when they feel attacked."

"What do you know that you haven't told me? What political connections and whose dirty money?"

"A couple of its board members don't have stellar reputations. There's a disgraced politician or two, that Bernie Madoff mentee who avoided prison by the skin of his teeth, and your father's old buddy Alexander Balducci. Rumor has it he's criminally connected to the mob and they've killed people for lesser offenses. But you already know those stories. You've prosecuted a few, if I recall."

Simone shook her head. "And you have all that information for me, right?"

Mingus pointed to a file folder resting on her dining room table. "Every dirty detail I've discovered since you've been gone." He suddenly broke out into song, riffing off his comment with the lyrics of the old Kelly Clarkson song "*Since U Been Gone.*"

"You are so stupid," Simone laughed, the moment of levity a welcome reprieve.

Mingus shrugged, the smirk across his face endearing. "I've been called worse!"

"I appreciate your help," she said as she turned on the lights in the living room. "I'm sure you have better things to do with the rest of your night."

"You really don't think I'm leaving you here alone tonight, do you?" Mingus double checked the lock on the front door.

"I'm sure I'll be fine, Mingus."

"I know you will," he replied. "Because I'm not leaving. You got anything to eat up in here or do I need to order us a pizza?"

She blew a soft sigh and Mingus stared, waiting for her to answer. When it became obvious that he had no intentions of leaving, or arguing with her, she asked, "Is Pizano's still open?"

"For another hour, I think. You want deep-dish?"

"No, thin crust with pepperoni and sausage."

As her brother dropped the box onto her dining room table and his large frame down onto her sofa, Simone disappeared into her bedroom. Closing the door, she sat against the edge of the bed and took a deep breath. Paul had said he loved her and for the moment, that was all she wanted to focus on because nothing else mattered.

Paul was still wide awake when his cell phone rang. Awake and angry. For a split second he thought about not answering the call, but he had a lot on his mind that he needed to say. When he answered, there was a lengthy pause before Simone finally spoke.

"I know you don't understand, but I had to leave. I needed to think, and I knew I wouldn't be able to focus if our attention was consumed by this pregnancy."

"You ran, Simone. We promised each other that we would talk things out and instead you ran."

"I didn't run, Paul."

"Did my saying I wanted our baby scare you?"

"You're damn right it did! Most especially because I don't know what I want, and I didn't want to say that and have you think I'm this horrible person."

"You didn't trust me."

"I didn't trust me, Paul! No matter what has happened between us, you've always been this rock. Consistent, predictable, and sometimes stubborn. You, I trust. I knew when you said you wanted this baby that you meant it with every fiber of your being. Just like I trust you when you say you love me."

"But you still ran." The annoyance in his tone was thick. "You took off like you always do when things get hard. This isn't how we fix our relationship, Simone. I need to be able to trust you when things get difficult. Most especially now!"

"But I'm not as confident as you are. Because all of this scares the hell out of me. Because you want to move to Morocco, and you can see this incredible life where our loving each other is enough to make it work. I was just getting comfortable with that idea, even knowing that there were things we still needed to work on. That I needed to work on for myself. Now suddenly, there's this whole other little person who'll be dependent on me to get it right and I'm petrified that I will fail you both. I'm not prepared to fail, Paul!"

Simone was sobbing and it was gut-wrenching. Paul wanted to reach through the telephone line to take her into his arms and hold her. But Simone didn't want to be held. She didn't want to be seen as vulnerable, or weak. She had known he would want to make everything better and she had done what she needed to do to stand on her own. To fix what she needed to fix to be an even better version of herself. She had left, hoping he would understand, despite knowing it would infuriate him.

Paul blew the softest sigh, a weight lifting from his spirit as his anger began to dissipate. Despite his frustrations he understood her. He knew her better than she knew herself sometimes. And he knew she had something to prove. Maybe even more so now that she was pregnant. But it still grated against his last good nerve that she was still quick to act impulsively, still quick to make assumptions, and always challenging the status quo when she didn't need to. But she was also the light of his life and the grasp she had on his heart was insurmountable. "I love you, Simone and whatever you want, I'll support your decision," he said begrudgingly. "If you're not ready to have this baby, I'll understand."

"I would never make a decision like that without you, Paul. Because I love you, too, and no matter what happens, it has to be what's best for us both. I just needed time to myself to figure it all out."

Silence filled the space between the phone lines. Both needed a moment to sit in the other's truth. Taking it all in was both cathartic and repressive, a wealth of emotion flowing between them.

"You should get some rest," Paul said. "You've had a long day."

"Mingus ordered pizza."

"Thin crust from Pizano's?"

"With pepperoni and sausage."

Paul chuckled and Simone felt herself smile.

"You need to come home," she said. "I have a plan."

"Do I even want to ask?"

"No. It will only start another fight."

"It'll probably take us another two, maybe three days

to finish testing the rest of the samples we have here. My box from Ghana arrived today."

"That's fine. It'll be more ammunition for us to work with and I still need to put some things here in place. Just come when you can, please. I miss you."

"I miss you, too, baby. I'll see you soon."

Chapter 13

When Simone exited the offices of Thurman, Brown and Taylor, she was ready to be done and finished for the remainder of the day. The prestigious law firm had made her a substantial offer weeks earlier and initially she'd been excited to accept, the prospect intriguing. Unfortunately, she had to respectfully turn them down. She had hoped to offer them the case, but at the last minute had chosen not to mention it. So now she needed a plan B and another law firm that was capable and interested in supporting the litigation she hoped to bring against Lender. But she was exhausted and in need of a serious nap and she had to wonder if this was going to last her entire pregnancy.

She was grateful for Mingus, who stood leaning against the car waiting for her. His arms were crossed over his chest and the dark shades on his face made him look only slightly menacing. But just the sight of her family lifted her spirits.

"You still here?" she questioned.

"I'm not going anywhere, Simone. Besides, we both know if you really wanted to ditch me, you would."

She gave him a slight smile. "Actually, I like having a personal chauffeur. You've come in handy."

"I may have found my calling. So, where to next, mademoiselle?"

"The law offices of Black, Turner and Hayes, please. Do you need the address?"

Amusement crossed Mingus's face. "Nah, I think I got that one," he said as he opened the passenger door.

Simone tapped her hand against his chest before she slid into the passenger seat. "See, you are good for something," she said teasingly.

Her brother laughed as he slid across the car's hood and into the passenger seat. "So, what's up? Why are we going to see your brother Ellington?"

"I have an interview with his law firm."

"When did that happen?"

"It hasn't yet, actually. He doesn't know I'm coming."

Mingus laughed. "And you call me impulsive!"

"I wish I could explain it, but I can't. Not yet. Let's see if Ellington will let us in first."

"Hey," Mingus said, as he maneuvered the car toward LaSalle Street. "It's whatever. You don't ever have to tell me anything and I'll be good."

Simone laughed. "I appreciate that. Thank you."

He reached for her hand and gave it a light squeeze. "Whatever you need, you know that, right?"

She felt herself getting emotional, so she nodded, then changed the subject. "How's Joanna? I need to call her, but with everything going on…"

"She's pulling her hair out! She's in Atlanta with her mother. Her aunt had to have surgery, so they went down to take care of her. She'll be back next week."

"She'll be bald next week. Her mother has that kind of effect on people," Simone said with a slight chuckle.

"Damn! I was just getting attached to her hair!"

"You're so stupid!" She tossed her brother a look. Mingus and her best friend, Joanna Barnes, had been together in a relationship for a few months. Ever since he'd been hired to investigate false charges that had almost gotten the history teacher incarcerated. He'd fallen head over heels for the woman and loved her almost as much as Simone loved the two of them together. Everyone in the family was ready for them to be married but her brother was taking his sweet time asking the beauty to be his wife. The couple had only been together a few short months and Simone knew they didn't feel they had any reason to rush. "So, when do you plan to make my bestie an honest woman?"

Mingus grinned. "When are you going to say yes and marry Paul?"

"Now you're hitting below the belt!"

"Turnabout is fair play. So, you tell me when you plan to get married and I'll let you know when I do!"

"That might be sooner than you think. You never know!"

"Oh, I know," her brother responded with a deep laugh.

Simone shifted against the leather seats, turning to stare out the window. The weather was questionable, the temperatures almost too warm for the time of year. It wasn't spring yet, but winter still had a hold on the season. The month before, there had been snow on the ground and now the trees looked like they were thinking about blooming.

Three turns and ten short minutes later, Mingus pulled the car into a parking spot in front of the law office of Black, Turner and Hayes. The glass-and-steel skyscraper was located in the three hundred block of LaSalle Street, with the offices occupying the sixty-fourth floor of the massive building.

After feeding the parking meter, Simone led the way into the building, which boasted floor-to-ceiling windows in the exterior offices, expensive contemporary decor and a library and conference room reminiscent of an old English library with polished wood-paneled walls, hardwood floors and three walls of leather-bound law books lined meticulously on shelves.

The two siblings stood together patiently as the young receptionist engaged the intercom and announced their arrival. There was no missing the surprise in their brother's voice when he repeated their names for verification.

"Yes, sir. They don't have an appointment but would like a moment of your time if it's possible."

Simone and Mingus shot each other a look, fighting not to laugh out loud.

A few minutes passed before Ellington Black came down the hall to greet them.

"This can't be good," he said as he shook his brother's hand before pulling Simone into a deep bear hug. "Where have you been? You've had the old people losing their minds."

"I didn't mean to," Simone said. "I told them not to worry."

"That's like telling them not to breathe," Ellington replied. He gestured for them to follow him to his office. "So, to what do I owe this honor?"

Mingus shrugged. "I'm playing bodyguard. Garnering favor from the parents being a good big brother. Until further notice, I go where she goes."

Ellington laughed. "They've got the fox watching the henhouse!" He pointed them toward two wingback chairs as he closed the office door. "So, what's up?" he asked, looking from one to the other.

Simone reached into her briefcase and pulled out a file folder. "I have a case I'd like for your firm to consider. And I want you to hire me to litigate it."

Ellington eyed her with a raised brow as he opened the

file and began to read. He shifted forward in his leather executive's chair as he slowly flipped through the pages. "How many patients do you believe have been affected?"

"There are thousands overseas and maybe a few hundred here in the United States."

"Have you filed your complaint yet with the FDA?"

"I'm just waiting for the results for the last tests Paul and his brother are doing now."

Ellington dropped the folder to the desk and tapped it with the palm of his hand. "What happened with John Thurman's firm? I understand they were certain you were going to sign with them. I'd think you would want to put this in their hands."

"We couldn't come to terms that we were both in agreement with. There was no point in even mentioning this to them."

Ellington folded her hands together, his elbows resting atop the desk. "What if I can't meet your terms?"

"You will have more invested in my demands than they ever will."

"So that begs the question, what do you want that they wouldn't agree to?"

Simone shot her two brothers a look and took a deep breath. "I'm pregnant and if I have this baby, I'll need some flexibility with my schedule because my baby's father is thinking about moving to Morocco. I'm fully committed to whatever my responsibilities will be, but I'll also need time to figure out this motherhood thing and a possible transcontinental relationship. I'll need you to work with me. Thurman wasn't interested."

The two brothers exchanged a look, shock and awe blessing their expressions.

Ellington sat back in his seat, turning his gaze to stare

at his sister. He cleared his throat, still allowing the news to sink in. "You said *if I have this baby...*"

"I can't wrap my head around it right now. I'm not even sure it's real," she said, taking a moment to tell her brothers about her last forty-eight hours.

"Damn, Simone! How do you just leave that man hanging like that?" Ellington exclaimed. "That would hurt my feelings!"

"Paul understands me," Simone said, sinking into a slight pout.

"That brother *loves* you. Anyone else would have left you ages ago! I know I would have!" Mingus interjected.

"Which is why I would never date either of you! It's a good thing we're related."

The trio laughed.

"Seriously," Ellington said, "you know we'll support you however you need us to. But I still don't know if I can give you a job."

Simone nodded. "I know, and I'm willing to bet that I can convince you to hire me."

Ellington gestured toward his brother. "Can you excuse us, please? We have some negotiating to do and knowing our sister it might get heated. Maybe come back in an hour?"

"Or two," Simone chimed. "I doubt he'll give in that easily."

Mingus nodded. "I'll be in the lobby! You two do your thing," he said. Rising from his seat, he leaned to kiss her cheek, pointed his index finger at his brother and disappeared out the door.

Simone shifted in her seat, she and Ellington locking gazes. "I want to be a partner," she said, "with a corner office."

Ellington laughed. "And so it begins!"

* * *

Almost three hours later Simone exited Ellington's law office and rode the elevator down to the first floor. Mingus was outside chomping on the last bite of a hot dog. He swiped at a dab of mustard that had fallen on his shirt as he balled up the foil wrapper and shot it into a wastebasket on the sidewalk.

"Y'all done?"

Simone nodded. "Done and finished. I'm ready to go home now."

Mingus nodded. "Must mean you've got a job!"

She laughed. "And a corner office!"

"Ahhh, the beauty of nepotism."

"Nepotism has nothing to do with it. I'm more than qualified and Ellington's been trying to get me to come work with him since I got my law degree. Now's just the right time. Of course, he still has to run it by his partners and there are two I will need to sit down and formally interview with, but I'm thinking what I bring to the table will help seal the deal."

"Okay."

"Why'd you say it like that?" Simone asked.

"I just said 'Okay.'"

Her eyes rolled skyward, a scowl pulling across her face. "You play too much. Take me home."

"Aren't you moody? Them pregnancy hormones done kicked in big-time!"

"Leave me alone, Mingus," she said as she slid into the passenger seat.

Mingus chuckled as he closed her door and rounded the car to the other side.

The ride was quiet, and it was obvious she was exhausted. She leaned her head against the window and closed her eyes. When she next opened them, Mingus was parked in the heart of Chicago's Gold Coast neighborhood in front of the Black family home. Situated on the large corner lot, the stone-and-brick architecture was a timeless reminder of a whole other era.

"Why are we here?" she asked, her head snapping in her brother's direction. "I said to take me home!"

"You need to have a conversation with your parents."

"Why the hell do I need to do that? I'm not ready to talk to them yet." Annoyance flushed her face.

Mingus passed her his phone, a text message filling the screen. Because your other brother doesn't know how to keep a secret and once he tells, it's probably a matter of minutes before Ma and Pa Black find out.

Her eyes narrowed as she began to read the message from Ellington, a mass text addressed to all her siblings.

I have news about Simone! Meet me for drinks at 7 if you want the details. And, it's good gossip, Vaughan! You pick the spot!

"I'm going to kill him!" Simone muttered between clenched teeth. She began to type furiously, responding to the message Ellington had conveniently forgotten to include her in. Mingus snatched his phone from her hands, a wide grin filling his face.

"Go tell them. Let them lay eyes on you so they can stop worrying about you being gone and go back to worrying about your screwing up your life. Then we can go cuss out our brother at seven o'clock. It'll be good for you to let us all love on you. We missed you!"

Simone lifted her eyes to meet her brother's gaze. She knew he was right, but she wasn't sure she was at all ready for the confrontation. She took a deep breath and watched as Mingus exited the car, moving to open the door for her.

"I don't know…"

"Yes, you do. But take a minute to think about what you plan to say. We've got time."

The solid wood-and-glass front door with its ornate iron details was rarely locked and the siblings entered without knocking. Stepping inside felt like entering the comfort and quiet of a family retreat. There was a quiet that was not typical, but the calm felt immensely welcoming.

Mingus called out. "Hey! It's just us! Who's here?"

Their mother's voice echoed down from the second floor. "Mingus? I'm in my office, son!"

Mingus gave his sister a nod and gestured up the marble staircase. "I'll let you take it from here. I'm going to go see what there is to eat in the kitchen."

"Didn't you just eat?" Simone questioned.

Her brother shrugged. "Stop stalling," he said as he moved toward the kitchen at the back of the home. "I'm looking for dessert!"

Simone shook her head and turned toward the stairwell. She moved through the home, past the walls papered in silk, the sparkling chandeliers, ornate wood moldings and fireplaces meticulously carved in stone. The windows were draped in sumptuous fabrics, and every detail, from the coffered ceilings to the highly polished hardwood floors reflected her parents' refined taste.

Her mother was in her office, seated behind her large glass-topped desk. When Simone walked into the room the matriarch looked up in surprise, uttering a loud gasp at the sight of her.

The Honorable Judith Harmon Black was a tall woman, nearly as tall as her sons. She towered above Simone, who hadn't gotten her height from either of her parents.

The judge had picture-perfect features: high cheekbones, black eyes like dark ice and a buttermilk complexion that needed little if any makeup. She was dressed casually, which was a rarity, but still donned her requisite pearls. A hint of blush to her cheeks complemented her fair skin and her lush silver-gray hair fell in thick waves past her shoulders. The sight of her mother suddenly had tears welling in Simone's eyes. Judith's smile leaped across the desktop to wrap Simone in a deep embrace.

Judith stood. "Simone!" she said as she moved around the desk and wrapped her youngest daughter in a warm hug. "Thank God! You're home!"

Simone suddenly felt as if a cloud burst, tears raining down her cheeks. She stood in her mother's arms and clung to her for a good few minutes. Her mother held her and allowed her to cry until she didn't have any tears left.

Judith cupped her hand beneath her daughter's face and lifted her chin. She wiped Simone's tears with her thumb, then reached for a tissue from a box on her desk, pressing it into the palm of Simone's hand.

"What's going on?" Judith asked. "This isn't like you. You were never a crybaby, so what's with all the boo-hoo-hooing?"

Simone shook her head. "I'm pregnant," she blurted, the words racing past her lips before she could catch them.

Judith's eyes widened as she pointed Simone into a cushioned seat. She moved back to her own chair and sat down. "When did this happen? How far along are you?"

"Paul says it's just a few weeks, but I have an appointment with Dr. Seymour tomorrow to confirm his test results."

"And how does Paul feel about this?"

Simone shrugged. "You know Paul. He's always ready to step up and do the right thing. It's why I love him. He's a standup guy! I don't know if I would want to do this without him."

"You don't need a man to do the right thing for you, Simone. You know full well how to be self-sufficient. Your father and I didn't raise any of you—most especially you and your sister—to have to depend on someone else for your own needs or happiness."

Simone held up a palm to stall the lecture she felt coming. "We wanted to try and work things out. We were making plans. Then this just happened and well, I'm not handling it as well as Paul is. I honestly don't know if I'm ready to be anyone's mother." Her voice dropped to a loud whisper. "I'm scared, Mom. I don't think I've ever been this scared of anything. But this has me petrified! I'm a hot mess on a good day. I don't want to screw up my child!"

Judith leaned back in her chair, twisting a silver ink pen between her fingers. A slight smile pulled across her face. For a brief moment she seemed to drift into thought as Simone sat staring. Simone suddenly felt like she was six years old again when she had poured bleach into the family fish tank wanting to clean the water. She'd been devastated when all the goldfish were suddenly floating on top and her siblings were screaming bloody murder at her. She'd sobbed like a baby then, too, ankle socks and patent-leather shoes swinging as she'd sat with her mother waiting to be told what a horrible person she was. But her mother hadn't called her horrible. In fact, she'd commended her for trying to do what she thought was right. Then she'd told her that learning about her fish and how to care for them would ensure future accidents didn't happen. "Educate yourself," Judith had admonished. "Be smart about everything you do."

Now all she could think was if she could kill her pet

fish what chance did a baby have in her hands? She didn't get a do-over if a well-meaning act went awry! Even if she did read every parenting book imaginable.

Judith seemed to read her mind. "I think you'll be an amazing mother, Simone," she said softly. "And together you and Paul will be incredible parents, whether you are in a relationship with each other or not. And I trust this because I know you will always put your child first and do whatever you need to do to protect her."

"Her?"

Her mother grinned. "A grandmother can dream, can't she?"

Simone laughed, shaking her head. Her mood seemed to lift, if only for a moment. "Paul wants to move to Morocco. He bought a house there."

"Why Morocco?"

"It's central to those places where he's established his medical missionary programs."

"I do admire his philanthropic spirit. He's a good soul."

"He's a little irritated with me at the moment," Simone said, explaining how she'd left him high and dry in Canada without so much as a warning.

Her mother shook her head. "I can't reiterate it enough, Simone—a relationship will not work if you don't communicate with your partner. Your father and I work because we've learned how to have the hard conversations. You can't run just because you don't like what Paul has to say. You need to sit in his truth and own yours. And you both have to be committed to doing that together."

"I know, but I needed to focus, and I couldn't do that. It was just easier to leave."

"No one said your relationship would ever be easy and you can forget about marriage being easy. It's hard, and it requires an investment of your time and energy and your commitment to work hard through the challenges when they come."

Her mother took a deep breath before continuing. "And what you did wasn't fair to Paul. Even if you decided to leave, he had a right to express how he felt about that, and you needed to hear it."

"I know," Simone said sighing softly. "And I'm working on doing better. I really am. Paul loves me, and I love him. But I don't think I can move to Morocco. Especially now with a baby coming."

"Then don't. But instead of looking at things so narrowly, allow yourself the luxury of being open to whatever the future holds. I'm sure Paul will help you figure it out. If being with him is what you want, then let him help."

"You'd be okay if I took your first grandchild to Africa?"

"It would mean your father and I would be doing much more international travel. We would make it work."

"Please don't tell Daddy about the baby yet. I think it's something Paul will probably want to have a conversation with him about first."

"I can respect that," her mother said with a nod. "So, what about the case you and Paul were working on? How's that going?"

"I'll be leaving the prosecutor's office to work the case in private practice."

Judith's brow lifted slightly. "You're planning to open your own firm?"

"No, ma'am!" Simone said with a shake of her head. "I'm joining Ellington's law firm as a junior partner. There, I'll have the full weight of the firm behind me when I file the class-action lawsuit."

"Well, you're just full of good news today, aren't you, baby girl?"

"Do you think Daddy will be mad at me and Paul? That we didn't get married before getting pregnant?"

Judith shrugged. "Your father wants you to be happy no matter what. I'm sure he'll hiss and scream at first, but probably not for long. His bark has always been harder than his bite. I have no doubts though that if he hears it from Paul first, Paul will get the brunt of it before your father gets to you."

Simone sighed. She stole a quick glance to her watch. "Then I need to run and go swear your other children to secrecy."

Judith laughed. "Who'd you tell?"

"Mingus and Ellington."

"You know Ellington can't keep anything secret!"

The two women chatted for a few minutes longer before heading down to the kitchen to check on Mingus.

Her brother was dozing in a recliner in the family room.

Their mother shook her head as she tapped him gently. "Are you okay, son?"

Mingus opened his eyes slowly, looking from his mother to his sister and back. "I'm good." He yawned, stretching his limbs up and out. "How about you two?" he questioned, looking toward Simone.

His sister smiled and nodded, her eyes shifting to his. The conversation between them was quick and silent, no words necessary. Because Simone did feel better, like the weight of the world had been lifted from her shoulders. She knew her baby would be fine because even if she screwed up, there was family supporting them. They would make sure her baby would be okay. Her whole face lifted in a smile. Her baby! She and Paul were having a baby! Suddenly the prospect of that didn't feel so daunting.

He reached into the breast pocket of his leather jacket and passed his mother an envelope. "That information you were looking for," he said. "Let me know if you need anything else from me."

The two exchanged a look and Simone could feel the energy between them shift as the moment became awkward. Her gaze swung from one to the other, but it was obvious it was not a conversation she was privy to. Her curiosity waved and she wanted to ask about their exchange but she knew better than to intrude. Mingus might share if she asked him when they were alone, but she knew her mother would not take kindly to her being nosy in business that was not hers.

Her mother slipped the envelope into the back pocket of her slacks. "Thank you," she said before changing the conversation. "Simone, do you want something to eat?"

"No, thanks. I'm headed to dinner to go kill Ellington and then I'm going home. It's been a long day."

Her mother laughed. "Tell your brothers and sister I expect them all here for Sunday dinner. It's important. And call your father, please, so he at least knows you are home." She wrapped Simone in one last hug.

"Thank you, Mom," Simone whispered.

Her mother kissed her cheek. "Trust your instincts, Simone. They will never lead you wrong. And please don't hurt your brother too badly. I like Ellington."

Mingus laughed. "You like us all!"

Simone giggled. "Nope, they *love* us all. Mom and Dad only like some of us. Me especially!"

"Glad I'm special, too!" her brother said as the two headed out the door, their mother smiling as she watched them exit the home.

Chapter 14

There was no denying the family resemblance as the Black siblings gathered for dinner at Thithi's Restaurant, one of their all-time favorite spots for Thai food. They were a pretty family with distinguished features and warm complexions indicative of their biracial heritage. Even seated, it was easy to tell that the brothers were all tall, with athletic frames, much like their father. The sisters had both gotten their mother's high cheekbones and dark eyes. They had inherited the best genetic material from their parents, and each wore it well, along with their jazz-musician names that spoke to their parents' aesthetic. Armstrong, Davis, Ellington, Parker, and Vaughan were laughing heartily amongst themselves. Ellington was sitting with a smug expression on his face that quickly bottomed out when he caught sight of them. "Hey, we weren't expecting you," he exclaimed as the hostess pulled up two additional chairs to the table.

"I'm sure you weren't," Simone said, her gaze narrowing. "It's hard to gossip about me when I'm here, right?"

Ellington laughed. "It wasn't like that, Simone!"

"Yes, it was," Vaughan said as she jumped from her seat to give Simone a hug, the two women holding tightly to each other. "I'm so pissed at you," Vaughan exclaimed when she finally pulled away. "Why didn't you call someone to let us know you were okay?"

"Because I *was* okay! Y'all don't call every day to check in with anyone."

"We didn't have people shooting and trying to kill us a few weeks ago, either," Parker said as Simone moved around the table to give them each a hug and kiss.

"When did you get back?" Armstrong asked.

"Last night."

Davis stood and hugged her, as well. "Missed you, sis!"

"Where's Paul?" Vaughan questioned, throwing a quick look toward the door.

"He's still…well…he…" Simone stammered. She wasn't ready to tell them that she had left Paul in Windsor. She wasn't in the mood for the judgment she knew would come from her brothers. She also wasn't ready to announce her pregnancy or explain plans she hadn't yet made. She shook her head. "I'm sure we'll all see him in a day or two."

Vaughan punched Ellington's shoulder. "So, this is the news you had? You could have just told us in a text that Simone was finally back home."

"He had more news than that," Mingus said, tossing in two cents as he reached for a menu.

Simone shot her brother a look.

"I did have more news," Ellington said, that smug look returning. "I am pleased to announce that attorney extraordinaire Simone Black has officially joined the law firm of Black, Turner and Hayes, eventually to be Black, Turner, Hayes and Black. After a quick discussion with the other partners and a vote in favor of meeting all her demands, she now reports to me! Once all the appropriate contracts are signed, of course."

There was a round of cheers as they all congratulated her, the warmth of it moving Simone to tears. She suddenly wished Paul was there to share in the joy with her.

"I guess I need to give the prosecutor's office my official resignation," she said, batting back the moisture in her eyes.

Ellington laughed. "Yeah, you need to do that. You can't stay on leave with them and work for me."

Parker leaned forward in his seat. "What's going on with that problem of Paul's? You two have any resolution yet?"

"It's why I'm back. I need to put some things in motion."

"And the two men that shot at you?"

"They didn't find us, so…" Simone shrugged.

"Which suggests you might not be safe," Armstrong snapped, their siblings nodding in agreement.

"You still need to come down to the station to give us a statement," Parker admonished. "And I mean it, Simone."

"I will! When Paul gets back, we'll both come right down to see you."

"No, Paul can give us his statement when he gets back. I expect to see you first thing in the morning."

"Really, Parker?"

"I mean it."

"I'll make sure she gets there," Mingus interjected.

Parker shot him a look as the others laughed.

"I mean it," Mingus said as he gestured for the waitress and ordered himself a drink. "I'll have her there bright and early. Won't I, Simone?"

"Yeah, whatever," Simone muttered, her focus on the menu and the chicken pad thai she wanted to order.

"Anything else you want to share with us?" Ellington suddenly questioned.

"Yeah," Mingus added. "Anything?"

The two brothers exchanged a look, Mingus clearly

fighting not to laugh out loud. The others were trying to figure out what was going on.

"What are these two fools talking about, Simone? What else aren't you telling us?" Vaughan asked.

Simon shot them a glare, swiping the smirks from her brothers' faces. "I have more news, but I can't share it until I've had a chance to talk to Daddy *first*," she snapped. "I hope all of you," she paused, glaring a second time at Mingus and Ellington, "will respect that."

"You and Paul got married!" Vaughan exclaimed. "You eloped!"

"You better not have," Parker interjected. "I can't speak for Paul, but I know you are not that crazy!"

"I know that's right," Davis added. "Pops would kill you and I don't even want to think what he'd do to Paul!"

"He'd bury Paul," Armstrong laughed.

"She's gonna wish she and Paul had eloped," Mingus mumbled under his breath.

Simone glared. "Y'all keep guessing. Have your little fun. I'm not paying you an ounce of attention. When I have something I want y'all to know, I'll tell you."

Ellington held up his hands as if he was surrendering. He leaned to kiss her cheek as he changed the subject. "Since we're all here, there's something that's been bothering me."

"What's that?" Parker asked.

"Is something going on between Mom and Dad that all of us don't know about?" Ellington asked, looking toward Vaughan. "Or a few of us don't know about?"

"I was wondering the same thing," Armstrong said. "Mom hasn't been herself lately."

Simone's gaze swept around the table. "I hadn't noticed anything. Did my being away cause a lot of friction between them?"

"It definitely didn't help," Mingus quipped.

"Something's going on," Vaughan answered. "But I don't know what it is. Any of you talk to Daddy lately?"

"I had lunch with him yesterday," Parker noted. "But he didn't say anything, and he seemed fine."

"Well, they're not fine together," Vaughan said. "They barely spoke to each other this past Sunday. And when they did, they bickered about everything."

They suddenly all turned toward Mingus, eyebrows raised as they eyed him questioningly.

"Either of them say anything to you, Mingus?" Parker asked.

"No," he answered, but there was a moment of pause just long enough for the rest of the brood to question how truthful he was being.

"You know something," Vaughan finally quipped. "What's going on?"

Mingus reached for his glass and took a sip. He didn't bother to give her an answer but the look he shot around the table spoke volumes. His silence was suddenly deafening and they all instinctively knew not to push the issue with him.

"Mom said to tell everyone that she expects us all to be at the house for Sunday dinner. Maybe we can figure out what's going on then," Simone interjected, genuine concern washing through her.

"Y'all need to stay out of it," Davis said. "It's not our business unless they want it to be."

Simone suddenly thought about her conversation with her mother. If something was going on with their parents, she trusted the two would talk it out and make it work. Because everything her mother and father preached, they lived whole-heartedly, and she was desperate to have that with Paul.

"Davis is right," Armstrong interjected. "Mom and Dad will work out whatever is wrong. *If* there is anything wrong at all."

A wave of silence draped the table as their server delivered the plates of food that had been ordered earlier. Simone reached for her sister's hand on one side of her and Mingus's hand on the other. Both squeezed her fingers, nothing needing to be said as Parker led the family in prayer, blessing the food and their good fortune. She was home, with family, and all was right in the world. For the first time in a good long minute she felt like things were beginning to look up. Now all she needed was for Paul to return to make it even more perfect.

Paul and Oliver had spent the better part of the day analyzing and testing the last drug samples they'd received. After recording the last results, he had secured the data and forwarded results data to Simone. They were finishing up in the lab when Paul's phone rang. He was about to answer the call when Oliver stopped short in the doorway and pulled his index finger to his lips to shush him. He shut off all the lights and they were suddenly standing in darkness, just the faintest hint of light shining through the door.

Paul felt the hairs on the back of his neck stand at attention. He silenced his phone instead of answering it and moved to Oliver's side, using the light from outside to peer around the open door. "What's wrong?" he whispered.

Oliver pointed to the house and a shadow moving past the family room window. "I think there are two of them," he said as he slowly closed the lab door and locked it. He engaged the flashlight on his cell phone. "They can't see inside here," he said, "but I didn't want them to see any light reflecting under the door. Who do you think it is?"

Paul shrugged, trying not to let the fear show on his face. His heart was suddenly racing, and he broke out into a cold sweat. "Whoever it is, I don't think they mean us any good."

"What do you want to do?"

"Well, we're not going down without a fight!"

Oliver nodded his agreement. He took a deep breath and moved across the room to one of the locked cupboards. Taking a key from his pocket and then opening the door, he pulled out two hunting rifles and passed one to Paul. "This place is a fortress, but if they breach that door, shoot."

Paul released the weapon's magazine and opened the chamber. "You keep them loaded?" he said, his voice a loud whisper.

"You're damn right I do! I live in the woods and most times I'm here by my lonesome."

"Is there a reason why you didn't put any windows in this space?" Paul questioned.

"Yeah, I didn't want anyone being nosy to see in."

"Makes good sense to me. But now we can't look out!"

Oliver shrugged. "What now?"

"If it's the men Lender hired and they're after me, there's nothing in the house for them to get their hands on. Simone took all the data. If this is some random robbery, they might walk off with that big-screen television of yours. Either way, I'm not going to go ask them what it is they want. We need to get to the car and get back across the border." He suddenly thought about Simone, grateful that she hadn't been there, inside, alone, when they'd intruded on the space. He couldn't begin to image what he would do if she were in harm's way.

"My passport's in the house. I'm also thinking they're probably parked down the road since we didn't hear a car pull up. That might be a problem if there's more than one of them."

Paul cussed, suddenly feeling trapped. "We need our passports."

"We need to live to tell this story to my niece or nephew," Oliver quipped.

Paul rested the rifle he was holding on the table and pulled his phone from his pocket. A missed call from Simone lit up his screen. Ignoring it, he dialed 911 and took a deep breath.

"What is your emergency?"

"Yes, ma'am. My name is Dr. Oliver Reilly," Paul answered, giving his brother's name and the home's address. "My brother and I just returned from a walk and there are intruders in our home. Can you please send someone?"

"Do you know how many there are, Dr. Reilly?" the operator questioned.

"We think there are two, maybe three men and it looks like they might be armed," he continued.

"I have a patrol unit in route, sir. Please do not engage with the men. Our officers will be there any minute now. Are you in a safe location?"

"Yes, yes we are. We're hiding in the barn behind the house," he concluded. "And we definitely won't engage them."

When he disconnected the call, Oliver shot him a look, his eyes rolling skyward.

"It was just a little white lie," Paul said, seeming to read his brother's mind. "But if they ask where we walked to, you'll have to answer. Make up whatever lie you need to."

"Like I've ever gone walking in the dark around here! We're both going straight to hell!" Oliver said. He turned and pulled the door open just a fraction to peek out. He noted the footprints in the light sprinkling of snow that covered the ground. They stopped just short of the barn and turned, heading back toward the other side of the house. He quickly closed the door and relocked it.

"Did you see anything?" Paul whispered.

Oliver shook his head. "No. Nothing good at least."

The next few minutes felt like an eternity. At the sound of sirens careening toward them, Oliver returned both rifles to the cupboard and relocked the cabinet. He and Paul moved back to peek out the door. Three patrol cars from the Windsor Police Service pulled into the parking area behind the home and several officers exited with their weapons drawn. As one officer moved toward the barn, a second on his heels, the others entered the house through the rear door.

Paul slowly pulled the barn door open, he and Oliver both exiting with their hands raised. He announced them both. "I'm Dr. Paul Reilly, and this is my brother, Dr. Oliver Reilly."

The officer recognized Oliver and greeted him with a nod. "Dr. Reilly, it's Liam Trembley, sir. Are the intruders still inside the house?" he questioned.

Dropping his arms, Oliver shook his head. "Officer Trembley! I'm sorry I didn't recognize you. We're not sure, but we didn't see them leave. Once we saw them walking through the house, we locked ourselves here inside my office. Then we called you."

The officer moved through the door and into the space. Oliver turned on the lights to give him full view of the room.

"This is some setup you have here, sir. What do you do?" Trembley asked, his gaze sweeping around the room.

"I'm a research scientist. Currently, I'm studying the impact of cancer cells on diseased tissue."

"You a scientist, too?" the officer named Liam asked, directing his question toward Paul.

Paul shook his head, folding his arms over his chest as he tucked his hands beneath his armpits. "No, I'm a physician. I practice medicine in the United States. I'm here visiting my brother for the week." Paul shot Oliver a look, beginning to sway nervously back and forth as he remembered the warrant with his name on it.

Another officer stepped out of the home and called out to them. "All clear! The house is empty."

Officer Trembley gave them a nod as he moved back to the entrance. "Why don't you go see if anything was taken? Officer Poole and I will take a look around out here."

The two brothers both blew a sigh of relief, but the emotion was tentative. They couldn't help but wonder if the two men were gone, where were they now and how long before they'd come back?

Paul knew what they'd been looking for and he couldn't help but be concerned that maybe this time it hadn't been their plan to let him survive. What would have happened if he and Oliver had been ambushed? Even thinking that things could have gone very wrong and he wouldn't have been able to get back to Simone and their baby had him feeling some kind of way.

Nothing inside was out of place. The televisions were still intact, and Oliver's gold watch rested on the counter. The police quickly eliminated theft as a motive for anyone to enter the home without permission. The brothers did as well, sensing the men Lender Pharmaceuticals had sent had invaded their space more interested in doing them harm than anything else. Paul had no doubt the drug company was still trying to shut him down.

"Is that your car parked down at the end of the road?" one of the officers questioned.

"No," Oliver said. "We saw it when we came in but figured someone had just broken down and left it there."

"One of my officers got the license plate and if we can't reach the owner, we'll have it towed to impound," he said.

"And you said you'd been out walking?" another officer asked, looking from Oliver to Paul.

Oliver nodded. "We just wanted some air, so we walked down to the main road and over to that lot that's for sale across the way. We're thinking about buying it. We were out longer than we anticipated because Paul thought he saw a coyote. I thought it was a dog, but we wanted to wait until it went on its way just to be safe."

"I'm pretty sure it was a coyote!" Paul muttered.

The two officers exchanged a look but said nothing. Officer Trembley stepped inside the home. "There are fresh footprints headed into the back woods, but they turn back around to the front of the house and cross through the yard. It looks like there were two people but there's no sign of them and the car that was parked at the edge of your driveway is now gone. One of my men is going to dust for fingerprints and I'll post a car at the end of the road tonight just to be safe."

Paul nodded. "We're actually headed back to the States tonight. I need to be back in Chicago tomorrow."

"And I'm flying to Atlanta after I drop him home," Oliver said. "I won't be back until next week."

"Just stay in touch with us," Officer Trembley said. "And, if we have more questions, we'll give you a call. There's no sign of forced entry and with nothing missing I'm not sure we know what's going on yet."

Paul shot his brother a quick look. "I think I might

have left the door unlocked. Do you think it could have been someone just being nosey?"

"That's possible. We still want to err on the side of caution, though."

"I appreciate that," Oliver said, extending his hand to shake the other man's.

Officer Trembley gave them both a slight smile. "My guys should be finished in about an hour, then we'll get out of your way."

"Take your time," Oliver responded. "Can I get anyone coffee?"

The officers all shook their heads no and continued about their business. The two brothers stared at each other.

"I'm going to go pack," Oliver finally said. "Let me know if they come up with anything."

Paul nodded, his anxiety level at an all-time high. All he wanted in that moment was to get back to Simone. To get Lender out of their lives, and finally be done with the mess. He wanted to trust that whatever she had planned had to be far better than what they were currently going through.

His voice dropped to a low whisper. "You do that, big brother. Because as soon as they're done, we're getting the hell out of Dodge!"

Chapter 15

Paul wasn't answering his cell phone and Simone didn't know whether to be angry with him or worried for him. She'd left a half-dozen messages and he hadn't bothered to respond to any of her calls. She'd even left a message for Oliver and that, too, had gone unanswered. It left an unsettled feeling in the pit of her abdomen, but she didn't know whether to attribute that to nerves or morning sickness.

Dinner with her family had lasted longer than she'd planned but it had felt good to be back in the presence of her siblings. They kept each other grounded and she trusted that if she needed them, they would be there for her. Even Mingus and Ellington trying to instigate trouble was done in love and the back-and-forth banter that kept them laughing was everything.

She'd been tossing and turning for hours, unable to drift off to sleep. Despite her exhaustion and the long day ahead of her she knew she wouldn't rest well until she heard Paul's voice and knew he was safe. She blew a soft sigh. Tossing her legs off the side of the bed and then standing up, she wrapped a flannel bathrobe around the T-shirt and shorts she was wearing and slid her feet into a pair of plush slippers.

Moving to the living room she found Mingus wide awake, reading a novel under the light of his Kindle, and sipping on a glass of bourbon. His bare feet were propped against her coffee table. He'd made himself at home and looked very comfortable.

"You can't sleep either?" she asked.

Mingus shrugged. "I wanted to finish this book," he said, gesturing with the paperback in his hand. "You not feeling well?"

Simone shrugged as she dropped down onto the sofa beside her brother. "I can't reach Paul. I don't know if I should be worried or not."

"Paul can handle himself if something comes up. That brother's gone into war zones to administer medical care to refugees. There's not a lot that can shake him. He's tough. He'll be all right."

Simone leaned her head against her brother's shoulder and extended her legs beside his. "I miss him."

"I'm sure he misses you."

Mingus reached for his glass and took a sip of his beverage. "Can I get you anything?" he asked.

She shook her head. "I just want to sit here for a minute."

He nodded and returned to his book, his sister settling against him to calm her nerves.

Mingus had left the window blinds open, the patio door reflecting the view from outside. There was a full moon and Simone stared out at the late-night sky spattered with stars. Her brother was right. Paul was one of the most resourceful men she knew. He'd be fine and she trusted they'd be back in each other's arms before she knew it.

She was just about to head back to her bed when there was a sharp knock on her front door. She sat up abruptly, shooting Mingus a quick look. Her brother gestured for her to stay put as he stood, pulling a large revolver from the waistband of his pants. He eased his way to the door and peered out the peephole. With a shake of his head, he secured his weapon and pulled open the door.

Paul stood anxiously on the other side. Simone jumped to her feet, excitement bubbling up as she threw herself into his arms. Her arms locked around his neck as he lifted her off the floor, her legs sliding around his waist and latching behind his lower back. The kiss was deep and intense, their two bodies so entwined that it was almost impossible for Simone to tell where hers began and his ended.

"I was worried about you," Simone gasped when she finally pulled herself from him. "Why didn't you return my calls?"

"Oliver and I ran into a little trouble. We had some unwanted company at the house."

"That's not good," Mingus interjected.

Paul shook his head. "No, it's not good. I don't know how they found the house, but we got lucky." He took a seat on the sofa and gave them a quick play-by-play of everything that had happened since she'd left Windsor.

Simone felt concerned. "Where's Oliver now? Is he safe?"

Paul nodded. "He should be landing in Atlanta as we speak. I dropped him off at Detroit Metro and made sure he got on a plane before I came here."

"He's not going to his house there, is he?" Mingus asked.

"No. He's going to stay with a friend."

"I'm going to put security on him until this is over," Mingus said as he began tapping a message into his cell phone. "When he calls, you tell him a man named Porter will contact him and will stay with him until I tell him otherwise."

"That's not…" Paul started before being interrupted.

"Yes. It is," Simone said firmly. "It's very necessary." She hugged him again, feeling immensely blessed to have him back with her. She had missed him, but until he had walked through the door, she hadn't realized just how much not having him there had actually hurt.

Mingus rolled his eyes skyward. "Well, on that note, I'm going to bed."

"You're staying?" Simone asked. "Now that Paul's here…" She paused, though seeing her brother's expression stalled her words.

"Until this is over, I am your personal bodyguard," Mingus answered. "And that goes for you, too, Paul. I'm the third wheel until further notice. And if you need to strike out on your own, someone from my team will be with you."

Paul extended his arm, the two men shaking hands. "Thank you," Paul said.

Mingus nodded. "She's got a full day tomorrow. You might want to make sure she gets some sleep." His comment was more of a demand than a casual statement.

"I swear!" Simone exclaimed. "You're not the boss of me, Mingus!" she yelled at her brother's back as he exited the room and disappeared down the hallway.

Paul laughed as he pulled her back into his arms and hugged her close.

"He's like having another father!" Simone quipped. "Even my dad's not that annoying!"

"Your brother is a great guy. I appreciate him being here to support us."

Simone shrugged. "Whatever!" She stepped out of his arms and took a step back. "Are you hungry? Do you want me to make you something to eat?"

Paul shook his head. "No, thank you. I'm exhausted. All I want is a shower and a bed."

Simone gave him a slight smile. "That I can make happen," she said as she moved to check the door lock one last time. "And I plan to personally tuck you in and kiss you good-night," she said, her voice dropping to a seductive tone.

As Paul smiled back, she grabbed his hand and pulled him along behind her to the master bedroom.

Hours later Simone's stomach was doing flips and her whole body convulsed with pleasure as Paul lay between her parted legs, his mouth pressed possessively to her most private place. His touch was determined, his tongue lapping at her greedily. Her body arched and then dipped as heat swarmed through her nerve endings and electricity fired through each sinewy muscle. His touch was wanton and intoxicating and Simone gasped for air at the intensity of it.

A shower had been reinvigorating for them both. Simone had joined him beneath the flow of warm water, needing to feel his body pressed closely to hers. She had dropped to her knees to worship at the fountain of his maleness until she had him unsteady on his feet, his whole body shuddering with gratification. Their need for each other had been volatile, something decadent and explosive rising with a vengeance between them. It was unexplainable and left them both drunk with wanting until they could barely see straight, and rational thought seemed virtually impossible.

She struggled not to cry out, the bedclothes clutched so tightly in her fists that her nails were digging deep into her flesh. Her back arched again and all her muscles vibrated like strings pinged on a violin. His name rolled past her lips, the sweetness of it melting like chocolate against her tongue. Her body exploded, her orgasm hitting with an intensity that had her shaking. Her temperature rose exponentially, perspiration bubbling against her skin. It was sheer bliss.

Paul crawled slowly up her body, a line of damp kisses teasing her flesh. He licked her belly button, one nipple, then nuzzled his face in the fold of her neck. The aftershocks still had her quivering and he helped her ride out the last waves of her orgasm before rolling onto his side to lie beside her. He adjusted a pillow beneath his head.

Simone muttered something, her words incoherent. She laughed, her back twisting against the mattress as she stretched her limbs. The lilt in her voice bounced sweetly off the walls.

Paul chuckled. "You okay?" he asked, his eyes lifting to stare over at her. He dropped his hand to her tummy and allowed his palm to rest gently against her.

"I'm better than okay," Simone finally answered. She shifted closer to him, needing to experience as much skin-to-skin contact as she could muster. She felt almost desperate for his body heat and the feel of his flesh against her own. Between missing him and worrying about him, her nerves had been frayed and she felt relieved to have him so close. "How about you?"

"I have no complaints," Paul said with just the slightest nod of his head.

He curled himself around her body, cradling Simone in his arms. His eyes were closed, and she could tell he was slowly slipping into that warm space between wake and slumber. His breathing began to slow, air coming in low, even gusts past his lips.

Simone settled into the comfort of each exhale, the sound not quite a purr as Paul began to snore softly. Just as she felt herself slipping into sleep with him, his deep voice vibrated through the late-night air.

"I need to speak with your father."

Simone nodded. "Okay."

"Okay, but before I do, now that you've had some time to think, I need to know what you want. Where are we going from here, Simone?"

Simone heaved a deep sigh, the conversation coming sooner than she'd anticipated. But she owed Paul answers and she couldn't continue to keep him hanging. He deserved better from her. Especially now that she was carrying his child.

"I owe you an apology," she said, her voice a loud whisper in the late night air. "Although I knew you'd understand why I left the way I did, I should have discussed it with you first. I know that you and I can't move forward if I'm not honest when things are off balance. And I was off balance. I was petrified and I didn't want you to see me be weak."

Silence filled the space between Paul reflected on her comment. He took a deep breath before he spoke. "Well, I didn't understand. I thought we were well past that point with each other. Don't you know that I don't see you as weak? Even when you're struggling with something? And even if you do experience a moment of weakness, I'm here to help you get through it! I'm not passing judgment."

"I'm flawed, Paul Reilly! Immeasurably flawed."

"You're dramatic, Simone. Overly dramatic!"

"I'm getting better. And, I'm committed to doing better. Because I want to be a great mother and a great wife. I want you to be proud of me. And I need you to trust that I will be everything our children need me to be."

"Children?"

"We need to plan at least one pregnancy. Like normal people do. Maybe when Junior here is five or six years old. That is, of course, as long as we don't have another accident when this kid is two or three."

"You can't run out on me again, Simone. If you do, I can't promise I'll chase after you. And you definitely can't run out on this baby if it gets hard. I can't promise what will happen if you do."

Simone swallowed, the emotion catching deep in her chest. Tears suddenly misted her eyes. "I swear, Paul. I will never make this mistake again! I love you! And I love our baby and I want us to be together, no matter where in the world it takes us."

Another moment of silence filled the air until Paul suddenly spoke again. "You know I love you, right?"

Simone shifted her buttocks against his pelvis. "Of course, I do. Why would you ask me that?"

"Just in case your father kills me after our conversation and I'm never able to tell you that again."

Simone giggled. "He won't kill you."

"You sure about that?"

"You're giving him his first grandchild. You'll be good as gold."

Paul's fingers danced warmly over the surface of her stomach, his thumb occasionally tapping against her belly button. Energy quivered with life beneath his touch. "We should go to sleep. We have to be up in a couple of hours," he finally whispered.

They both drifted back into the quiet, trading easy caresses as sleep began to consume them. Without anything else needing to be said, the decision had been made. They were having a baby, planning a future, and only needed to get past the problem that was conveniently being ignored.

"I'm filing the formal complaint with the FDA this afternoon and tomorrow we're holding the press conference to announce that we're bringing a civil lawsuit against Lender Pharmaceuticals." Simone made the pronouncement the next day over a bowl of yogurt and granola and a cup of morning coffee.

Paul was about to take a drink from his own cup of coffee when he paused midsip, suddenly feeling uneasy about the next steps. He knew they were opening a big can of worms and he was fearful the tactic might come back to bite them. It was one of the only times the unknown felt like it might be a challenge he wasn't equipped to beat.

"So, what can go wrong?" he asked. "Because I'm thinking something might go wrong."

Simone placed her cup onto the table, pushing it from her. "Nothing is perfectly fail-safe. We're not going to know what will happen until we take action. But we have the full support of my brother's law firm and that's going to bode well for us. Ellington has even agreed to personally sit second chair."

Paul nodded. "And you're good with working for your brother? I know how excited you were about the other law firm."

"I was excited, but when I reasoned what would be in the best interest of the case, and our family, joining Ellington's firm made more sense."

She took a breath before she continued. "Announcing the lawsuit will draw attention to Lender that I'm sure they're not going to be happy with. But I fully intend to shine a very bright spotlight on what they've done. I'm also going to shine a light on you."

"On me? Why me?"

"Because if you're the face of the complaint and the lawsuit, Lender is less likely to continue to try and come after you. How would it look if you publicly call them out for their wrongdoing and then something happens to you? That's not the kind of publicity they want. Trust me. That's also why we're holding the press conference at the hospital. I've already made the arrangements. I have every intention of doing whatever it takes for this to make national news and inevitably go viral and get international attention."

"The hospital has probably fired me by now."

"No, you're still very much employed. In fact, you're about to be their local hero. The crown prince of everything that should be right with medical care in today's environment. You'll need to present your studies to the board before we talk to the press, but that's just about giving them the facts of the case. You'll take a stand, defend the science, and our lives will go back to being normally dysfunctional."

Paul blew a heavy sigh, staring intently at Simone. She seemed unfazed, totally focused on a plan she was certain would put things right. She swallowed the last bite of her yogurt and stood up from the table, clearing away their dirty dishes.

"I need to get dressed," she said. "I have my doctor's appointment and then we need to get that arrest warrant lifted."

"That won't happen until Daddy lays eyes on you," Mingus interjected, moving into the room. "Good morning."

Paul shook his head. "Good morning."

"Parker can lift it, can't he?"

"Nope! The superintendent filed it. Only the superintendent can unfile it. There's also the option of an overly eager rookie pulling you over and taking you in. You might even get tased if you're lucky," Mingus said sarcastically.

"So, after we leave the doctor's, we need to go see your

father," Paul said, rising from his own seat. "I can't afford to get arrested."

"Well, we also have an appointment with the hospital administrator this afternoon and I need to run by my new office so I can start delegating the workload so we can prepare for tomorrow's press conference."

Simone took an inhale of air, holding it deep in her lungs. She already felt taxed from everything that needed to be accomplished before the day ended. She anticipated the next day would be equally exhausting. Despite her body functioning with a mind of its own, Simone was determined to push though and do what she needed to do. She couldn't afford to fail. Everything Paul held near and dear depended on her succeeding.

Paul moved to her side, seeming to read her mind. "Everything's going to be fine. We'll get through it and if it becomes too much for you, you need to let me know." He leaned and kissed her cheek.

Simone tapped her fingers against his chest. "I'm going to get dressed. You need to practice."

Paul looked confused. "Practice?"

"Begging. I'm sure my father won't accept anything less."

Mingus and Simone laughed heartily.

Paul nodded. "Yeah," he said, joining in with the laughter. "Today is going to be a very long day!"

Simone and Paul left the doctor's office with a prescription for prenatal vitamins, a lengthy list of follow-up appointments and well wishes from her favorite physician and his staff. Once his diagnosis had been confirmed, Paul sat with his chest pushed forward, gloating like it was his greatest accomplishment in the whole wide world. Simone was equally excited but determined not to let it show. Just in case. Nothing was certain in life and if the past few weeks were an indication of what might lie ahead of them, she didn't want to tempt fate and be disappointed.

Mingus drove them from the medical center to their brother's law offices and waited while the two went upstairs to see Simone's new space and meet her staff. Paul stood back, pride painting his expression as she threw herself right into the fray, giving orders. It took no time at all for everyone to know that she was living up to her reputation. She was known for being a fierce litigator: well-prepared, fair-minded and tough as nails. She expected one-hundred-percent from anyone working for her because she always gave that and much more. She was impressive, and watching her, Paul understood how passionate she was about the work she did. She loved her job as much as he loved his. As she settled in, he excused himself, taking the elevator back down to the lobby.

Mingus was leaning against the car, his arms crossed over his chest. Paul joined him. Standing side by side, the two looked like perfection sculpted from clay. It didn't escape Paul's attention that passersby were taking notice of them, some staring blatantly. He was acutely aware that a few women gawked, and they were drawing attention that neither had anticipated.

"Well, now," Paul said, as a young woman wearing skin-tight leggings, wedge sneakers and a bomber jacket stopped to press her telephone number into the palm of Mingus's hand.

Mingus winked his eye at her and when she rounded the corner out of sight, he tore the sliver of paper into tiny pieces and dropped them to the ground. "These women will get you hurt out here," he muttered.

Paul laughed. "I don't typically have problems like that."

"Give it time. I bet as soon as you're in the park pushing little junior around in his stroller, the women will be all over you."

Paul laughed. "And Simone will definitely hurt someone."

"Starting with you," her brother added.

A moment passed before Mingus spoke again. "You know, if you were anyone else, I'd kick your ass for knocking up my sister. But since she loves you, and the rest of us actually like you, I'm going to give you a pass."

Paul chuckled. "Do you think your father will give me a pass?"

"Oh, hell no! You're a dead man walking."

Paul stole a quick glance down to the cell phone in his hand for the time. It wasn't quite the lunch hour and he anticipated Simone wouldn't be finished anytime soon. He sent her a quick text message, advising her to stay put until he returned. When she replied, asking where he was going, he told her a little white lie, not wanting her to worry. Knowing that she was already stressed had shifted him into protective mode, wanting to ensure he did nothing to add to her anxiety. There was a quick back-and-forth exchange before she seemed to be content with his answers.

He turned his attention to Mingus. "Do you know where I can find your father right now?"

Mingus nodded. "Yeah, why?"

"I think I need to speak with him without Simone. She said she'd like to work until we have to meet the hospital administrator and I could use a ride."

Mingus reached for his own cell phone, shooting Ellington and Simone both a message. He suddenly gestured toward two men parked in a car on the other side of the street. The passenger nodded, then exited the vehicle and crossed over to where they stood.

"If she tries to leave, send me a message," Mingus said.

The man nodded, shooting Paul a quick look before moving into the building to take up space in the lobby.

"They work for you?" Paul questioned.

"Yeah. Backup. Just in case. You have a target on your back, remember?" He rounded the car to the driver's side and opened the door.

Paul shot a look over his shoulder as he slid into the passenger seat. "It's hard to forget," he muttered.

Minutes later they pulled into a parking space on Forty-Seventh and King Drive. As they stepped out of the car, both men stole glances around the block, looking up one side of the street and down the other. Mingus pointed toward the entrance to Peach's Restaurant.

Paul shot his friend a look. "You're really making me interrupt your father's lunch?"

Mingus shrugged, his grin a mile wide. "You asked me where he was, and this is where he is. Every other Thursday from eleven thirty until two. Meeting with the other Southside Heavies."

Paul's gaze narrowed. "Southside Heavies?"

"You'll see," he said as he moved toward the restaurant's entrance and pulled open the door.

The two men stepped inside, and Mingus pointed Paul toward the back of the room and a table surrounded by eight men in deep conversation. Paul recognized Simone's father, Jerome Black, and Pastor Randolph Hinton from Mount Episcopal Baptist Church, one of Chicago's most renowned megachurches. The others looked equally prestigious and intimidating.

"The man seated next to my father is Darryl 'T-Dog' Rockman. He's a lieutenant with the Disciple Kings. Beside him is Alderman Lincoln Haynes and next to him is real estate mogul Maxton Price. He owns a good third of the property on the south side of the city."

"I recognize Pastor Hinton and the man beside him looks familiar, but I can't place where I know him from."

"That's Illinois House Speaker Mike Zell. And on his left is Floyd Mac of Mac's Barbershop, and last, but not least, Dr. Gregory Graves, founder and director of The Graves Boys Academy."

Understanding fell against Paul's shoulders. The men around that table were renowned for their activism in the community, each impacting the lives of its citizens in ways that weren't always visible to the public. They were highly respected by their core base and carried significant weight in what did, and more important, what *didn't* happen on the South Side of Chicago. It was a truce of major proportions to have them all seated around a table breaking bread together.

Paul nodded, slightly awe-struck. The magnitude of what was going on was not lost on him. The men around that table were iconic, superheroes to the Chicago masses. He aspired to accomplish a third of what most of them in the room had already accomplished in their lifetimes. He found himself hoping that his work to right the wrongs of Lender Pharmaceuticals would have as significant an impact to those who had trusted him with their health. "Southside Heavies!"

Mingus grinned. "You know Miss Nanette, don't you?"

"Yes," Paul said. Nanette was a fixture in her Chicago neighborhood, a community mother of sorts. Everybody on the South Side who knew her, loved her. She was known to feed the neighborhood to help pay her mortgage, selling plates of her home-cooked offerings. Her home was considered neutral ground for the gangs, and at any given time the lowest of the city's downtrodden and Chicago's most elite could be found dining together at her table.

"Miss Nanette coined the phrase. In fact, she instigated the first meeting of the Southside Heavies. Periodically, the faces change. Members drop or are added but they all come to the table with the same mission. To do what's best for the residents they serve."

A pretty woman with a satin-smooth complexion suddenly stepped forward to greet them warmly. "Table for two, gentlemen?"

Paul shook his head. "We just need Superintendent Black's attention for a quick minute."

She threw a glance toward the table of men and then turned back toward him. "They really don't like to be disturbed."

"It'll be fine," Mingus said as he pushed past the woman and headed in his father's direction.

Paul grinned sheepishly. "Sorry about that," he said, "but it won't be a problem. I promise."

The woman's eyes were wide as saucers as her gaze floated after them. Jerome Black looked up, only slightly surprised as the two men stopped at his table. "Mingus! I wasn't…" he started just as Mingus side-stepped and Paul slid front and center. The patriarch sat back in his seat, eyeing Paul intently. "Dr. Reilly."

"Good afternoon, sir," Paul said, acutely aware that every eye was suddenly focused on him. His nerves felt fried and his knees were shaking as he struggled not to let his anxiety show.

There was a moment of hesitation and then the Simone's father introduced them. "Gentlemen, I'm sure you all know my son Mingus."

There was a round of nods and greetings, Mingus

shaking hands with the pastor and dapping fists with the gang leader.

"And this is Dr. Paul Reilly."

"Good afternoon," Paul responded, moving to shake hands as each man introduced himself. He turned his attention back to Simone's father. "I apologize for the interruption," Paul said, "but I was hoping to have a quick word with you, sir. Or if I might schedule some time to speak with you later?"

"No. We need to talk now!" Superintendent Black snapped. He stood up, excusing himself from the table. He gestured for Paul to follow behind him. As the two men disappeared toward the restaurant's kitchen, Mingus slid into the seat his father had just vacated.

Laughter rang out warmly behind them as the two men sauntered through the kitchen area and out the back door to the alley in the rear. Jerome turned, both hands clutching his sides. The patriarch was a distinguished man with salt-and-pepper hair, a rich, chocolate-brown complexion and a full beard and mustache. He was tall and the two men stood eye to eye evenly. His expression was stoic, and Paul knew he was in a mood, and clearly not happy. For a split second Paul would have preferred going hand-to-hand in combat with the two men from Lender than the conversation he was about to have with Simone's father.

"Where is my daughter?"

"She's safe, sir. At the moment, she's at Ellington's law office, working."

Jerome gave him a slight nod, seeming to file that bit of information away. "How dare you put my child in harm's way? Have you completely lost your mind?"

"No, sir, and I did everything I could possibly do to ensure Simone was safe."

He shouted, "You should have never left the state with

her! You should have turned yourselves in to the police so that we could have protected you both. That's what you should have done!"

Paul didn't respond as the man continued to rant. There was nothing he could say to defend his actions, or Simone's. They had worried her parents, and her father was spewing that back at him. Paul understood his fear because he had also felt it, unable to shake the emotion, even when he and Simone had been going through it together. Most especially after discovering she was pregnant, their unborn child inadvertently in danger as well. There was nothing he could do but apologize.

"I'm very sorry, sir. It was never my intention to put Simone in harm's way. We were just reacting to the situation to the best of our ability. The decisions we made were done with no ill will intended, sir."

Jerome snapped, "I expected you, of all people, to have an ounce of sense more than Simone. I know how impulsive my daughter can sometimes be. I expected you would be able to keep her in line. I was depending on you!" He swiped a hand across his brow as he turned, inhaling deep, swift breaths to calm his nerves.

"Again, sir, I regret how things happened. We never meant to worry you or Judge Black. But Simone is safe and well." He took a breath as Simone's father turned back around to stare at him. His eyes were narrowed, and his brow was furrowed. Paul imagined that if looks could kill he might actually be standing there dead. He persisted.

"Superintendent, I love Simone. Your daughter is my entire world and I would give my own life to protect hers."

Jerome grunted, his eyes rolling skyward.

Paul continued, "I know that there is nothing I can say right now that will help you to understand why we did what we did, so I'm not going to try. But I need you to believe me when I tell you how much Simone means to me. I hope to make her my wife and for that to happen, sir, we both need your blessing. Simone would never have me if she didn't have your permission. She respects your opinion, sir, and it would not sit well with her if you didn't approve of me, or our being together.'

Jerome took another deep breath, but he didn't say anything. The muscles in his face, though, had relaxed significantly and the vein that had been pulsing with a vengeance just minutes earlier had calmed significantly. Paul took that as a good sign. He continued to talk.

"Simone wanted to be here when I spoke to you, but I knew I needed to speak with you first. Man to man. Because I love Simone as much as I do, sir—it's just as important to me that you support our being together. Not just for Simone, but because I don't ever want you to doubt that I have your daughter's best interests at heart. Or that I won't do whatever it takes to protect and take care of her."

Jerome stared at him intently, his head bobbing in a slow nod. "I guess she could do worse," he finally muttered, a hint of levity returning to his tone.

Paul smiled, feeling his mouth lift in an easy bend. "Let's just hope she can't do any better!" he said.

Jerome laughed heartily. "I'm still pissed," he said after the moment of flippancy passed.

Paul took another deep breath. "Then I should probably share our other news with you now."

"Do I even want to hear this?"

There was just the briefest moment of hesitation and then Paul said, "Simone and I are pregnant. We're expecting a baby. I'm excited about it, but she still has some reservations. She needs your support now more than ever. I need your support because Simone and that baby are my family and I don't want to lose them."

The silence grew full and thick as Jerome just continued to stare Paul down. Paul sensed that the levity that
had risen between them had been quickly extinguished.
He suddenly wished he could find a hole to crawl into,
something like fear piercing his midsection. He watched
the patriarch's jaw tighten as he ground his teeth together
and that vein was pulsing like it was trying to sync with
a marching band.

Jerome suddenly snapped, "I swear! I should just
lock your ass up and throw away the damn key!" He did
an about-face, moving back through the door into the
kitchen, the fixture slamming harshly behind him.

Paul hesitated before he followed, thinking he might
have pricked the man's last good nerve. Wondering if he
had just overshared before the patriarch had been ready.
He clearly wasn't happy or excited by the news and Paul
wondered if he was rethinking whether or not he approved
of Paul being with his daughter. He blew a heavy sigh,
his hands clutching his sides. He leaned his head back,
his eyes closed as he whispered a quick prayer skyward.

Minutes later Paul reentered the dining room, moving
back to the table, and Mingus, who stood at his father's
side. The superintendent had retaken his seat. The others
around the table all turned to stare, giving him a harsh
look. Paul was suddenly very uncomfortable and then
just like that, they broke out in laughter. Simone's father
was shaking his head from side to side.

The two men said their goodbyes and exited the restaurant. As they made their way to the car, Mingus slapped
him against the back. "Dad said to tell you he expects you
at Sunday dinner. He also said I should kick your ass if
you even think about not showing up."

Paul blew a sigh of relief and grinned. "Trust and believe, my brother, that won't be a problem. By the way,

did he by chance mention whether or not he's lifted that warrant he issued for my arrest?"

When Paul walked into Simone's law office, she was on the phone being harangued by her father. Jerome had gotten to her, reiterating his displeasure with the two of them. Simone was listening, unable to get in a word as her father bellowed over the phone line, as Paul dropped down onto the small sofa that decorated the space, empathy painting his expression.

Simone shot him a look, her eyes rolling skyward. Annoyance flooded through her, compounded by frustration as her to-do list played in rotation in her head. She didn't have the time or the energy for her father's tantrum, but she also knew she needed to let him vent because he was really pissed with her and Paul.

She nodded into the receiver. "Yes, sir… No, sir… but… I didn't…yes, sir…we were planning…" Simone sighed and pulled the phone from her ear. She cupped her palm over the mouthpiece. "Did he scream at you, too?"

Paul nodded. "He ripped me a new one! My ass still hurts!"

With a slow shake of her head, Simone pulled the phone back to her ear. "Yes, Daddy… I promise…we will… I can't…okay…okay…yes, sir…yes… I love you, too, Daddy!"

After disconnecting the line, Simone tossed her phone to the desktop and joined Paul on the sofa. For a brief moment they sat staring at each other and then both laughed.

"That was rough," Paul said. "I really thought he was going to lock me up and forget where he put the key."

"He still might. He hasn't yelled at me like that since I was in high school. I felt like I was six years old all over again." It hadn't been often that her father had yelled when she'd been a child, but Simone had always dreaded those moments. As she'd gotten older, she realized his bark was worse than his bite and if she simply sat and listened, those moments would pass quickly and she'd be his favorite baby girl again.

"I think he still likes me, though," Paul said.

Simone laughed. "I know he likes you. You've been summoned to Sunday dinner. He likes you a lot." She lifted her face to kiss his lips.

"That's good, because I really wasn't planning to go anywhere," Paul said as he kissed her back. "So, how has the rest of your day been?"

"Busy, but I think we're ready for tomorrow. You and I need to go through the data one last time. Then we'll send our formal complaint to the FDA with copies of all our documents. When we leave here, we'll go sit down with the hospital administrator and their legal team, present our case so that they are aware of what you are doing and why, then I just want to go home and put my feet up."

Paul nodded. "If you're up to it, I'd like to make one more stop. I'd like to run by our friend Liza's to see if she can look something up for us. There is something that's been bothering me."

Simone laughed. "She's a hacker, Paul, not a library!"

He shrugged. "She's good at what she does and if she finds what I think she can find, it will further support our case."

"Then we run by there. Are you looking for something in particular?"

"I need the FDA test data for those three Lender drugs that were banned."

"Is any of that public data?"

"I'm not sure. I can call and ask first, but I'm thinking it probably isn't. But I need to see the numbers and compare them to the results Oliver and I got from some of our tests. Your theory that maybe those drugs and Halphedrone-B are actually one and the same has been gnawing at me. If those drugs are contaminated and the contaminant is the same, it may be enough to prove they simply changed the name and knowingly repackaged a tainted product."

"I was just throwing it out there as a what-if."

"I know, but if you're right…" His voice trailed off as he considered the possibility.

Simone finished the thought for him. "If we're right, then Lender purposely poisoned patients and sheer greed was their motivation. Bottom line, if they knowingly sold drugs that had been previously banned, that's criminal and I want to do whatever we can to shutter their doors."

"I honestly find it unfathomable that no one in that company would have found this to be wrong on every level imaginable."

Simone gave him a nod. "Well, let's go see what we can find out. Let me send my brother a text so he can warn Liza that we're coming," she said as she rose from her seat and moved to reclaim her telephone.

"If Ellington doesn't mind, I'd like to borrow an empty office," Paul said. "I need to place some calls to my colleagues overseas. They need to be aware of what's going on. I think if I tell them that we've gone forward with filing the complaint and that we're announcing our intent to sue the drug company the doctors will be more inclined to pull the drugs voluntarily instead of waiting for an official recall."

"Follow me," Simone said. "I'll find you some space. I actually have a little juice in this joint."

Paul laughed. "Simone, please don't get yourself fired. It's only your very first day!"

* * *

The office receptionist waved for Simone's attention as she and Paul were headed out the door. Excitement bubbled from the young woman's cheery spirit, her exuberance a refreshing greeting to clients. Her name was Candace, and like Simone, she was new to the firm.

"Attorney Black, there's a package here for you. It was just delivered." Candace pushed a white container across the marble counter toward Simone. It was the size of a large shoe box and nondescript, with no identifiable markings.

"For me?" Simone's eyes widened in surprise, the delivery unexpected. "Do you know who it's from?"

"One of the local delivery services dropped it off, but there was no card attached to the outside."

"Did you have to sign for it?"

Candace suddenly looked nervous that maybe she'd done something wrong. "No, ma'am. He just said he had a package for you and then he turned around and left."

"Were you expecting something?" Paul questioned, suddenly on guard. He stepped between Simone and the box, the gesture instinctively protective.

Simone shook her head. "No. Unless someone in the family sent it. Maybe a welcome gift? Parker and Armstrong had flowers delivered earlier today to say congratulations."

"Text everyone and ask," Paul said as he lifted the box from the counter and moved swiftly to the conference room, setting it in the center of the table.

Within minutes of Simone pushing Send on the text message, Mingus and one of his associates stepped off the elevator, both moving swiftly to where they stood in the conference room door. "Did you try to open it?"

her brother questioned, looking from them to Candace and back.

Simone shook her head. "Paul just carried it from the reception desk to there."

"I shook it," Candance interjected, her voice a loud whisper as she stood twisting her hands together nervously. "I don't know if that's important."

Mingus nodded, then moved to the table, spinning the box in a slow circle.

"Be careful," Simone admonished. "Maybe we should call Parker and have him send over a bomb team?"

Paul shot her a look. "You need to stand back, please."

"You both need to stand back," she snapped back.

The man with Mingus pushed past the couple and closed the door, leaving them standing on the outside of the room.

Paul inhaled a deep breath. "We're not doing this. This is ridiculous," he said, turning to face Simone. "We can't live like this. You and the baby are my life. If anything happened to either of you..." The words caught in his chest as he choked back hot tears that threatened to fall from his eyes.

Simone was crying, her anxiety level having finally spilled over. She stepped into his arms, grabbing at the front of his shirt as he pulled her against him.

The door to the conference room suddenly flew open, Mingus's associate moving swiftly past them back toward the elevator. Mingus stood in the corner of the room on his cell phone. His expression was stone, no hint of emotion across his face.

They moved into the room, their gazes questioning as he disconnected the call.

"What is it?" Simone asked.

"Where do you two need to go from here?" Mingus asked.

Paul answered. "The hospital for a meeting and then I wanted to swing by and see Liza."

Simone asked again. "What's in the damn box?"

Mingus shook his head. "Parker's on his way to get the box. He wants to dust it for prints. I doubt he'll find anything, though. My guy is headed to see if he can track down that delivery man."

"Is it something bad?" Simone persisted.

"I need to put a few more of my people in place and then we'll leave," he responded, ignoring her question.

Simone shook her head, moving closer to the table. "Why won't you tell me…" she started.

"Leave it alone, Simone," Mingus said.

"Is it bad?" Paul asked, his anxiety level still rippling with a vengeance.

Simone flipped her hand at her brother as she moved to the box. The top was askew and she pushed it off to peer inside, pulling the box toward her.

The cry that echoed around the room was gut-wrenching. It was a dull wail that sounded like pain and fear twisted in a tight knot. It pierced the quiet in the room with such turmoil that Paul and Mingus both rushed to Simone's side.

"Damn, Simone!" Mingus admonished.

Paul reached for her, trying to pull her close, but Simone pitched forward back toward the door and dropped to her knees, vomiting into the trash can in the corner. Tears streamed down her face and she was shaking.

The two men exchanged a look as Paul turned to see what Simone had seen. A small kitten lay inside the container, its little head severed from its tiny body and its white fur matted with dried blood. Paul closed his eyes, fighting the urge to rage. The cruelty of the act was beyond reason. He turned and moved to where Simone sat sobbing. He pressed his hands to her shoulders and pulled her from the floor.

"I need to take her home," he said to Mingus. "I'm canceling the meeting."

"No," Simone said, swiping at her eyes as she fought to regain her composure.

"Simone, you're not safe. They were clearly sending us a message. So, we're finished. We're not doing this."

"Yes, we are," she said, sniffling loudly. "We have to, Paul. We can't let them scare us off."

"Well, I am scared. I'm scared to death that something will happen to you and the baby. I would never survive that, Simone."

Simone wrapped her arms around his neck and kissed his cheek. She pressed her palm to his chest and tapped gently. "I'm going to the restroom to freshen up my face. Then we need to leave or we're going to be late for our appointment. We didn't come this far to quit," she said.

"Besides, we have a whole police department behind us," Simone continued as she pointed toward the lobby and the officers who were headed in their direction.

Paul and Mingus locked gazes. "Can you talk some sense into her?" he asked.

Mingus shrugged. "Not my fight, bro! I'm just here to protect and serve."

As Paul watched her walk away, disappearing down the length of corridor to the restrooms a wave of despair washed over him. Simone wanted to push forward, and he knew nothing he could say would deter her. She would get her way. But this message had been way too close for comfort and he had to make sure he stopped the threat to their safety in its tracks. He just wasn't sure how.

Chapter 16

When Simone woke the next morning, Paul was still poring over the documents Liza had found for him the previous day. Piles of paper were strewn around her living room and he sat at the kitchen table entering data into a program on his computer. He hadn't gotten an ounce of sleep and he was clearly singularly focused on finding an answer to questions that hadn't been asked yet.

He looked up as she moved into the room, heading to the kitchen for a cup of coffee. A bright smile pulled across his face. "Good morning, beautiful!"

"Good morning! Did you come to bed at all?"

Paul shook his head. "No. I had to weed through this information. Plus, after that delivery yesterday, I had a lot on my mind."

Simone nodded her understanding because she hadn't rested well, either. "Did you find anything?" she asked, gesturing toward the papers in his hand. She inserted a decaffeinated K-Cup coffee pod into her Keurig coffee maker and pushed the start button.

"As a matter of fact, I did," Paul said, a smug smile crossing his face. "I compared the lab results from those products that were rejected to the products we studied, and the similarities are undeniable. The contamination is even worse in some cases. I think we can prove Lender renamed and relabeled contaminated products and has been selling them as Halphedrone-B. Looking back over some of their financial records, the costs for the initial production of the drug cut deep into their bottom line. I think they stopped production after the second year and replaced it with merchandise that had been previously rejected. Product that's been stockpiled in a warehouse in Mumbai because if they had destroyed that excess drug it would have crippled their profit margins. They'd already gotten Halphedrone-B approved and no one was looking hard at subsequent product. I believe we can make the case and connect many of the dots."

Simone sat down at the table, bringing two freshly brewed cups of coffee. She passed one to Paul who took it eagerly, his excitement abundant. He obviously felt like he'd struck gold and the joy was written all over his face.

"So," she said, her mind beginning to race. "I now have to figure out how we introduce stolen evidence. Because we're not supposed to have this data, so we can't just say *look at this* without them questioning how we came into the information."

Paul took a large sip of his coffee. "You'll figure it out. I believe in you! And if not, maybe they can give us side-by-side prison cells."

Simone smiled. "I may have to call in a few favors because I don't look good in convict stripes."

Paul laughed as he took a second sip of brew. "What time is the press conference?"

"Three thirty. We need to be at the hospital before then, though. I have a few loose ends to tie up and obviously I need to figure out how to include or not include this new information. I should probably run it by Ellington when I get into the office."

"Please, do that. Please!"

Simone rolled her eyes. "What are you going to do between now and then?"

"I need to get a few hours of sleep, then I'm heading over to the hospital. I need to get updated on a few patients and hopefully start to get back to work. I should already be there in plenty enough time for the press conference."

"Just don't be late."

"I won't be late, Simone."

"Just to be sure I'll send Mingus back to get you."

"I can drive. I know he'll have one of his guys tailing me, but he definitely doesn't have to go out of his way," Paul said.

"Yes, he does. It's necessary. Just to be safe."

"Just to make sure I show up?" he shot back.

"I know how much you hate public events."

"I hate giving speeches and I definitely don't plan to speak this afternoon, so do not put me on the spot."

"Would I do that?" she asked.

"I mean it, Simone!"

She giggled. "No worries, baby! I got you!"

Paul shook his head, his look skeptical. "I need a shower and then I need to lie down. How soon before you leave?"

"I'm going to finish my coffee, then get dressed. I'll leave right after that. If you're asleep, I won't wake you. But make sure you set your alarm."

Paul stood up and shuffled his papers into a neat pile. He leaned to kiss her cheek. There was just a moment of hesitation, his lips lingering against her skin, as if a question on the tip of his tongue, as if he suddenly felt uncertain about asking it.

Simone sensed his trepidation as she pressed her palm to the side of his face, leaning back to stare into his eyes. "We've got this," she answered. "Everything's going to be fine. I promise."

As Paul headed toward the bedroom, Simone sat back

in her chair, dropping into reflection. They were going through the motions, pretending all was well, even as doubt and uncertainty kept rearing its head. What had happened in the office had left her battered. And angry. She hated being threatened and she didn't take the warning lightly, but she refused to let it beat her. Because for as much as she needed Paul and his strength to forge ahead, he needed her to be equally as strong. They were both on emotional overload and her hormones were spinning her in a hundred different directions. But she was determined to be the rock he needed, an immovable boulder barreling against anything that threatened their future.

Despite concerns about his safety and that of his patients, Paul had finished his rounds at the hospital and was going through patient charts when Nurse Grace knocked on his door. She poked her head inside to see if he was busy.

"I'm sorry. I didn't mean to disturb you, but you have a visitor."

Paul looked up from the lab results he was reading. "A visitor?"

"Vivian Lincoln would like a minute to speak with you. And I apologize, I don't remember which drug firm she's with."

"Is she alone?"

Grace nodded. "She is. If this isn't a good time, I can send her away. I already told her you have an appointment with Dr. Cartwright, so you won't have much time for her," she said, referring to the hospital administrator.

After a moment of consideration Paul nodded. "That's fine. You can send her in," he said. With Mingus's men positioned outside the door and in strategic locations on the hospital floor, Paul doubted highly that he needed to be worried about Vivian trying anything. He had to wonder, though, what she wanted and why she was there. He closed the files he'd been reviewing and placed them on the credenza that sat behind him.

He reached for his phone, debating if he should text Simone. He decided to wait until he saw her and could answer the mountain of questions he anticipated would be coming.

There was a second knock on the door. "Come in," Paul called out as he moved onto his feet and rounded the desk to stand in front of it.

Vivian moved through the entrance, closing the door behind herself. "Dr. Reilly."

Paul nodded, noting the formality in her tone. He responded likewise. "Ms. Lincoln. What brings you here?"

Her gaze swept the length of his body, shifting from his head to the floor and back. "May I sit down?"

Paul gestured toward a seat with his hand. "Please."

"Thank you."

Paul returned to his own seat, still eyeing her cautiously. An air of tension had risen in the room, feeling like thick mud weighing him down. "So, to what do I owe the honor?"

"Let's not play games, Paul. You need to call off this witch hunt. There is absolutely nothing wrong with our product and your lies will only serve to discredit you."

"Excuse me?"

She continued, "We have people at the FDA, so we're fully aware of the complaint you lodged this afternoon. And I understand you have questions and concerns, but you're blowing this well out of proportion. Lender is in the business of saving lives and you're trying to criminalize our efforts."

Paul bristled, indignation rising with a vengeance. The

audacity of her statement was laughable. That she honestly thought he'd file a complaint without proof would have been insulting if he had cared about her opinion.

"I have people at the FDA as well, and I trust there will be a thorough investigation into any and all claims I may have. I'm trying to hold Lender accountable for their actions. If everything is as copasetic as you claim, then you shouldn't have anything to worry about."

"You really don't want to do this. If you know what's good for you…" Her eyebrows lifted, her head tilting slightly as she glared at him.

"Is that a threat?"

Vivian stood back up, her high heels clicking against the tiled floor. Her lips were pursed as if she'd sucked on something sour. "We don't make threats, Dr. Reilly. But I assure you, this will not go the way you think it will."

Paul smiled, narrowing his gaze. Clearly, he had struck a nerve and he found it interesting that Vivian Lincoln, of all people, was trying to strongarm him. "I consider myself warned."

She moved to the door, pausing to stare back at him. "By the way, I don't take kindly to being stood up."

"Well, I don't take kindly to being *set* up," Paul quipped.

Still looking like she'd swallowed spoiled milk, Vivian hesitated in the entrance, as if there was one last thing she needed to say, but she didn't, instead, slamming the door closed as she made her exit.

Paul felt his heart racing and he released the breath of air that he'd swallowed. He wasn't sure whether to be concerned or not, but he knew it was too late for them to retract their complaint or to withdraw the lawsuit Simone had filed during her lunch break.

He thought about the children and families still suffering because of Lender and he didn't care what Vivian, or her company, thought about what they were doing. He was determined to stop them, no matter what it took.

The alarm on his Apple watch vibrated against his wrist. The hospital Powers That Be were waiting for him. Although they would remain neutral with relation to his legal actions, they stated at their meeting the previous evening that the administration and the hospital's board had vowed to stand behind him in support. Paul knew it had less to do with him and much to do with reducing their liability to the patients impacted by the drugs that had been prescribed by their staff. After the cat incident it had been welcome news, and as Simone had succinctly pointed out, they were better served standing on the side of what was right than supporting what was very wrong.

Hanging his white coat on a hook in the closet, Paul changed into his suit jacket. With one quick adjustment of his necktie, he took a deep breath to calm his nerves and headed to the conference room on the top floor of the medical facility.

An hour later, after a brief meeting, Paul followed the hospital's board members and legal team out to the south side of the building. The warm temperatures felt more like early fall than the last of winter; the sun was still shining brightly in a clear blue sky, and Paul imagined it was very much a seasonal calm before an unexpected storm.

The meeting had been brief, and most of their time had been spent waiting for everyone to arrive. The discussion had been to reiterate the hospital's position and to ensure everyone was on the same page when the press asked questions. He hadn't had much to say, still mulling over his conversation with Vivian. He also still had doubts that this was the right route to go, but there was no turning back from the decision.

He was surprised by the crowd that stood on the hospital's steps. Simone must have gotten the attention of every news affiliate that reported on the city of Chicago. Reporters, podcasters and journalists stood closely together. A few were doing sound bites to lead into the story. Others were jotting notes into well-worn composition books or dictating into handheld recorders.

There was also a very visible police presence. Uniformed officers were maintaining crowd control. The superintendent himself stood toward the back of the crowd, his wife standing by his side to show their daughter support.

Simone stood at the podium, Ellington by her side. The two looked cucumber cool, unfazed by the flurry of activity around them. There were last-minute microphone checks and one of the paralegals was passing out envelopes of information that included the press release and an assortment of supporting documents.

At one point Simone turned, searching him out, and when their gazes connected, she gave him the sweetest smile and a nod of her head. For reasons he knew he would never be able to verbalize, he was taken aback by the confidence she exuded. She wore it like a badge of honor that complemented the winter-white suit draped around her body. It was paired with an emerald-green satin tank and green suede pumps, and she was stunning. In his heart he saw a warrior woman: fierce, determined and a force to be reckoned with. It was Simone at her very best; the woman he had always known was there even when she herself hadn't been sure. Just the sight of her calmed every ounce of his nervous anxiety.

Simone gestured for him and his colleagues to come

stand on the step directly behind her. He took a deep breath, knowing that they were minutes away from sharing what he had been haunted by for close to a year. It was a moment of reckoning and he could only pray that fate would serve them well as he walked to Simone.

Paul had just reached her side, Simone placing a hand on his forearm as she reached to whisper in his ear, when he heard gunshots ring out. The harsh explosions rattled the calm, the too familiar *bang, bang, bang* sounding loudly through the afternoon air.

Paul was unprepared for the chaos that suddenly ensued, most in the crowd taking flight. He looked left and then right as he grabbed Simone by the shoulders and threw himself around her, pushing her down to the ground. The protective gesture was second nature, her safety his only concern. Beside him, Ellington was shouting but the words were undiscernible, nothing resonating in Paul's ears but the echo of gunfire and the loud screams of panic.

Out of the corner of his eye he saw Mingus racing in their direction, his gun drawn. Other officers were also rushing toward the danger, searching for whomever had fired the shots. It was then that Paul felt the warm flow of blood pouring over his hand, the offending ooze spreading like a Rorschach inkblot across Simone's white blazer. Her body had gone limp and as he turned her in his arms, he realized Simone had been shot; bullets presumably meant for him had struck her instead. Shock wafted through his spirit, holding hands with panic like he'd never known before. He gasped loudly, then screamed her name.

He swept Simone up into his arms and raced toward the hospital's entrance. Muscle memory kicked into action as Paul shifted into doctor mode, screaming out triage instructions. As he reached the doors he called for a gurney and medical supplies, his hands pressed against Simone's two bullet wounds to help stall the bleeding. For Paul the doctor, the moment should have been no different than any other experience he'd had in various war zones. But this was Simone and their unborn baby! This was everything he valued in life. That moment would forever haunt him if he got it wrong and he was determined to get it right, calling on every ounce of medical training he had ever had.

It took less than three minutes before Simone was being rushed into an emergency room bay, a nurse cutting away her new suit so that they could inspect her injuries.

Minutes later, after conducting an assessment of her vital signs and getting an IV started, Paul was still shouting out instructions as another doctor, the surgeon on call, pushed him out of the way and took charge. For a split second Paul lashed out, refusing to relinquish control. Desperation was fueling his efforts, his need to bring Simone back from the brink exponential. Adrenaline coursed through his blood stream and he stood toe to toe with the other man, shaking with rage in his leather shoes.

"Dr. Reilly, we need you out of the way, please. We'll take good care of your wife," he said.

Paul nodded, seeing no need to correct the man. Simone wasn't his wife, but she would be. It might not have been official, but she was his, heart and soul. She was the air he breathed, the water he drank, the sweetest dreams when he slept, the lifeline that kept him standing. She was so much more, and he didn't have the words to tell the other man so. Then suddenly he did.

"She's pregnant," he advised. "Approximately six weeks or so along. We're having a baby. You need to save them both!"

The other doctor nodded as he issued an additional list of instructions as they were pushing Simone out of the emergency room toward the surgical wing.

It was all too surreal. Paul stood still as stone. He was shaking and he held out his blood-streaked hands, fighting to stall the quiver of adrenaline that had consumed him. He wasn't quite sure where next to turn.

"Dr. Reilly? Dr. Reilly?"

Paul did an about-face toward the emergency room nurse calling his name. "I'm sorry, do you need me?"

"The family is gathered in the waiting room, wanting an update. I didn't know if you wanted to give that to them yourself or if you'd prefer Dr. Kennedy do it."

Paul took a deep breath, shaking himself from the trance he'd fallen into. His emotions were raw, and he had no sense of time and place. He only wanted to be in the operating room. He wanted to trade places with Simone, to move her far from the hurt that had rendered her helpless. He needed to be useful and he was feeling everything but. He suddenly couldn't get enough air into his lungs and he bent forward, hands pressed against his thighs as he sucked in oxygen. He felt broken and he had to dig deep to find the strength he knew Simone needed from him.

"Are you okay, Dr. Reilly?" the woman asked, moving swiftly to his side.

He nodded. "I just need a minute to clean myself up," he said to the nurse who was still standing there, staring at him. "Get me an update from the surgical team and then I'll go speak with the family."

"Yes, sir," she said as she turned and exited the room.

Paul moved to a supply closet and found a clean set of hospital scrubs to change into. He didn't want Simone's mother to see his suit covered in her daughter's blood. Quickly discarding his clothes on the floor, he washed his hands and face, then moved back to the nursing station and the nurse he'd spoken to just moments earlier. She held out the telephone for him to speak with the operating room, the words barely registering as he listened to the surgical resident on the other end give him an update on Simone's status.

"Thank you," he said finally as he disconnected the call. He took two deep breaths still trying to calm his nerves.

"Can I get you anything, Dr. Reilly?" another nurse questioned.

Paul shook his head. "Thank you. No. I'm good."

The two women exchanged quick looks. "The family was moved to the private waiting room outside the surgical area. They're waiting for you there," the first nurse said.

Paul nodded and turned, moving swiftly in that direction.

The Black family were all sitting anxiously. Simone's father was pacing the floor, Parker trying to get him to calm down and sit.

The patriarch snapped. "I'll sit when I know what's going on with my daughter," he was saying as Paul moved into the room.

At the sight of him, they all jumped to their feet, throwing questions in his direction faster than he could catch them. He held up a hand to stall the comments and gestured for them to all take a seat. He moved to the empty chair beside Simone's mother and took the woman's hand, squeezing it gently.

"Simone is still in surgery," he started, pausing as he felt the emotion bubble in his throat and tears burn hot behind his eyelids. He took a swift inhale to regain his composure. "She was shot twice in the back. One bullet lodged centimeters from her heart and the other exited out of her abdominal area. There is a lot of internal damage. She has a wonderful team supporting her but it's going to be a while before we know anything. Dr. Dayton is the premier cardiothoracic surgeon here at the hospital and he is working with Dr. Kennedy, who heads our surgical department. I trust them both with my own life, so she's in the best hands. They're doing everything they can to save Simone. Right now, she's stable, but her condition is…is critical," he said, his voice breaking.

Judith pressed her free hand against the back of his and squeezed his fingers. Paul lifted his gaze to meet hers evenly. "What about the baby?" she asked.

"Baby? What baby?" Vaughan snapped, taking a step forward. She shot a look around the room, then glanced back toward Paul.

Paul looked from one face to the other, as well. Simone had planned to tell the rest of her siblings about the pregnancy at Sunday dinner. She'd been excited about sharing her news and had only hoped Ellington and Mingus— mostly Ellington—wouldn't spoil the moment for her.

"Simone is pregnant," he said. "We were planning on telling you all this weekend. But we won't know anything for a while. She's lost a lot of blood and with her injuries and the stress on her body, they're not sure she'll be able to maintain the pregnancy." His voice cracked a second time, hot tears burning against the back of his eyelids. Even as the words had left his mouth, Paul couldn't begin to fathom what he would do if anything happened to either of them. But he knew it would break them both if they lost the baby.

"That baby comes from good stock," Jerome said. "He's a fighter. He'll be fine."

Paul smiled ever so slightly. Simone had already declared their child a girl so he could just imagine what she would have to say about her father's proclamation. He welcomed Jerome's optimism, no matter what the baby's sex.

"How long do they think the surgery's going to take?" Mingus asked.

Paul shook his head. "It might be a few hours. We just don't know."

Silence filled the space and Paul realized he was struggling not to cry. He suddenly felt a hand on his shoulder and looked up to see Simone's father fighting back his own tears.

"We gotcha, son. You can trust that. There's not a soul here in this room, in this family, who isn't here to support you. But Simone is going to need you more than she is ever going to need any of us, so have your moment, then pull yourself together. I have never trusted my baby girl with anyone before but I'm trusting her with you. Don't make me regret that!"

"Thank you, sir," Paul said softly. He swiped at his eyes with the back of his hand.

Parker stepped forward. "Can you give me a statement, Paul? It won't take long," he said. gesturing toward the door with his head.

Paul nodded, rising from his seat. He followed Parker, Mingus, Armstrong and their father into the hallway.

Parker paused for a moment as a family of three strolled past, then he turned his attention back to Paul. "What do you remember? We have a few witnesses who say they think the shooter was a woman. The hospital's security cameras caught a glimpse of the car, but everything happened so quickly, we don't have many leads."

Paul thought back to that moment and what he could recall. He'd been singularly focused on Simone, her hand pressed against his arm, her smile bright. Just the near-ness of her had calmed his nerves and then all hell broke loose.

But he did remember the car that had careened off, a late-model Jaguar, and only because he had looked up just as it sped toward the highway spinning rubber along the way. He hadn't seen the driver, but he knew enough to give Simone's brother a name.

"Vivian Lincoln," he said. "I'd bet my last dollar that if she didn't pull the trigger, she knows who did," he added, filling them in on all that had happened just an hour earlier.

"Find her and bring her in for questioning," Jerome commanded, "and call Judge Preen for a warrant to do a search of every place she's shown her face in the last forty-eight hours. Make it as broad as you think you need it to be to get the job done."

Parker nodded. "Yes, sir. The media is also looking for a statement. What do you want me to tell them?"

"We have no official comment at the moment. I am personally focused on my daughter's recovery," Jerome said. He turned toward Mingus, his voice dropping to a harsh whisper. "Call your reporter friend. Leak what-ever you think will help us get the most traction about this Lincoln woman and that damn drug company. Put the word out that if they had anything to do with this, I will be coming for them."

Mingus gave his father a nod and turned on his heel, disappearing toward the end of the hallway.

"I need to stay with your mother, but I want you on this," the patriarch said to his sons. "We'll call you as soon as your sister gets out of surgery. Until then, you find who did this. Use whatever resources you need."

Armstrong and Parker nodded, both men exchanging a look. Each one extended his hand toward Paul, then bumped shoulders in a one-armed embrace. As he watched them disappear behind Mingus, Paul realized he was suddenly privy to the inner workings of the Chicago police force that few others were privileged to see.

He recalled a previous conversation with Simone once, when the media and local politicians were in an uproar about their newly minted superintendent. People were in a furor about her father's stance on police tactics. In a community with a historic distrust of law enforcement, he followed the law as long as the law allowed him to do his job to the best of his ability.

When necessary, Jerome and company didn't hesitate to walk a very fine line and the family didn't always follow the rules of protocol to get the job done. For them, the ends justified the means. And unapologetically, they were determined to do whatever was needed to get justice for Simone. Paul was grateful for them because in that moment all he could focus on was Simone's recovery.

Jerome gave Paul a look. "My wife's a strong woman but she's having a hard time with this. She feels helpless and she just wants to do something to help Simone get past this. I should be out there looking for the shooter, but I need to stay close. Just in case," he said.

Paul nodded his understanding. "I know how she feels," he said as they moved back through the door.

Inside the waiting room, Judith sat with her legs crossed, her top one bouncing with nervous energy. "One of the nurses brought us coffee," she said. pointing to a half-dozen paper cups filled with French roast. "If either of you is hungry, she said someone would gladly go get us something to eat."

"I don't have much of an appetite," Jerome said.

"None of us do, Daddy," Vaughan interjected. She rose

from her seat to give her father, and then Paul, a hug. "Are you okay?" she questioned, eyeing Paul with visible concern.

Paul gave her a look. He wasn't okay. He was nowhere near being okay. He felt lost, and broken, struggling with being on the outside when he wanted to be by Simone's side, ensuring everyone else was doing their job and doing it well. He shrugged his shoulders. "I'll be better when your sister is back in my arms, safe and sound."

Vaughan gave him a smile. "I have faith that will happen sooner than you realize."

Paul moved to the seat beside the matriarch. "Is there anything I can do for you, Judge Black?"

"You can start by calling me Judith. We're family and family doesn't stand on formality." She gently tapped the back of his hand with her palm.

"Yes, ma'am."

The Blacks chatted casually together, everyone clearly trying to mask their concerns and frustration. Paul appreciated being able to catch up with Simone's siblings, their discussions giving him something else to focus on. And even with the company to distract him, he still found himself wondering what might happen if surgery didn't go well. The mere thought of losing Simone kept him on edge and barely able to function.

It was almost five hours later when the two surgeons, the head of the obstetrical department and the hospital administrator came to speak with them. Everyone's anxiety rose tenfold, the air so thick in the room it could have been cut with a knife.

Paul jumped from his seat first, moving forward to meet them. His gaze shifted from one to the other trying to read their expressions. His heart raced, his blood pressure sky high. "How did it go?" he questioned anxiously.

"How's my daughter?" Judith asked at the same time, her hands wringing nervously together.

Paul reached for the matriarch's hand, tangling his fingers with hers. Judith gave him a slight squeeze, a gesture meant to calm them both. Jerome moved to his wife's other side, an arm sliding around her waist as they all stood holding each other up.

"If you don't mind, why don't we all take a seat?" Dr. Dayton said. "We've been on our feet for a good little while. Now, are you all related to Simone?"

"We're her parents," Jerome answered. "Dr. Reilly is the father of our daughter's baby and these three are her siblings." He pointed toward Vaughan, Ellington and Davis who hovered behind them.

Paul seemed to read the man's mind. "You can speak freely. I'm sure Simone's mother, Judge Judith Harmon Black, will confirm they have Simone's healthcare proxy. And I'll personally attest that Simone would want you to disclose her information to her family.

The hospital's administrator nodded in agreement. "It's fine," Dr. Clarke said. "I know them personally and the Black family have been long time supporters of the hospital."

As the family moved to sit back down, Dr. Kennedy picked up the conversation. "Simone came through the surgery nicely. She's still in recovery and we plan to keep her there a little longer before we move her to ICU. There was significant internal damage and bleeding but luckily the bullet in her abdomen didn't hit any vital organs."

"The bullet lodged near her heart was trickier," Dr. Dayton said. "It was just a millimeter away from puncturing the left chamber. We also didn't realize until we got in there that she had a third bullet lodged just an inch from her aorta," he continued. "We successfully removed them both and don't anticipate any residual complications."

"What about the pregnancy?" Paul questioned, his gaze turning to the third physician in the room. Anxiety flooded through him, the nervous energy spilling out of him.

Dr. Mabel Tripodi smiled, the gesture consoling. "Only time will tell. But you've got a strong little guy there and his mother is even stronger. We are going to treat her pregnancy as a high risk for now. You need to understand that Simone's body has been through major trauma. And it's also still very early in this pregnancy. Right now, I'm concerned about her blood pressure. It's been a little sketchy and that doesn't help. If it becomes too much on Simone and the baby, with everything they've both been through, there is always the risk her body will spontaneously abort, and she'll miscarry."

There was a collective gasp as that news settled in. Paul took a deep breath, his knees beginning to shake and the muscles across his back tightening. The news wasn't anything he hadn't expected, but hearing it stated out loud wreaked havoc on his already shaky nerves and he struggled to maintain his composure. He had questions, many of them, but he wanted to be respectful of her parents and the concerns he knew they had.

"When can we see her?" Jerome questioned.

"It'll probably be at least another hour and only two of you at a time for a few short minutes. The ICU nurses are a tough bunch, so don't be offended if they throw you out at any time," Dr. Kennedy said.

Dr. Clarke interjected. "Superintendent Black, Judge Black, I want you to know that your daughter is receiving the best medical care. I'm sure Dr. Reilly will attest to the fact that she has the best team rooting for her recovery. And if there is anything at all that I or my office can do for you, please do not hesitate to contact me. We hate that this happened. And Superintendent, I'm sure you know better than any of us how much we all wish we could do more to combat the tragic shootings that occur daily here in Chicago."

Jerome nodded. "I appreciate you and your staff cooperating with my men. We definitely want to get as many guns off our streets as we can."

Paul stood up, about to burst out of his skin. "I'd like to check on Simone, please."

"She's still in recovery," Dr. Dayton said. "That's really not…"

"I know the protocols," Paul replied firmly.

Simone's physicians exchanged a quick look with the administrator.

"That should be fine," Dr. Clarke said. "As long as you have no objections, Superintendent? Judge Black?"

"None at all," Judith answered. "Dr. Reilly is the father of our daughter's baby and one of her emergency contacts. She trusts him explicitly and he is privy to all her medical concerns. He has our permission to advocate for her health however he sees fit."

"Thank you," Paul said.

"I'll walk with you," Dr. Tripodi said. She shook hands with everyone in the room and she and Paul made their exit.

When they were out of earshot, the family behind them, Paul asked, "Colleague to colleague, Mabel, what's her prognosis? Are we going to lose this baby?"

"Paul, you know better than any of us that I can't answer that with any certainty. Simone has a long recovery ahead of her. This pregnancy isn't going to make that easy. Only God knows for certain what will happen from here.

Friend to friend, I will do everything in my medical power to help you both see this pregnancy to term. But if I were you and you believe in a higher power, I'd start praying."

Paul nodded his head slowly. "Praying is the only thing I've been able to do."

Chapter 17

Hours after surgery ended, Paul was back in his hospital office when the Black brothers came strolling in. It was well after midnight and Paul had been there most of the day. He'd spoken to his brother twice, Oliver promising to be there on the next flight headed out of Atlanta. Simone was resting comfortably in the intensive care unit and they had specific instructions to contact him immediately if there was any change to her condition. Her mother had refused to leave, and the last time Paul had gone down to check on her, they had made Judith comfortable in a reclining chair in the corner of the room.

The brothers all found a seat, making themselves at home. It didn't take rocket science for Paul to figure out they were there about the case and he was eager to hear what they had learned.

"Have you seen the news?" Ellington questioned.

Paul shook his head. "No. Why?"

"You need to," Davis responded. He reached for the remote control on the small television in the corner of the office and turned the device to the local news station.

The evening newscaster was standing on the steps of the hospital, a microphone in hand. The hospital signage was just over his left shoulder, the angle just so to capitalize on the location and put him screen center. The lights from the emergency entrance illuminated the shot.

"This is Wesley Wallace and I am here at Northwestern

Memorial Hospital where a thirty-four-year-old attorney and former state prosecutor is in critical condition, suffering from gunshot wounds and struggling to survive!"

The camera transitioned to a shot of the hospital steps where the offense occurred; multiple police officers stood around assessing the scene. The reporter continued. "Right now, a community is sending up prayers for the daughter of the Chicago police Superintendent, Jerome Black. His daughter, Simone Black, was critically wounded by gunfire in a drive-by shooting this afternoon. Friends and family posted these images of Ms. Black, a local attorney now in private practice, on social media. Her parents and family are by her side in the hospital tonight and are asking for prayers."

The camera spotlighted two nurses, capturing their comments in quick sound bites.

"My heart goes out to the family. I can't begin to imagine what they must be feeling."

"This was such a senseless crime!"

There were more shots of the crime scene and the police as the reporter continued to narrate the story.

"Police say Ms. Black was preparing for a press conference to announce a class-action lawsuit against drug giant Lender Pharmaceuticals and the hospital's decision to pull the drug Halphedrone-B and two other blood-pressure medications pending the results of an FDA investigation into contamination allegations. Right now, police are looking to see if cameras picked up the assault and images of the shooter who is still out there. They are not saying whether or not Ms. Black was targeted."

The camera returned to the reporter. "Witnesses say that a silver Jaguar was seen speeding away from the scene. Chicago police are asking people to come forward and call Crime Stoppers if they have any information. This is Wesley Wallace for ABC 7 Chicago. Back to you, Mark."

The scene shifted to the studio and the news desk.

"Thank you, Wesley. And in related news, John Mitchell Lender, CEO and founder of Lender Pharmaceuticals, was found dead this evening in what is believed to be a self-inflicted gunshot wound. Police are not saying if the two shootings are in any way connected. Lender Pharmaceuticals develops and produces medicines and vaccines for a wide range of medical disciplines and has a net worth in excess of fifty-four billion dollars. We will keep you posted as we learn more information."

Davis turned off the TV, and all the brothers turned back to stare at Paul.

Paul sat back in his chair, not knowing when he'd shifted forward in his seat. Hearing them talk about Simone had made him cringe with hurt, hating that what had happened had been reduced to an assortment of emotionless soundbites. But the revelation that John Mitchell Lender was dead suddenly splayed his curiosity wide open. "Was it a suicide?" he questioned, turning toward Parker.

Parker and Armstrong exchanged a look. "We don't think so," he answered. "It's just too convenient and the initial forensics don't support that story. But someone has gone to great lengths to make it look like one. And conveniently, the gun found beside him was the same caliber as the weapon used to shoot Simone."

"We're still waiting on the ballistics report, but I'm betting it's the same gun," Armstrong said.

"Which would tie the two cases together and put Simone's shooting on him. And attribute his death to guilt," Parker surmised.

"But you don't think that's what happened?" Paul asked again.

There was a loud pause, no one saying anything.

"If it were that neat, it would allow your friend Vivian Lincoln to slide right into the CEO position," Mingus interjected. "She stands to inherit all of his stock, which would give her controlling interest in the business and make her a very wealthy woman."

"So, the bigger question then becomes," Ellington added, "what do you believe, Paul? Do you think Vivian Lincoln's hands are clean in all of this?"

Paul shook his head emphatically. "Hell, no. Not at all," he answered without hesitation.

Parker nodded. "We don't think she's innocent in all of this, either."

"So how do you prove it?" Davis asked.

Silence filled the space a second time. The quiet felt stifling, nothing but the sound of a ticking clock and the scuttle of nurses on their evening rounds outside the door.

"How about a confession?" Paul suddenly asked.

"We always welcome a confession," Parker answered. "How do you propose to make that happen?"

Paul stood. "I have an idea."

The decision to keep Simone sedated in a drug-induced coma had been for her benefit, giving her body time to simply rest and heal. Another two hours had passed before Paul was able to relieve her mother and sit by Simone's side. The matriarch hadn't wanted to move, but Armstrong had insisted, finally convincing his mother that she needed as much rest as her youngest daughter.

Paul anticipated being with her most of the morning until Judith returned, wanting to stay with her baby girl. He fully understood because until Simone opened her eyes and gave him one of her snarky comments, he knew there was little else he'd be able to accomplish. He needed to sleep, but rest avoided him, in case he closed his eyes and missed something. He reached for her medical chart outside the room's door, reading through all the doctors' notes. He had a question or two and he made a few mental notes to follow up with them once the staff changed shifts and they made their new day rounds.

She looked fragile, he thought as he stood staring down at her. Her mother had brushed her daughter's hair, wrapping it with a pretied silk slip-on scarf. He knew Simone would appreciate the gesture. Cords connected her to machines that were monitoring her vital signs. Her blood pressure was still erratic and a cause for concern, but the doctors were still optimistic about her having a full recovery.

Paul blew a soft sigh as he drew the backs of his fingers down the side of her face. She was tough as nails and he trusted that in no time at all she'd be back to herself and giving him a hard time. He didn't have the same trust about their baby but as one of the nurses had pointed out, they'd seen things happen that none of them could ever explain. It would be God's will and he continued to pray that God knew his and Simone's hearts.

He leaned to kiss her cheek then moved back to that recliner. He pushed it closer to the bed so that he could reach out to hold Simone's hand. It was only hours later, when Judith returned and woke him up, that he'd realized he'd been sleeping soundly, his fingers still locked tightly with Simone's.

Paul's decision on calling Vivian Lincoln to offer his condolences on her loss came with its own level of anxiety. After spending time with Simone and her mother, he'd gone back to Simone's house to shower and change. Beginning to feel like himself again, he sat down and ate a bowl of cereal and milk. After calling the hospital to check once again on Simone, he sat down to set things in motion, hoping what he planned wouldn't come back to bite him in the ass.

Vivian had been surprised to hear from him, or she pretended to be. Paul had used that to his advantage because he was pretending. Pretending to be a concerned friend as he spun a web of lies as he talked to her.

"I do have some compassion, Vivian. Mr. Lender was a leader in the drug business. His initial efforts in the game served many people well. I believe in giving credit where credit is due. I was also concerned about you. I know this can't be easy."

"That's kind of you to say. He was dedicated to the business. I hate that he was in so much emotional pain that he would take his own life!"

"I also wanted to apologize," Paul continued. "During your visit the other day we both said some pretty awful things to each other."

"I agree and I want you to know that I was just talking out of frustration. The lawsuit and all…" Her voice trailed off, leaving the comment open for interpretation.

Paul took a breath. "Let's not talk about that. Hopefully, with everything that's happened, we can resolve it privately and make it all go away."

"If it could be that easy," Vivian gushed.

"I understand. I also need to apologize for standing you up when we ran into each other in Detroit. My schedule blew up on me and I just needed to take off."

"I admit, Paul, that did hurt my feelings."

"I would never purposely hurt you. I'm not that kind of man. In fact, if I'm honest, I must admit that I was a little intimidated. You're a beautiful woman and you've dated some very eligible men, if I believe what I've read in the tabloids. I've questioned if I would be able to measure up." Paul was grateful they weren't face-to-face. He pretended to gag, pointing his index finger toward the back of his throat.

Vivian giggled. "Fake news," she said. "Most of it anyway. And if I didn't think you'd make the cut I wouldn't have shown any interest." She giggled again.

Paul rolled his eyes a second time. If he could have reached through the phone line he would have pulled her through the device and wrung her thin neck. He'd never been a violent man, but it was taking everything in him not to rage, wanting to punish her for putting Simone in that hospital bed. He took a deep and held it before he spoke. "Well," he said, another lie rolling off his tongue, "I hope we can still be friends and move forward."

"About that lawsuit…" she started.

Paul interrupted her. "I regret that as well, but what I was seeing frightened me."

"I so wish you had come to me first. I'm sure I could have explained everything so that your concerns would have been alleviated. But not to worry. Our team here is handling things."

"Well, I'm not sure what's going to happen. I don't know if you heard, but the attorney on the case was shot in a drive-by yesterday afternoon. They're not sure she's going to make it."

"Tch, tch, tch!" Vivian exclaimed. "I did hear that and it's such a shame. Have you heard whether or not they have any leads yet?"

"No," Paul responded. "I do know they're questioning whether or not Mr. Lender's death was related. Because of the lawsuit, of course."

"I do know he was very upset about the allegations against him. But I don't want you to blame yourself. You couldn't have known he'd take things so personally."

"No, I couldn't have known that," Paul replied.

There was suddenly an awkward silence and Paul knew he needed to do something to change that. He took a deep breath.

"I don't want to take up any more of your time, Vivian. I'm sure you need to get back to your family. Perhaps we can get together for a drink sometime soon?"

"How about tonight?" she asked.

The question stunned him, coming out of the blue. He didn't know what he had expected, but he hadn't expected her to jump at the bait so quickly. Now he wondered if maybe she had plans for him that he hadn't anticipated.

After agreeing to meet her, he was even more conflicted when she insisted he come to her home. Her excuses as to why she couldn't go out had run the gamut from her not being dressed, to the fact she didn't feel like going out, and each excuse escalated with a hint of sexual innuendo. When they'd settled on a time, he disconnected the call, turning to look at Mingus and Armstrong and feeling like a deer caught in headlights.

"Let's get a mic and camera on you," Armstrong said.

"Are you sure she won't be able to tell that I'm wired?"

"The only way she's going to know is if you take your clothes off to show her."

Mingus laughed. "I wouldn't let that happen if I were you." He jostled his brother's arm. "Can you see him trying to explain that one to Simone?"

Paul shook his head. "Not funny. You both know Simone would kill me!"

"That's putting it mildly. Simone would crush you like

a bug, revive you and do it again just to make sure you suffered!"

"Well, since y'all are putting me up to this, I can't do anything that will get you killed, too. Because she would crush all of us!"

"I know that's right!" Mingus quipped, still chuckling under his breath.

"Just try to relax," Armstrong emphasized. "If you get nervous and start sweating you might short out the system and electrocute yourself."

Paul laughed, the nervous chuckle sounding awkward to his own ear. He was suddenly having second thoughts, questioning if he could do what was needed without showing his hand. Not wanting Simone's brothers to see his discomfort, he deflected. "So, is this how you all get rid of your sister's boyfriends?" he asked, trying to ease the tension that had risen in his heart.

Mingus shook his head. "Nah! I just tell them to go away."

Armstrong nodded. "We all do. We can be very convincing."

There was a moment of pause and then the three burst out laughing. The moment of levity eased the tension, necessary so that they weren't all consumed with rage and sorrow, worrying about what would happen next.

"If you get into trouble and need our help, just say your safe word. We'll be there before you know it."

"Safe word?"

"Something easy that lets us know you're in trouble. A word you won't forget in a pinch," Armstrong added.

Paul nodded, a slight smile pulling at his mouth. "French toast."

Mingus grimaced. "French toast?"

"It's the only thing your sister can cook and cook well."

Laughter filled the room a second time.

The next few minutes were spent taping a microphone and battery pack to his upper torso so that it wouldn't be easily exposed. Armstrong explained how the micro camera hidden in his lapel pin worked. After checking all the connections and testing the volume levels, the two brothers wished him good luck and sent him on his way. They followed behind him in an unmarked van.

The ride to Vivian's was fraught with nervous energy. Paul talked into the microphone the entire time, fighting to dispel the anxiety that had him wanting to turn around and change his mind. The idea of playing on Vivian's romantic interest in him had sounded like a good idea at first, but now he was having second thoughts. Maybe, he mused, she wasn't as enthralled as he sometimes imagined. Perhaps she was wanting to get him before he was able to get her. Maybe they were all wrong and Vivian didn't have anything to do with Simone's shooting. His cell phone rang, lighting up on the car's dashboard. He depressed the answer key, the Bluetooth connection filling the vehicle's audio system.

"Stop talking," Armstrong admonished. "You're driving yourself crazy."

"You're driving us crazy," Mingus yelled.

Paul laughed. "Sorry about that. I was just trying to pass the time."

"Just practice your pick-up lines. This woman is looking to get into your pants. Work that and make it work for you. Show us that romantic side Simone is always bragging about."

"Just don't screw this up," Armstrong chided. "This may be the only opportunity we get to nail this broad."

Paul nodded, even though neither man could see him. "I know what I'm doing," he said. He took a deep breath, thinking of Simone and the baby and what had put them all in this position in the first place. After a quick call to the hospital to make sure nothing had changed with her condition, he stepped out of his car. His jaw tightened and his anger rose tenfold, fueling his objective. "I've got this," he said, signaling he was ready. "You don't have to worry about me."

Vivian's luxurious residence was located in Lakeshore East, in one of Chicago's newest high-rise apartment buildings. Paul was slightly taken aback when Vivian opened the door wearing a sheer red negligee that was super short and cut extremely low. Double D breasts looked like they were about to explode past the expensive lace and the hem barely covered a matching lace thong. He suddenly broke out into a sweat, fighting not to let his disgust show on his face. Armstrong's comment about him electrocuting himself suddenly flooded his thoughts.

"Wow!" he exclaimed, as he stepped through the entrance, his grin like a mask settling in place. "I wasn't expecting…"

Vivian pressed her index finger to his lips to stall his comment. "I thought I'd surprise you."

"Well, I'm definitely surprised," Paul said. "You look incredible."

"You are exactly what I need tonight!" she said as she grabbed his hand and pulled him inside to the living room. "Let me pour you a drink. I make a mean cocktail. Just tell me what your booze of choice is."

"No. Thank you. I don't drink."

"How can you not drink?"

"It's not a habit I ever picked up because I'm usually on call at the hospital."

"The hospital is *why* I drink," she said. "I've always

hated pushing meds at doctors, going from door to door like some snake-oil salesman. And everyone there is always sick with some horrible disease."

"That's why it's a hospital!" Paul chuckled. He bit back the snarky comment at the tip of his tongue, wanting to rail at her about the "snake-oil" she and Lender had been peddling to patients.

She shrugged her narrow shoulders. "Whatever." She moved to the bar and poured herself a tumbler of scotch. "I'm glad you came," she said.

Paul faked another smile as he sat down. "Me, too."

Vivian moved to the sofa and dropped down beside him. "I've had a rough few days."

"I understand. Losing someone you care about is always hard."

She waved a dismissive hand, but she didn't say anything.

Paul spoke instead. "I'm glad I can be here to support you."

"I'm a little confused about that. Every time I tried to hook up with you before, you weren't interested. Why now?"

"I told you. I was intimidated. I've never been a big ladies' man and I don't date much."

"What happened with you and that woman you were dating?" Her brow lifted as she stared at him.

Paul felt the muscles in his face slide into a deep frown, a nervous twitch pulling at his eye. "It didn't work out," he lied.

A look crossed the woman's face. Like she had questions, or maybe knew something he didn't. Instead of commenting, she took another sip of her beverage. When she spoke, her tone had changed. "You disappoint me, Dr. Reilly."

Revelation simmered in Paul's heart. He instinctively knew he had made a mistake as she stood up and moved back to stand in front of the bar. He knew he needed to think fast, still unsure what was going through her head. He took a breath. "Why's that?" he asked.

"Why don't you just tell me why you're really here?"

"You invited me."

"It's more than that. You're here pretending to be interested in me and we both know you're not."

Paul continued to play dumb. "Why would you say that?"

"Why did you lie about your girlfriend? I know you were dating that attorney."

Paul hesitated, meeting her gaze evenly. Something unspoken shifted between them, a battle of wills coming to a head. "Why did you shoot her?" he finally asked.

Vivian stared at him. Her eyes narrowed, the lids hooded as she eyed him. "You really have become a problem," she answered. She reached for her cell phone and began to text someone a message.

Paul went on the offense, his anger painting every word. He snapped, "You don't really think you're going to get away with it, do you?"

Vivian laughed, resting her phone back on the bar as she took another sip of her drink. "I've already gotten away with it and you'll never be able to prove otherwise."

"You believe that?"

"Haven't you heard? My poor, depressed father-in-law shot that woman. Then he killed himself. It's so sad."

"So, you killed him, too?"

"You can't prove that, either."

"I could go to the police."

Vivian laughed a second time, her tone bordering on histrionics. "You could, but I'll never let that happen."

"Why? Why did you do it?"

"Why wouldn't I? I now *own* this company. I can afford to make you and the problems you've caused me just go away just like that." She snapped her fingers to emphasize her statement.

"So, you plan to kill me, too?"

"Of course not, you, silly boy!" she said facetiously. "You showed up on my doorstep, raging about what John Mitchell had done. You became violent and I had to defend myself."

"No one's going to buy that."

"You sure about that?"

"I've never been violent toward a woman a day in my life," Paul retorted.

"Then maybe we were having an affair and I tried to break it off? You didn't know how to take rejection well. You broke in when I wasn't expecting you and I thought you were a burglar! Oops! Wouldn't that be tragic?"

It was only then that Paul saw the gun lying on the polished bar top. He suddenly hoped the camera had picked it up and the police team had seen it, too. He refocused his attention on Vivian, assessing how erratic she was becoming, her behavior fueled by too much drink.

"You're quite the storyteller."

"A girl has to be creative."

"I still don't understand. All of this because I discovered you were selling a contaminated drug?"

Vivian shook her head. "Because I was making the company money and you and your do-good histrionics threaten that almighty dollar. Yes, we sold those drugs. And yes, we knew they were no good, but we needed that financial boost. We'd taken a hit with products that had continually been rejected. Millions of dollars sitting in a warehouse rotting away!"

She took another gulp of scotch before continuing. "And John Mitchell, bless his soul, was ready to retire. I had to prove myself worthy of assuming the helm because he wanted to hand the reins of the company to the current chief operating officer. I couldn't let that happen. So, I did what I had to do."

"Those drugs killed innocent people. Children who trusted us to help them." Paul's voice rose slightly.

"It's a hazard of doing business," she quipped.

"And you had to shoot Simone?"

"I had to stall that information from becoming public knowledge until I could get ahead of it. Shifting the dialogue becomes easy when you toss guns and gun violence into the conversation. Had my guys gotten the two of you the first time, we wouldn't be having this conversation!" She shrugged her shoulders.

"And you pulled the trigger on Simone yourself?"

"Don't be stupid. Why would I get my hands dirty when I can pay people to do that for me? All I did was speed past the hospital after you and I talked. It was a nice distraction, don't you think?"

"And killing Lender?"

"He was a dead man walking. Stage four pancreatic cancer. But I couldn't risk him finding out what I had done. That might have gotten me cut from the will."

Paul suddenly wanted to slap the smirk off her face. He clenched his fists tightly, containing the emotion. "So, what now?"

Vivian moved behind the bar, pouring herself another drink. She gulped it down, then slapped the tumbler against the wood surface. Movement in the doorway caught Paul's eye and he turned to see the two men from the night he and Simone had been shot at standing there with their guns raised. Vivian threw the duo her own look.

"Make it look like an accident," she said, as she moved toward the other door.

"Wait!" Paul exclaimed, holding up his hand as he turned toward her.

She turned back around, eyeing him smugly. "Yes?"

"Doesn't a dying man get one last meal? Because I could really use some French toast right about now!" Then everything went black as pain exploded in the back of his head.

Paul later discovered he'd missed most of the excitement. When he came to, Mingus was staring down at him as EMS checked his vital signs. A dozen or more police officers were milling around the apartment and Vivian was in handcuffs.

"Nice job!" Mingus said, giving him a thumbs-up. "And you didn't have to take your clothes off."

Paul groaned as he sat up, a hand clutching the back of his head.

"Sir, you need to lie still," the paramedic intoned.

"I'm good. I'll be all right," he said. He turned back to Simone's brother. "What happened?"

"You said your safe word and the cavalry came running." Mingus shrugged nonchalantly.

"What about Moe and Larry?" he asked, referring to Vivian's two-man goon squad.

"Moe took a bullet, but he'll live. Larry wasn't feeling quite so froggy. He gave himself up without incident."

Paul nodded. "Did you get everything on tape?'

"Audio and video. It should play out nicely in court. If it even gets that far."

Superintendent Black suddenly entered the room. He shook his son's hand and then gave Paul a look. "We're going to need a statement from you, son, as soon as you're feeling up to it."

"Yes, sir."

"That was some nice police work. You made the family proud. And the city of Chicago is indebted to you."

"Thank you, sir."

The patriarch turned back to Mingus. "What about that confession?"

"Parker has the tape. It was all by the book so you shouldn't have any problems with it. Captain Black made sure he got everything he needed."

Jerome nodded. "I need you to escort Dr. Reilly to the hospital, unless he wants to ride there with EMS?"

Paul shook his head. "That's not necessary. I really am good," he said.

"It's necessary," Jerome answered. "Simone's awake and she's asking for you."

Although everyone kept telling her to relax, Simone was finding that difficult. The monitors kept beeping in response to her anxiety and a nurse hovered over her to scrutinize the spikes in her blood pressure.

"Where's Paul?" she questioned again, unhappy with the previous answers to her question. "Why isn't he here?"

Her mother sighed, frustration furrowing her brow. "Paul is on his way, Simone."

"He was shot, wasn't he? Is he dead? You're not telling me something."

"Baby girl, Paul is fine. He needed some rest and he ran home to take a shower. He's on his way. I promise. Now, you need to relax. Your getting upset is not good for you or the baby!"

Simone closed her eyes, focusing on her breathing. She inhaled slowly through her nose and then exhaled out of her mouth. Comprehending that she'd been shot and was in the hospital recovering felt surreal. Knowing that she and her baby had survived was a blessing and all she wanted was for Paul to be there, holding her hand, so she could believe it wasn't just a dream she couldn't escape from. She took another deep breath.

"That's much better," the nurse said, her head bobbing up and down. "Keep thinking good thoughts and I'll be back in a few minutes to look in on you." The woman made one last check of Simone's IV and then she exited the room.

Judith moved back to her daughter's side, pulling up a chair to the bedside. "You had us worried."

"Do they know who did this?"

Her mother nodded. "Your father said they're following up on a few leads and they have their eye on a suspect. But don't you worry about that. You know your father."

Simone nodded. She shifted against the bed's mattress, trying to make herself comfortable. She ached, but the pain was being dulled nicely by some seriously good meds. "Are you and Daddy good?" she suddenly asked. "With each other, I mean."

Judith smiled. "Why would you ask me something like that, Simone?"

Simone didn't miss the slight twitch in her mother's face, the muscle above her eye constricting. "We've all been worried about you. You two have secrets and that scares us sometimes."

Her mother chuckled, her tone slightly strained. "Your father and I have issues like every other married couple. But we love each other, and we love our family. There is nothing between us that any of you need to be concerned about."

Simone gave her mother a slight nod. "Okay. Tell Vaughan. She and Ellington are scared."

"I will. But you need to rest. We want you home and you can't come home if you don't take care of yourself."

"I want Paul. He should be here."

"Paul's coming, baby. He'll be here very soon."

Simone closed her eyes and seemed to drift off for a split second. She suddenly opened them again, reaching for her mother's hand.

"I think this baby is a boy."

Her mother's smile widened. "What makes you think that?"

"I saw him. I was holding him in my arms, and he was smiling up at me. He said his name is Nino Jerome Reilly."

"Nino?"

"For Nina Simone. Like his mommy!"

"That's a beautiful name."

"He's a beautiful baby!" she muttered as she drifted back off to sleep. "He's so beautiful! Just like his daddy."

The next time Simone opened her eyes Paul was sitting in the chair by her side. She could feel a wide grin spread across her face. He smiled back as they locked gazes, taking each other in. Everything in their small world felt right again, joy rising like a phoenix from the ashes.

"Hey there, sleepyhead!" Paul whispered loudly.

"Hey yourself! I was starting to think that you were dead," Simone replied. "They couldn't find you!"

"I'm not going anywhere, and neither are you. How are you feeling?"

"Like I've been run over by a tractor trailer."

"That's to be expected."

"Tell me the truth—how's our baby? And I want the

doctor answer, not the boyfriend-trying-to-be-protective answer."

Paul nodded. "Tough as nails. He's hanging in here, too. He needs you to be strong for him, though. So, you need to rest and do what the doctors tell you to do." Paul squeezed her hand, entwining their fingers together easily.

"Someone shot me," she said, an air of surprise in her voice.

"I think they were trying to shoot me," he answered.

"It was that witch Vivian, wasn't it?"

He nodded again. "Your father and brothers slapped the handcuffs on her a few hours ago. It's over. We got a full confession about her involvement with the drug scheme, your shooting and the murder of John Mitchell Lender."

"She killed John Mitchell Lender?"

"Sadly, yes she did."

"I told you she was crazy. We are lucky to be alive."

"Yes, we are."

"You need to listen to me more often."

"Yes, dear."

"I mean it, Paul! I am a great judge of character and everything about that woman screamed there was something not right about her."

"I know."

"I saved you. Just imagine what might've happened if I hadn't come back into your life."

Paul smiled. "You are the best thing that has ever happened to me, Simone Black!"

Simone reached for the front of his shirt and pulled him toward her to be kissed. "And don't you ever forget it," she said as she captured his lips with her own.

Chapter 18

Simone spent six weeks recovering from her injuries. All six of those weeks were passed in the hospital to alleviate concerns with her pregnancy. Paul never left her side, every waking moment spent encouraging her to do what the doctors ordered. Simone had proven herself to be a difficult patient at best, wanting only to return to her job to follow the prosecution of Vivian Lincoln and get back to work on their lawsuit.

Lender Pharmaceuticals was still trending in social media. Halphedrone-B had been recalled and surviving patients had been provided with free medication from one of their competitors. Their stock had plummeted and virtually overnight Vivian's gold mine had become completely worthless, overrun with lawsuits and legal entanglements that would eventually shutter its doors.

Overseas, Paul's patients were invigorated, suddenly thriving in ways many had thought unfathomable. Hope was renewed in communities that had lost sight of such months earlier. Vaughan had arranged a week-long media blitz for Paul to tell his story and shed light on the broader problem of health care challenges in the United States and abroad, and the medical community, politicians and social activists were all stepping up to help. Everyone knew the spotlight wouldn't last long before something or someone else took over the front pages, but they were determined to make the most from the moment as they could manage.

The city of Chicago had honored Paul for his help in bringing down Vivian, and the hospital lauded him as a hero for his efforts to expose Lender Pharmaceuticals for their criminal endeavors. He'd taken a short leave of absence from his patients to devote himself exclusively to Simone's recovery. Their time together was golden as they negotiated their future life together and imagined what life would be like when their son was born.

"Simone, I'm not giving up my mission work."

Simone threw up her hands in frustration. "I'm not asking you to give it up, Paul. But I am saying you need to cut back once Nino is born. He needs his father around. Who's going to teach him how to be a man if you're halfway around the world?"

"First, I'll be around to teach my son how to be a man. You can trust that! And secondly, have you met your father and your brothers? Nino will not lack male role models."

"Well, I'm only agreeing to traveling with you on two mission trips per year."

"Well, that's something. But I'm willing to bet that once you do those two, you'll want to do more, and it'll be a great way to teach our son how to look out for others who might not be as blessed as he is."

"You'll have to tell my parents. But I warn you, my father isn't going to be happy about any of it."

Paul laughed. "Your father loves me. He and I are great friends. He will be just fine! Now, are you ready for them to bring the wheelchair so we can get you out of here?"

"I've been ready. I don't know what's been taking you so long."

Paul shook his head. "Good, because we're late for Sunday dinner. I'm sure your mother is ready to send out a search team for us."

"For me maybe. I am carrying the heir to the Black family throne. You just knocked up their daughter!"

Paul laughed. "You are in for such a surprise after that baby gets here and you no longer get any attention!"

Simone rolled her eyes skyward and then she laughed with him, joy resonating warmly through the room.

An hour later Paul held her hand as they entered the Black family home. They called out in greeting as they maneuvered their way toward the family room and the back of the house. Loud cheers greeted them as they stepped into the space. Vaughan, Joanna and Armstrong's wife, Danni, had decorated the room with balloons and streamers and an oversize welcome-home sign hung from the ceiling.

Simone's parents stood together arm in arm, tears streaming from her mother's eyes. The matriarch stepped forward to give them both a hug.

"I can't tell you how happy this day makes me!" Judith said. She swiped at her eyes with her fingers.

"We missed you, kid," Vaughan echoed.

"Yeah, yeah, yeah!" Davis said teasingly. "We missed you like a fungus!"

The room laughed as everyone stepped up to embrace Simone and welcome her back into the fold.

Oliver stepped forward to give her a big bear hug.

"I'm so glad you made it," Simone exclaimed. "I was afraid you were stuck in Atlanta!"

"I wouldn't miss this for anything in the world," he said as he and Paul bumped fists.

Oliver gestured to a man standing behind him. "Let me introduce you to my new friend," he said as he gave her a wink of his eye. "He's a police officer!"

Simone grinned.

"Simone, this is Liam. Liam, this is my brother's fi-ancée, Simone."

The man named Liam stepped forward to shake her hand."

She shook her head. "We're huggers around here," she said as she wrapped her arms around the man's shoulders. "It's very nice to meet you!"

She gave Oliver a look and a thumbs-up over the man's shoulder.

The brother laughed heartily.

Simone laughed with them as Paul guided her to a seat and insisted that she sit down. "You'd think I haven't seen you people in months, the way you all are acting," she teased.

"Baby girl, we're just glad we don't have to go back up to that hospital to see your pretty face," her father in-terjected.

Simone blew her father a kiss. "I love you, too, Daddy!"

"Well, I don't know about anyone else," Ellington said, "but now that Simone isn't holding up the meal, I'm hun-gry!"

They all laughed.

"The food is ready. We can all eat," Judith said.

Laughter was infectious as it spread from one room to the other, everyone filing into the dining room to eat. Simone sat back and took it all in. Her hand rested on her abdomen and she sensed that her little bundle of energy was as excited for the experience as she was. She felt Paul looking at her and when she turned to meet his gaze, there was an overwhelming look of love across his face.

"You good?" he asked, leaning to kiss her cheek.

She nodded. "I'm better than good. And as soon as I get some of my mother's lasagna I'm going to be great!"

"I love you," he said, every ounce of his emotion shimmering through his expression.

Simone lifted her face to his, kissing him gently. "I love you, too!"

Jerome suddenly slammed a palm against the table. "Since there's so much love going around the room, someone tell me when you plan to make an honest woman of my daughter. And Mingus, what the hell are you waiting for? Women like Joanna don't grow on trees, son!"

Mingus choked on the glass of tea he'd been drinking. He shot Joanna a look, amused by the heat that colored her cheeks a vibrant shade of red. "How did I get drawn into this?" he said, laughing.

"Well, someone needs to do something. Your mother's ready for another wedding. And more grandchildren!"

The low murmur in the room rose to a thunderous ruckus as they continued to tease and joke with each other. Another thirty minutes passed as they finished off the vegetable lasagna, Caesar salad and homemade crusty bread. Dessert was peach cobbler topped with vanilla ice cream.

As forks dropped against empty plates Judith cleared her throat for their attention. She and Jerome exchanged a look and as Simone watched them, she sensed the mood had suddenly turned serious. Her siblings sensed it as well, quiet rising through the room like a morning mist.

"What's wrong, Mom?" Davis asked, eyeing both of his parents with concern.

The matriarch shook her head. "I'm very happy," she said softly. "Nothing could bring me greater joy than to be surrounded by my family and our friends."

"Then why so melancholy?" Vaughan questioned, she and Simone exchanging a look.

Jerome stood, moving to stand behind his wife's chair.

He pressed his hands to her shoulders, and you could feel her fall back against his strength for support. "Your mother has something she wants to share with all of you."

Oliver held up his hand. "Judge Black, Liam and I can excuse ourselves if you'd prefer. We wouldn't want to intrude…"

Judith shook her head. "Oliver, you're as much family to us as Paul is. And I have a good feeling about Liam." She gave the two men a smile. "In fact, I imagine we might be planning your wedding before I can get Simone or Mingus to even consider the idea."

Everyone around the table laughed. Neither Mingus nor Simone was amused.

"I've considered it," Mingus muttered as he pulled Jo-anna into his arms and hugged her warmly.

Judith continued. "I'm being blackmailed," she said, the words falling from her mouth with a loud clatter.

Her children all sat upright, shifting forward in their seats.

"I'm telling you this because I have no intentions of giving in to the demands. Your father and I have reached out to the FBI and they're working on the case, but you all need to be prepared because you're going to hear some things about me."

"What kind of things?" Ellington questioned.

"Things in my past that I had hoped would never come to light."

Jerome gently kneaded her shoulders. He pressed a kiss to the top of her head.

"But Daddy knows, right?" Simone asked.

Jerome nodded his head. "Yes, I do," he said.

Armstrong reached for his mother's hand. "What are we going to hear, Mom? You know you can tell us anything, right?"

A tear rolled over her cheek. "Recently, I asked Mingus to find someone for me. A young man named Fabian Scott. Mingus discovered he lives very near here, in Saint Louis."

"So, who is this Fabian Scott and what does he have to do with you being blackmailed?" Parker asked.

Judith swept the table with her eyes, pausing to give them each a look. "Fabian is my son. My eldest son. I gave birth to him when I was seventeen and I gave him up for adoption."

"Whoa," Davis muttered, everyone else falling silent as shock swept through the space.

"Someone has been threatening to expose that information if your mother doesn't vote favorably on a case that's coming up in her jurisdiction," Jerome said. "Your mother wants to reach out to the boy so that he isn't blindsided by the news."

"I don't know if that's a good idea," Ellington said.

"Me, neither," Simone added. "If the adoption was closed and he's not listed in the mutual consent registry, he may not want to be contacted. That might blow up into an even bigger problem for you. And, if your methods to find him were slightly shady…" She hesitated, shooting her brother a look.

"He's registered," Mingus interjected. "He filed to have his information released to his birth parents ten years ago."

"Who's his father?" Davis suddenly questioned.

Judith shook her head. "That's not important right now."

Her youngest son persisted. "I think we have a right to know."

"I think you better check your tone," Armstrong snapped at his brother.

Jerome gave his youngest son a look that sat him back in his seat.

Contrition washed over the younger man's face and he apologized. "I'm sorry," Davis said softly.

"We'll support whatever you need to do," Vaughan said. She rose from her seat to give her mother a hug.

Judith pressed a cloth napkin to the moisture that dampened her cheeks. "I know you all have questions and I'll answer them for you in due time. I promise. Right now, though," she turned toward Ellington, "I need you to sit down with me and your father so we can decide the best way to approach this."

"Yes, ma'am," Ellington replied.

Judith rose from her seat, turning to wrap her arms around her husband's shoulders. Jerome hugged her tightly before she pulled herself from him. She rounded the table to give each of them a hug.

She paused to whisper in Simone's ear. "No matter what your circumstances, you will always do whatever you need to do to protect your child. Just keep trusting your instincts and you, Paul and Nino will be just fine! I love you!"

Simone nodded, fighting back her own tears. She turned to kiss her mother's cheek. Minutes later her parents and Ellington had disappeared up to her office, the door closed firmly behind them.

Parker directed his attention to Mingus. "How long have you known this?"

"A few weeks. Mom asked me to do a little digging and she swore me not to discuss it with anyone."

"What do you know about him?"

Mingus shrugged. "He's an English teacher and he's written a few books."

Vaughan was suddenly looking up Fabian Scott's name

online. "I don't see anything published by anyone called Fabian Scott."

"I never said he published under his name."

"Is he married?"

"Where did he go to school?"

"Does he have any kids?"

They were all throwing questions at Mingus like wild darts being tossed at a country bar. But it quickly became obvious that he had nothing else left to share. He stood up, extending his hand toward Joanna. "We're out of here. I'll catch up with you all later."

"We're leaving, too," Danni said as she and Armstrong exchanged a look. "I'm working a case tonight, so I have to get to the precinct."

"I'm staying," Parker said. "I want to know what the FBI is doing about mom being blackmailed."

"I have questions, too," Davis said. "And she owes us some answers. How could she just give up her child?"

"Don't do that," Vaughan said. "Until Mom's ready to share the details with us you have no right to judge her!"

"Like hell I don't!" Davis snapped.

"What's wrong with you?" Armstrong questioned, eyeing his baby brother suspiciously.

Mingus was still standing in the doorway, Joanna leaning into his side. "You need to tell them," he said, the comment directed at Davis.

"Shut up, Mingus!" his brother snapped.

"Tell us what?" Vaughan asked.

"Nothing!" Davis said. He grabbed a stack of plates from the table and headed into the kitchen to do the dirty dishes.

Silence descended on the room, everyone looking at each other but no one saying anything. The awkward moment passed as quickly as it had arrived.

Paul nodded, changing the subject. "Well, Simone needs to go get some rest. So, we're headed home, too."

"We'll catch a ride back to the hotel with you, if you don't mind," Oliver added.

"I don't recall anyone asking Simone what she wanted," Simone quipped.

Paul met the look she was giving him. "You can't stress yourself out, Simone. You haven't been out of the hospital a full day yet."

"I still want me another piece of cobbler and ice cream," she said.

Vaughan laughed. "She is eating for two now!"

"Simone has always eaten for two," Parker said. "Now she's eating for an army!"

"Whatever! One of you just put me some more dessert into a container, please!"

The ride home was relatively quiet. No one mentioned Simone's mother or the bomb she'd tossed into the room leaving everyone reeling from the fallout. Instead, Simone peppered Liam with questions and by the time they reached their hotel destination, she too was convinced that Liam was a keeper. She liked the man and it was obvious he cared about Oliver.

After saying good-night to the two men, Paul turned the car toward home. He'd just exited off the interstate when Simone grabbed his arm, startling him out of the calm that had surrounded them.

"What's wrong?"

"Nothing. I feel fine. But I don't want to go home."

"Excuse me? Simone, you need to rest."

"I need to be married. How far are we from Vegas?"

Paul laughed. "We are not driving to Vegas!"

"Why not? Don't you want to marry me?"

"You know I want you to be my wife more than anything else in this world. You don't need to even ask that question."

"Then let's just do it. Let's elope! Make an honest woman out of me!"

"Is that even possible?" Paul asked, chuckling softly.

"Your father said that," Simone replied, speaking at her stomach. "Never let him forget it, Nino!"

Paul reached a warm palm out and placed it against her tummy. She still wasn't showing but both were acutely aware that their future lay snugly beneath the palm of his hand. Simone was typing into her cell phone, waiting for a page to load. She suddenly waved the device excitedly.

"Okay, so a road trip might be a bit much but there's a nonstop flight leaving at seven tonight. We can be there in four hours and married in five!"

"You're serious?"

"I'm very serious. If I'm going to be divvying up my time going around the world with you, we might as well start now."

"You don't want your family there?"

"They'll be there with us in spirit and we can always Skype them in."

"What about your mother?"

"What about her? My mom has everything handled. You can bet that telling us tonight was only a formality. She already knew what she was going to do and how all of this is going to play out. I'm sure we'll meet my new brother in due time."

Paul hesitated. "I don't know, Simone…"

"Paul Reilly, I love you. I want to be your wife. Will you marry me?"

"I love you too and yes, I will definitely marry you."

"Then you better do it now before I change my mind," Simone said definitively.

Laughter rumbled from Paul's midsection. "Okay, but I'll do all the packing. Let's go to the house—you need to put your feet up, and I'll throw some things into a bag for us."

Simone began to type again into her device. "Good! That's settled. Tickets have been purchased. We can pick them up at the gate."

"And I have one more condition."

"Really, Paul? These tickets are nonrefundable."

"Send a message to your family, and my brother, please. If anyone wants to join us, I'll pick up the tab for their plane tickets, too. We might as well make this a party!"

Simone grinned widely, her smile spreading like a canyon across her face. "I do like how you think, Dr. Reilly!"

Shortly before midnight on the fourteenth of the month, Paul Reilly married Simone Black at The Little White Church in Las Vegas, Nevada. She wore a champagne-colored satin gown borrowed from her mother's closet and courtesy of the hotel's concierge and a talented tailor named Alberto, it fit her to perfection. She carried a bouquet of classic red roses to match her red-bottomed high heels and her mother had finger-waved the short length of her hair into a style reminiscent of the 1920s flapper era. She was stunning and Paul proclaimed her the most beautiful bride he had ever seen in his lifetime.

Paul looked dashing in the one black tuxedo he had owned since forever. As he stood at the chapel altar, waiting for her to descend the aisle, he knew beyond any doubt that he was the luckiest man in the whole wide world. His brother Oliver stood beside him as his best man. Simone's sister Vaughan was her maid of honor.

Her parents had been the first to accept the invitation and they had flown back immediately after the ceremony. Simone's brother Armstrong and his wife were the only ones unable to make it to Vegas, their responsibilities to the Chicago Police Department claiming their time. But they watched the ceremony on their iPads in Armstrong's office at the police station as Davis streamed it to them live.

It was everything any of them could have ever imagined and Jerome giving Paul his blessing just minutes before the ceremony was icing on some very sweet cake. Hours later they lay side by side in the Piazza suite at The Venetian Resort. The luxury accommodations, with marbled floors, oversize king bed and jetted tubs, were the epitome of grace and elegance and afforded them the highest level of comfort. Simone had already decided they wouldn't leave that bed for at least a week.

"You have to be exhausted," Paul said, as he lifted himself up on his elbow, resting his head in his hand as he stared down at her.

"I'm tired, but I feel amazing."

Paul leaned to kiss her lips. "I'm glad we did this. It was the most perfect wedding and I'm happy our family could be here to celebrate with us."

"I love my people and I'm glad they're now your people, too!"

Paul kissed her again, leaning over her gently as she pulled him down against her.

Outside, a partial moon was beginning to disappear behind a cluster of clouds. The evening air was warm, and a gentle breeze blew through the opened balcony door.

Breaking the kiss Paul rolled from her, lowering himself against her side. He wrapped his arm around her torso and hugged her to him. His hands danced lightly against her back and waist, his fingers teasing like the easy caress of a down feather. Simone's eyes closed and then opened and closed again. She turned, pressing herself tightly to him as she tossed her leg over his hip, her naked body kissing his sweetly. Heat billowed between them feeling like someone had lit a match to the furnace.

A few short minutes passed before she was sleeping soundly, whispery snores blowing past her parted lips. Paul took a deep breath as he watched her, feeling his own body beginning to slide into a gentle state of warmth and calm. His own eyes fluttered back and forth, open and then closed. Like every night prior, he lifted her in prayer and thanked God for the blessings that had been bestowed on them. He was grateful. Love had torn them apart and love had reunited them. Life just didn't get any better.

* * * * *

*Don't miss the previous volumes in
Deborah Fletcher Mello's
To Serve and Seduce miniseries:*

Tempted by the Badge
Seduced by the Badge

Available now from Harlequin Romantic Suspense!

Get 4 FREE REWARDS!

We'll send you 2 FREE Books plus 2 FREE Mystery Gifts.

Harlequin® Romantic Suspense books feature heart-racing sensuality and the promise of a sweeping romance set against the backdrop of suspense.

FREE Value Over **$20**

*State Trooper Kelly Roberts joins Special Agent
Tony Lazzaro's task force, determined to bring down
a cybercriminal preying on young victims. Solving
this case is a chance for redemption. If Kelly catches
the killer, she'll be one step closer to solving her best
friend's abduction. She never expects to fall for Tony...*

*Read on for a sneak preview of
Dana Nussio's next book in the True Blue miniseries,*
Her Dark Web Defender.

"Ready to try this again?"

"Absolutely."

Kelly met his gaze with a confidence he didn't expect.
Was she trying to prove something to him? Trying to
convince him he'd made a mistake by shielding her
before?

"Okay, let's chat."

The conversation appeared to have slowed during the
time he'd gone for coffee, but the moment Tony typed
his first line, his admirers were back. Didn't any of these
guys have a day job?

It didn't take long before one of them sent a private
message at the bottom of the screen. GOOD TIME GUY
wasn't all that shy about escalating the conversation
quickly, either. Kelly took over the keyboard, and when

the guy suggested a voice chat, she didn't even look Tony's way before she accepted.

"Hey, your voice is rougher than I expected," she said into the microphone.

Only then did she glance sidelong at Tony. He nodded his approval. He'd been right to give her a second chance. Dawson and the others didn't need to know about the other day, the part at the office or anything that happened later. Kelly would be great at this.

When the conversation with GOOD TIME GUY didn't seem to be going anywhere, they ended that interaction and accepted another offer for a personal chat. She navigated that one with BOY AT HEART and even a repeat one with BIG DADDY with the skill of someone who'd been on the task force a year rather than days.

Her breathing might have been a little halting, and she might have tightened her grip on the microphone, but she was powering through, determined to tease details from each of the possible suspects that they might be able to use to track them.

Tony found he had to admit something else. He'd been wrong about Kelly Roberts. She was stronger than he'd expected her to be. Maybe even fearless. And he was dying to know what had made her that way.

Don't miss
Her Dark Web Defender *by Dana Nussio,*
available November 2019 wherever
Harlequin® Romantic Suspense
books and ebooks are sold.

Harlequin.com

HRSEXP1019